Weezy laid the object on the ground between them and began to examine it, tilting it a little this way and a little that.

Jack knelt opposite her. "What do you think it is?"

She shook her head, looking as baffled as he felt. "I don't know. Some kind of stone—onyx, maybe? It's got no writing on it, but I get this feeling it's . . . old." She looked up at him. "Know what I mean?"

Jack couldn't say why, but he knew exactly what she meant.

"Yeah. Very old."

"And where there's one there's probably others." Her eyes were wide with wonder and excitement. "Help me, Jack?"

He laughed. "Try and stop me."

He wanted one of those cubes for himself.

So they started digging—not easy in the wet sand. But they kept coming up empty. Frustration was beginning to nibble at Jack when his fingertips scraped against a hard surface.

"Got something!"

He dug his fingers down on each side of whatever it was and pulled it up.

He stared in mute, openmouthed, grossed-out shock. Beside him, Weezy screamed.

BOOKS BY F. PAUL WILSON

JACK
SECRET HISTORIES

F. PAUL WILSON

A TOM DOHERTY ASSOCIATES BOOK
NEW YORK

TOR®

This is a work of fiction. All the characters, organizations, and events portrayed in this novel are either products of the author's imagination or are used fictitiously.

JACK: SECRET HISTORIES

Copyright © 2008 by F. Paul Wilson

All rights reserved.

A Tor Teen Book
Published by Tom Doherty Associates, LLC
175 Fifth Avenue
New York, NY 10010

www.tor-forge.com

Tor® is a registered trademark of Tom Doherty Associates, LLC.

ISBN 978-0-7653-5811-0

First Edition: June 2008
First Mass Market Edition: January 2010

Printed in the United States of America

0 9 8 7 6 5 4 3 2 1

JACK: SECRET HISTORIES

They discovered the body on a rainy afternoon.

1

"Aren't we there *yet*?" Eddie said, puffing behind him.

Jack glanced over his shoulder to where Eddie Connell labored through the sandy soil on his bike. His face was red and beaded with perspiration; sweat soaked through his red Police T-shirt, darkening Sting's face. Chunky Eddie wasn't built for speed. He wore his sandy hair shorter than most, which tended to make him look even heavier than he was. Eddie's idea of exercise was a day on the couch playing *Pole Position* on his new Atari 5200. Jack envied that machine. He was stuck with a 2600.

"Only Weezy knows," Jack said.

He wasn't sweating like Eddie, but he felt clammy all over. With good reason. The August heat was stifling here in the Pine Barrens, and the humidity made it worse. Whatever breeze existed out there couldn't penetrate the close-packed, spindly trees.

They were following Eddie's older sister, Weezy—really Louise, but no one ever called her that. She liked to remind people that she'd been "Weezy" long before *The Jeffersons* ever showed up on the tube.

She was pedaling her banana-seat Schwinn along one of the firebreak trails that crisscrossed the million-plus acres of mostly uninhabited woodland known as the Jersey Pine Barrens. A potentially dangerous place if you didn't know what you were doing or where you were going. Every year hunters wandered in, looking for deer, and were never seen again. Locals would wink and say the Jersey Devil snagged another one. But Jack knew the JD was just a folktale. Well, he was pretty sure. Truth was, the missing hunters were usually amateurs who came ill equipped and got lost, wandering around in circles until they died of thirst and starvation.

At least that was what people said. Though that didn't explain why so few of the bodies were ever found.

But the Barrens didn't scare Jack and Eddie and Weezy. At least not during the day. They'd grown up on the edge of the pinelands and knew this section of it like the backs of their hands. Couldn't know all of it, of course. The Barrens hid places no human eye had ever seen.

Yet as familiar as he was with the area, Jack still got a creepy sensation when riding into the trees and seeing the forty-foot scrub pines get thicker and thicker, crowding the edges of the path, and then leaning over with their crooked, scraggly branches seeming to reach for him. He could almost believe they were shuffling off the path ahead of him and then moving back in to close it off behind.

"See that sign?" Eddie said, pointing to a tree they passed. "Maybe we should listen."

Jack glanced at the orange letters blaring from glossy black tin:

NO FISHING
NO HUNTING
NO TRAPPING
NO TRESPASSING

No big deal. The signs dotted just about every other tree on Old Man Foster's land, so common they became part of the scenery.

"Well," he said, "we're not doing the first three."

"But we're doing the fourth."

"Criminals is what we are!" Jack raised a fist. "Criminals!"

"Easy with that." Eddie looked around. "Old Man Foster might hear you."

Jack called to the girl riding twenty feet ahead of them. "Hey, Weez! When do we get there?"

She usually kept her shoulder-length dark hair down but she'd tied it back in a ponytail for the trip. She wore a black-and-white—mostly black—Bauhaus T-shirt and black jeans. Jack and Eddie wore jeans too, but theirs were faded blue and cut off above the knees. Weezy's were full length. Jack couldn't remember if he'd ever seen her bare legs. Probably white as snow.

"Not much farther now," she called without looking around.

"Sounds like Papa Smurf," Eddie grumbled. "This is stupidacious."

Jack turned back to Eddie. "Want to trade bikes?"

Jack rode his BMX. He'd let some air out of the tires for better grip in the sand and they were doing pretty well.

"Nah." Eddie patted the handlebars of his slim-tired English street bike. "I'm all right."

"Whoa!" Jack heard Weezy say.

He looked around and saw she'd stopped. He had to jam on his brakes to keep from running into her. Eddie flew past both of them and stopped ahead of his sister.

"Is this it, Smurfette?" he said.

Weezy shook her head. "Almost."

She had eyes almost as dark as her hair, and a round face, normally milk pale, made paler by the dark eyeliner she wore. But she was flushed now with heat and excitement. The color looked good on her. Made her look almost . . . healthy, a look Weezy did not pursue.

Jack liked Weezy. She was only four months older, but his January birthday had landed him a year behind her in school. Come next month they'd both be in Southern Burlington County Regional High, just a couple of miles away. But she'd be a soph and he a lowly frosh. Maybe they'd be able to spend more time together. And then again, maybe not. Did sophs hang with freshmen? Were they allowed?

She wasn't pretty by most standards. Skinny, almost boyish, although her hips seemed to be flaring a little now. Back in grammar school a lot of the kids had called her "Wednesday Addams" because of her round face and perpetually dark clothes. If she ever decided to wear her hair in pigtails, the resemblance would be scary.

But whatever her looks, Jack thought she was the most interesting girl—no, make that most interesting *person* he'd ever met. She read things no one else read, and viewed the world in a light different from anyone else.

She pointed to their right. "What on Earth's going on there?"

Jack saw a small clearing with a low wet spot known in these parts as a spong. But around the rim of the spong stood about a dozen sticks of odd shapes and sizes, leaning this way and that.

"Who cares?" Eddie said. "If this isn't what you dragged us out here to see, let's keep going."

After hopping off her bike, she leaned it against a tree and started for the clearing.

"Just give me a minute."

His curiosity piqued, Jack leaned his bike against hers and followed. The knee-high grass slapped against his sweaty lower legs, making them itch. A glance back showed Eddie sitting on the sand in the shade of a pine. Jack caught up to Weezy as they neared the spong.

"They just look like dead branches someone's stuck in the sand."

"But why?" Weezy said.

"For nothing better to do?"

She looked at him with that tolerant smile—the smile she showed a world that just didn't get it. At least not in her terms.

"Everything that happens out here happens for a reason," she said in the *ooh-spooky* tone she used whenever she talked about the Barrens.

He knew Weezy loved the Barrens. She studied them, knew everything about them, and had been delighted back in 1979, at the tender age of eleven, when the state passed a conservation act to preserve them.

She gestured at the sticks, not a dozen feet away now. "Can you imagine anyone coming out here just to poke sticks into the ground for no reason at all? I don't—" She stopped, grabbed Jack's arm, and pointed. "Look! What'd I tell you?"

Jack kind of liked the feel of her fingers gripping his forearm, but he followed her point. When he saw what she was talking about, he broke free and hurried forward.

"Traps! A whole mess of traps."

"Yeah," Weezy said, coming up behind him. "The nasty leg-hold type. Some dirty, rotten . . ."

As her voice trailed off Jack glanced at her and flinched at her enraged expression. She looked a little scary.

"But they've all been sprung." He started walking around the spong. "Every single one of them."

"Whoever did this is my hero," she said, following close behind. "Didn't I tell you that everything that happens out here—"

"—happens for a reason," Jack said, finishing for her.

Clear as day that someone had set up a slew of traps around the perimeter of the spong, planning to trap any animals that stopped by to drink from the water in its basin.

And just as clear, someone else had come by with a bunch of dead branches and used them to tap the trigger plates, springing the traps and making them harmless. In some cases the steel jaws had snapped right through the dead wood; in others it had only dented it, leaving the branch upright.

"Got to be at least a couple dozen along here," Jack said.

"Not anymore."

She bent, grabbed one of the trap chains, and started working its anchor loose from the sand.

"What are you doing?"

"Watch."

As the coiled anchor came free, Weezy grabbed it and the trap itself, then hurled the whole assembly into the spong. The two ends swung around on their chain like a boomerang before splashing into the shallow water and disappearing beneath the surface.

She turned to him, brushing the sand from her hands.

"Come on, Jack. We've got work to do."

He stared at her, surprised by the wild look in her eyes . . .

"But—"

"These rats don't check their traps for three or four days at a time."

"How do you know all this?"

"I read, Jack."

"So do I."

"Yeah, but you read fifty-year-old magazines. I read about what's really going on in the world." She pointed to a trap. "Three days in one of those. Think about it."

He did, imagining himself a fox or possum or raccoon with a broken leg caught in the steel jaws, hungry and thirsty, with water just a couple of dozen feet away but unable to get to it. It made his gut crawl.

Without a word, he bent and worked an anchor free of the ground, then followed Weezy's example and tossed the trap into the water.

"Two down. How many more to go?"

He found her staring at him with a strange light in her eyes.

"About thirty."

"Then we're gonna need help." He turned and waved to Eddie. "Over here! You gotta see this!"

As Eddie made his way toward them, Jack and Weezy bent again to the task of ripping out the traps and hurling them into the drink.

Eddie arrived and gawked at what they were doing. "Are you guys *crazy*? You can't do that!"

Jack held up a trap. "Really? Watch."

He tossed it into the water.

Eddie slapped his hands against the side of his head. "What if Old Man Foster comes along and catches us?"

Weezy said, "Well, his signs do say, 'No Trapping.' We're just helping him out."

"That means no trapping by anybody *else*. We could be in hellacious big trouble."

Jack doubted that. Old Man Foster was just a name. No one had ever seen the guy. Everyone knew he owned this big piece of the Barrens and that was about it. Though nobody saw them go up, fresh *No Trespassing* signs appeared every year. Sometimes poachers would take them down, but before you knew it they'd be back up again.

Another mystery of the Pine Barrens. A very minor one.

As for Eddie, Jack wasn't sure if he was acting as the voice of good sense, or trying to duck the work of pulling out the traps. He hated anything more strenuous than working a joystick.

"Look," Jack told him. "The sooner we get this done and get on our way, the less chance we'll have of being caught. So come on. Get to it."

Eddie obeyed, but not without his trademark grumbling.

"Okay, okay. But I don't have to ask whose idea this was. It's got my crazy sister written all over it."

In a flash Weezy was in his face. "What did you say?"

Eddie gave her a sheepish look. "Nothing."

"You did! I heard you! Hasn't this been talked about a million times?" Eddie nodded without looking at her. "Right," she said. "So you keep your mouth shut or someone's going to hear about this."

Eddie sighed, saying, "Okay, okay," and returned to working on a trap.

Baffled, Jack caught Weezy's eye as she turned from her brother. "What—?"

"Family matter, Jack." She turned away. "Don't worry about it."

Jack wasn't worried. But he couldn't help but wonder. He'd known these two all his life. What was this all about?

2

"Okay," Weezy said, stopping her bike. "Here we are."

After sinking all the traps, they'd pedaled like mad away from the spong. Along the way, Jack had wished for a few clouds to hide the sun and cool the air, but the sky ignored him. At least now they'd arrived at their original destination.

Jack followed her gaze. "It's just some burned-out patch."

Fires were common in the Barrens during the summer. Tourists and nature lovers came to camp and sometimes got careless with their campfires or Coleman stoves or cigarettes. Same with poachers. And many times Nature herself took the blame, setting a tree ablaze with a bolt of lightning.

Usually a ranger in a fire tower, like the one on Apple Pie Hill, would spot the smoke and send out an alarm. Then the local and county volunteer fire companies would go racing to the scene along the fire trails. But the smaller fires started during a storm often would burn only an acre or two before being doused by the rain.

"Not just any burned-out patch." She motioned Jack and Eddie to follow. "Come on. I'm going to show you something no one else—except for me—has seen in a long, long time."

Eddie said, "Aw, come on, Smurfette—"

She stopped and turned to him. "And you can cut the Smurfette bit. Unless you like 'Pugsley.'"

"Okay, okay. But what about the firemen who put out the fire? They must have seen it."

"No firemen for this one."

Eddie snorted. "You psychic now?"

"Check it out." She gestured around them. "What's missing?"

Eddie and Jack did full turns.

"Green trees?" Jack said.

Weezy shook her head. "Litter. There's no litter. Firefighters always leave coffee cups, candy wrappers, Coke cans, Gatorade bottles, all sorts of stuff. But not here. Ergo . . ."

Jack knew from his father that *ergo* was Latin for "therefore," but a glance at Eddie showed he hadn't a clue.

He checked the ground again. Not even a gum wrapper. Weezy didn't miss a trick.

As they followed her into the burned-out area, Jack noticed how the pine trunks had been charred coal black. The remaining needles high up were a dead brown, and the usual spindly little branches sticking out here and there lower down the trunks had been burned off. But the trees weren't dead. Every single trunk was sprouting new little branchlets, pushing them through the scorched crust of the bark and sporting baby needles of bright green. Everyone had heard of the Sears DieHard battery. These were nature's die-hard trees.

As she'd done all day, Weezy led the way, winding through the blackened trunks until she came to a break in the trees.

"Here's where the mound begins."

"Mound?" Eddie said. "Where?"

But Jack saw what she meant. They stood at the tip of where two linear mounds, each a couple of feet high and maybe a yard wide, converged to a point. Both ran off at angles between the blackened trees.

"Like some giant gopher," Eddie said.

Weezy shook her head. "Except look how smooth they are. And how straight. Nobody knows it's here, and I never would have noticed it if the fire hadn't cleared all the undergrowth. I haven't explored the whole thing, so I—"

"You were out here alone?" Jack said.

She nodded. "You know me. I like to explore. Who else is going to come along? You?"

His two part-time jobs didn't leave Jack much time to explore the Barrens, especially not to the extent Weezy did. She'd spend hours digging for arrowheads or other artifacts. The only reason he was out here today was because Mr. Rosen closed his store on Mondays.

He smiled and shrugged. "Beautiful teenage girl alone in the woods . . . might meet a Big Bad Wolf."

She grinned and punched him on the shoulder. "Get out! Now you're making fun of me."

"Maybe a little, but you've got to be careful, Weez."

She sighed. "Yeah, you're right. But they've got to find me first." She shrugged. "Anyway, I got a little spooked here before I could explore the rest of the mound, so that's—"

"You? Spooked?" Eddie laughed. "You *are* a spook. Nothing spooks you."

"Well, this place does." She pointed along the lengths of the two ridges to where they faded into the trees. "See how nothing grows on the mounds? I mean, isn't that weird?"

Jack saw what she meant. Low-lying scrub—most of it scorched and blackened—crowded around the trees and spread across every square inch of sand between them. Everywhere except on the mounds.

Yeah. Weird, all right. Sand was sand. What made the mounds different?

Or was it a single mound, angling in different directions?

"Feel it," she said, patting the surface. "It's still sand, but it's hard. Like it hasn't been disturbed for so long it's formed some kind of crust."

Jack ran his fingers along the surface, then pressed. The sand wouldn't yield. But something else . . . an unpleasant tingle in his fingertips. He pulled them away and looked at them. The tingling stopped. He glanced at Weezy and found her staring at him.

"So it isn't just me. You feel it too."

"Feel what?" Eddie said, rubbing his hands over the hard surface. "I don't feel anything."

Weezy was still staring at Jack. "Now you know what spooked me."

She reached around to a rear pocket and pulled out the small spiral notebook and pencil she never went anywhere without.

"I'll bet somebody designed this in a special shape. Let's see if we can figure it out."

"What do you mean, 'special shape'?"

"A lot of these mounds are ancient—thousands of years old."

"You mean, like, burial mounds?"

Jack had heard of those. The Lenape Indians used to inhabit the pines.

Weezy shook her head. "Some of the most mysterious mounds have nothing to do with burials. Take the Serpent Mound in Ohio. It curves back and forth like a snake for over a quarter mile. And get this—nobody knows how old it is. This could be something like that." Her face brightened as she smiled. "And *I* discovered it. I've *got* to get this diagrammed."

Wondering how she knew all this stuff, Jack watched her draw a few lines on her pad, then move off, weaving through the trees as she followed the mound to the right. Jack and Eddie followed close behind through air heavy with the smell of burned wood. This was Weezy's show, but Jack was getting into it. Something about these mounds and the way nothing grew on them gave him a funny feeling in his gut, but he had to admit he was fascinated.

"Oh, look at this," she said after she'd gone maybe twenty feet. "Another mound crosses here." She drew some more lines. "This is getting confusing."

"Hey," Eddie said.

Jack turned and saw him standing atop the mound with his arms spread.

"Eddie—" Weezy began

"You want to map these mounds, right? Well, instead of ducking through all those trees, doesn't it make more sense to follow the mounds themselves? It'll be a lot less boracious."

Jack to turned to Weezy. "You know, that's a great idea."

Weezy hesitated, then shrugged. "I guess everybody has a good idea in them," she muttered. "Even Eddie."

Jack bowed and made a flourish toward the mound. "Ladies first."

She smiled and faked a curtsy. "Why, thank you, kind sir."

As the three of them began walking the mound, the sky darkened. Jack looked up and saw a menacing pile of clouds scudding in from the west, blotting out the sun. Weezy shaded her eyes as she stared skyward.

"Shoot. We've got trouble."

"Looks like a thunderhead," Eddie said.

She nodded. "Cumulonimbus—piled high. Going to be a bad one."

"'Cumulonimbus'?" Jack had to laugh. Weezy never ceased to amaze him. "How do you *know* this stuff?"

She frowned. "I'm not sure."

"Do you sit down and memorize everything you read?"

She shook her head. "I don't have to. If I read something once, it's *there*. I never forget it. Ever. At least not so far."

No wonder she got straight A's. Jack would give anything—*anything*—for that power.

Thunder rumbled in the distance.

"Hurry," she said. "I want to get this done before the downpour."

She started quick-walking along the mound until she came to another intersection. As she stopped to mark in her notebook, Jack looked around for Eddie and spotted him a couple of dozen feet back. He was down on one knee, fiddling with his sneaker lace.

"Come on, Eddie. Don't want the Jersey Devil to catch you."

He grinned. "You kidding? I have JD sausages for breakfast every morning."

He jumped up and started trotting toward them. When he neared he jumped and landed inches in front of Jack.

"Boo!"

More thunder then, but another sound too. As Eddie's feet thumped onto the surface of the mound, they kept on going, breaking through the outer shell with a crunch.

Jack looked down and saw Eddie's sneakers sunk ankle deep in the softer sand within.

"Jeez, man! What'd you *do*?"

He heard Weezy hurry up behind him and gasp. "Oh, Eddie! How *could* you?"

Eddie's face reddened—whether with anger or embarrassment, Jack couldn't tell.

"Hey, I didn't—"

"You are the most unbelievable klutz! This mound's sat here undisturbed for hundreds, maybe thousands of years, and you're here, what, ten minutes, and already you've desecrated it!"

"It was a soft spot! How could I know?"

Lightning flashed, followed quickly by a roar of thunder that rattled Jack's fillings. He looked up at a sky completely lidded with dark clouds looking ready to burst. Jeez, this storm was coming fast.

"Time to take cover, guys," he said.

He grabbed Weezy's arm and started pulling her back toward the bikes. He knew if he didn't she'd probably stay in the open, storm or no storm, drawing her diagram. She didn't fight him. Eddie followed.

Just as they reached the bikes, the sky opened like a bursting dam. They huddled in the center of a thick copse of young pines.

"Under a tree," Weezy said. "The worst place to be in a storm."

Jack knew that, but didn't see as they had much choice. Even under the trees they were getting soaked.

"In case you haven't noticed, Weez," Jack said, "we're in the middle of the Pine Barrens. If you know of a place without trees, I'm all ears."

Weezy said nothing more, just crouched on her haunches, her eyes closed and her fingers in her ears. Eddie too. They both jumped with every thunderclap.

Jack didn't get that. He *loved* thunderstorms—their fury, their unpredictability, their deafening light shows fascinated him. Same with his father. Many a summer night they'd sit together on the front porch and watch a storm approach, peak, and move on. Sometimes Dad would drive him over to Old Town where they'd park within sight of the Lightning Tree. For some reason no one could figure, the long-dead tree took a hit from every storm that passed overhead.

The thunder grew louder, the lightning flashed brighter, the rain fell harder. The world funneled down to the copse and little else. Nothing was visible beyond their clump of trees. Water cascaded through the branches and swirled around their feet. Might as well have been in the shower—except Jack wished he could have cranked up the hot water handle.

He felt his Converse All-Stars filling with water.

Swell.

3

After a couple of forevers, the storm tapered off. When the rain finally stopped they stepped out of the copse and shook themselves off.

Jack took off his T-shirt and wrung the water out of it. Eddie followed suit. Weezy didn't have that luxury. Her Bauhaus shirt was plastered to her; she pulled it free of her skin as best she could. Her soaked hair looked almost black, her bangs were plastered to her forehead, and her ponytail had become a rattail.

"Look at us," she said. "Three drowned mice."

"At least we didn't get hit by lightning," Eddie said. "Let's get home. I need to dry off."

"But I haven't mapped the mound yet."

Eddie rolled his eyes. "You've gotta be kidding! You can come back any time—"

"Just give me a few minutes."

"Come on, Eddie," Jack said, nudging him with an elbow. "What difference is a few more minutes going to make?"

"Okay, okay. I'll stay with the bikes."

She pulled out her notepad and regarded it with dismay. "Soaked!"

But that didn't stop her. She hurried ahead, hopped on the mound, and began retracing her steps. The sun popped out as Jack followed. Now he welcomed it.

Weezy stopped where Eddie had broken through the crust and pointed to the edges.

"See this? I was so mad at him I didn't notice before, but it's really weird."

Jack saw what she meant. Eddie had shattered a four- or five-foot length of the crust into about a zillion irregular pieces, but the edges of the broken area—the near, the far, and both sides near ground level—were perfectly straight. Could have been cut by an electric saw.

The rain had done a number on the soft sand within the mound, washing it out and fanning it around the break like a cloud. Jack didn't know what kind of cloud it resembled, but he was sure Weezy could tell him.

He kicked over a random shard of crust and spotted something shiny and black beneath it. Before he could react, Weezy was on her knees and all over it.

"What's *this*?"

She started scooping away the surrounding wet sand, gradually revealing a black cube the size of a softball. Gently, cautiously, she wriggled her fingers beneath it.

"Why don't you just pick it up?" Jack said.

"Because it may be attached to something." Her fingers must have met on its underside because suddenly she lifted it free and held it up. "Heavy!"

She laid it on the ground between them and began to examine it, tilting it a little this way and a little that.

Jack knelt opposite her. "What do you think it is?"

She shook her head, looking as baffled as he felt. "I don't know. Some kind of stone—onyx, maybe? It's got no writing on it, but I get this feeling it's . . . old." She looked up at him. "Know what I mean?"

Jack couldn't say why, but he knew exactly what she meant.

"Yeah. Very old."

"And where there's one there's probably others." Her eyes were wide with wonder and excitement. "Help me, Jack?"

He laughed. "Try and stop me."

He wanted one of those cubes for himself.

So they started digging—not easy in the wet sand. But they kept coming up empty. Frustration was beginning to nibble at Jack when his fingertips scraped against a hard surface.

"Got something!"

He dug his fingers down on each side of whatever it was and pulled it up.

And found himself looking into the empty eye sockets of a rotting human head.

He stared in mute, openmouthed, grossed-out shock. Beside him, Weezy screamed.

4

Jack spotted a sheriff's patrol car rolling down Quakerton Road, Johnson's main drag, just as he, Weezy, and Eddie raced into town. Johnson—often confused with Johnson Place, fifteen miles northeast of here—wasn't big enough to rate its own police force, so the Burlington County Sheriff's Department patrolled the streets.

Trouble was, the cruiser was moving away.

Jack threw extra muscle behind the pedals and started waving an arm and yelling as he chased it. Whoever was behind the wheel must have spotted him because the cruiser pulled over and waited.

He skidded to a halt beside the driver's window and saw Deputy Tim Davis behind the wheel. Jack knew him from when Davis used to date his sister, Kate, back in their high school days. He looked up at Jack through super-dark aviator sunglasses.

"Hey, Jack. How's that beautiful sister of yours?"

Jack had pedaled so hard on his way back from the mound that it took him a second or two to catch enough breath to reply.

"Greatwefoundadeadbodyinthepines!"

He laughed. "Did you say '*dead* body'? What? As opposed to a live one?"

"I'm not kidding, Tim." He might be "Deputy" to everybody else, but he'd been "Tim" to eight-year-old Jack back when he'd gone out with Kate and so he'd always be "Tim" in Jack's mind.

"It's true!" Weezy puffed as she pulled up beside him. "I saw it too!"

Tim's smile vanished as he stared at Jack. "This had better not be one of your practical jokes."

Jack gave him a wounded look. "Who, me?"

He'd pulled a couple of pranks on Tim and Kate when they were dating—innocent little tricks like resetting Tim's watch and his car clock ahead so they'd get home an hour early. Truth was, even though he'd liked Tim, he hadn't wanted Kate dating anyone.

"Look at us." Jack pointed to his face, then Weezy's. "Do we look like we're joking?"

People were discovering bodies all the time in the mystery-thriller-adventure stories Jack devoured. He'd always thought he'd be pretty cool if ever in that situation.

Uh-uh.

He could still feel the dry, rotted flesh against his fingers, see those empty eye sockets, the grinning teeth, the matted hair. Ugh. It made him queasy to think about it. He tried to push it from his mind but it kept slithering back.

He wasn't sure but he thought he might have screamed right along with Weezy. If so, he hoped she hadn't heard him. That would be majorly embarrassing.

Tim got on his radio. "This is A-seventeen requesting backup. I have a report of a corpse in the Pines near Johnson."

A burst of static followed, choking a voice saying *Roger that* or *Ten-four* or whatever.

Tim opened his door, unfolding a map as he stepped out. He spread it on the hood of his car.

"Where exactly did you find this body?"

Jack looked at the angled lines of the fire lanes and the winding old Piney roads and didn't know where to begin. He'd been following Weezy's lead and hadn't been paying attention.

Weezy stepped forward and jabbed her finger onto the map. "Right about here."

Tim looked at her. "That's Zeb Foster's land."

Weezy went all wide-eyed and innocent. "Is it? Oh, my goodness. We had no idea. We were just following this fire trail, then we took the right fork here, and the left fork here . . ."

Jack spotted Eddie standing by the rear bumper, leaning on his bike and looking annoyed. Jack wheeled over to him.

"You guys weren't kidding, were you," he said. "All the way home I half thought you were putting me on. Wouldn't be the first time you sucked me in."

"But we wouldn't be putting on the sheriff's department, right?"

He shook his head. "I guess not. So if it was real, why didn't you let me see?"

"Nobody stopped you. You could've gone over."

"Yeah, but I thought you were kidding and you'd laugh at me."

"We're a little old for 'made-you-look' stuff, don't you think?"

Jack hadn't pulled anything on Eddie since this past winter when he'd pulled the ancient trick of rubbing some black grease around the edges of the eyepieces of a pair of old binoculars. After Eddie had taken a look, he'd wandered around his house for hours with two black eyes. Hadn't a clue until Weezy came home and cracked up at the sight of him.

Eddie pounded a fist on his handlebar. "Man, some people have all the luck."

"Trust me, if you'd seen it, you'd be thinking 'yuck' instead of luck."

Eddie's eyes took on a faraway look. "Yeah, but a *dead body*. Awesomacious."

Jack turned back to Tim and Weezy.

He heard her saying, "You follow those trails and look for a burned-out area on your right. That'll be the place."

Tim was nodding. "Sounds easy enough. Anything else you can tell me?"

Jack caught Weezy's eye and nodded to the black box in the bike basket. She returned a frantic *No-please-don't!* look. So he said nothing.

Tim looked at Jack. "We'll probably need a statement from you three sometime tomorrow."

Another sheriff's car pulled up then. Tim and the newcomer talked for a minute, then the two of them roared off toward the Pines.

Jack, Weezy, and Eddie stood there, looking at each other.

"Now what?" Eddie said.

Weezy pulled the black box from her basket. "We go back to my place and see if we can open this."

Jack said, "What makes you think it opens?"

She handed it to him. "Check the edges. Don't those look like seams? This could be some kind of ancient puzzle box."

Yeah, the edges did look seamed . . . or creased.

"Sounds like fun but . . ." Jack handed it back. "I promised Mister Courtland I'd mow his lawn today."

"You can mow it tomorrow."

"Tomorrow I'm at the store. Besides, I promised him today."

Weezy sighed. "Okay. Stop by later and see what we found." She looked at the box, turning it over in her hands, then back at Jack. "Thanks for not mentioning it to Deputy Dog."

"Tim's okay."

"Yeah, but he would've wanted it for evidence or something." Her expression was fierce as she clutched it against her chest. "This is *mine*."

Jack dramatically cleared his throat. "Um, if I remember, we found it together."

Her expression faltered. "Yeah. Okay. I guess we did. You want it?" Her eyes said, *Please don't say yes.*

"Nah. You keep it."

She grinned her relief. "You're a good friend, Jack. The best."

She leaned close and touched his arm, and for an instant he feared she might kiss him. Not that it would be so bad in itself, but jeez, not in front of Eddie. He'd never hear the end of it.

He said, "Just let me know if you discover any ancient secrets—like eternal life, or how to turn lead into gold. I get an equal share."

"Deal. As for secrets . . ." She stared again at the box.
". . . the world is *full* of secrets."

Eddie rolled his eyes. "Here we go again. 'The Secret
History of the World.'"

"Stop it, Eddie. There *is* a secret history. And who knows?
This just might hold one of those secrets."

She replaced it in her basket, then waved and started
pedaling off.

"See ya."

Eddie followed. "Later, Jack."

As Jack watched them go, Weezy's words echoed in his
head.

You're a good friend, Jack. The best.

Am I? he thought as he hopped on his bike and headed
home.

Was anyone really his friend? Sure, he hung out with
kids. Not very many. Just a few, in fact. Mostly Weezy and
Eddie, and lately Steve Brussard. But he didn't feel they were
true friends. More like acquaintances. The only one he felt
any connection to was Weezy, and she was a girl. And even
that wasn't a real *connection*. He simply found her unique.
No one he knew looked at the world the way she did. She
was always finding weird links between seemingly unrelated
things or occurrences.

He saw himself, on the other hand, as pretty dull. Whatever he liked to do tended to be something done alone. Like
reading. Like mowing lawns. Like swimming—he was on the
Johnson swim team, and yeah it was called a *team*, but he
couldn't think of many things more isolated than stroking
back and forth the length of a pool where the only thing to
hear was the splash of his arms and legs, and the only thing

to see was the black lane strip on the bottom. Except maybe cross-country running, which he also liked.

Where did he fit? Where did he belong?

Maybe high school would be different. Dread tinged his anticipation. Meeting new kids. Being at the bottom of the pecking order. SBC Regional had kids from all over the area. Maybe he'd find a bunch he could connect with.

And maybe he'd follow the same pattern as he had in middle school.

The difference between loner and loser was one letter.

Which was he?

5

"Oh, Jackie!" his mother said as she hugged him for the umpteenth time since he'd dropped the bomb about finding the body. "Will my miracle boy be able to sleep tonight?"

"It's Jack, Mom. *Jack*, okay. Please?"

He'd been called Jackie—at least at home—for most of his life. But he was heading for high school now where he wanted to be *Jack*. His mother was proving the hardest to break of the habit.

As for "miracle boy"—forget about it. He'd come along when she'd thought she was through with having children, thus the name. She'd no doubt call him that on her deathbed.

Mom dying . . . he brushed the thought away. He couldn't imagine it. He expected her and Dad to live forever.

He had her brown hair and brown eyes, and her love of music, although their tastes were nothing alike. She listened to the same Broadway albums over and over—*South Pacific* was playing now—while Jack was firmly into rock. His current faves were Michael Jackson's "Beat It" and the eerie "Synchronicity" off the new Police album.

She used to be thin but now complained about putting on weight these past couple of years. He'd heard her blame it on "the changes."

"Okay, yes," she said smiling at him. "*Jack*. I'm trying, honey, but old habits are hard to break, you know."

"Just think: Whenever you're about to say 'Jackie,' cut it in half."

She laughed. "I'll try, I'll try."

She turned on the dishwasher and headed for the living room to read. She loved novels and belonged to both the Literary Guild and the Book-of-the-Month Club. He'd noticed she was reading something called *Master of the Game* by Sidney Sheldon.

Jack had the kitchen with its dark cabinets, Formica counters, and Congoleum floor to himself. The house had started as a three-bedroom ranch and probably would have remained so if not for Jack. Not so many years after his arrival, his folks had added dormers and finished off the attic into a master bedroom suite. They moved upstairs, leaving the downstairs bedrooms to the kids.

He retrieved a bag of pink pistachios from a cabinet and sat down at the kitchen counter to shell them. Rather than eating one at a time, he liked to collect a pile of twenty or so and gobble them all at once. As he shelled, he thought about dinner, just recently finished.

The hot topic of conversation around the table had been—no surprise—the body. Tons of speculation on who it was, how old it was, whether it was an ancient Lenape Indian mummy or the victim of a mob hit transported down here from New York in a trunk and buried where they thought it would never be found. Or that maybe it was Marcie Kurek, the sophomore who'd disappeared from SBC Regional last year and never been heard from since. That idea had silenced the table.

Otherwise it had been kind of fun listening to all the theories. One of those increasingly rare family dinners when everybody was present. What with Tom back and forth to Seton Hall law school and Kate getting ready to start med school at UMDNJ in Stratford, that hardly ever happened anymore. Most nights lately it had been just Mom, Dad, and Jack.

Of course the event wouldn't have been complete without the inevitable lecture from Dad about the dangers of kids wandering through the Pine Barrens without adults. Jack had listened patiently, trying to look interested, but he'd heard it so many times he could recite it by heart. Dad was a good guy, but he just didn't get it.

Yeah, the Barrens had its dangers. Some of the Pineys were what they called inbreds—what his brother Tom liked to call "the result of brothers and sisters getting too frisky with each other"—and maybe a little unpredictable. And you could come upon a copperhead or timber rattler, or lose some toes to a snapping turtle if you dangled a bare foot in the wrong pond. But you learned to keep your eyes open . . . you became Pine-wise.

Old Man Foster might have a deed that said he owned a whole lot of acres and the state conservation agency might pass all sorts of regulations, but as far as Jack was concerned, the Pine Barrens were an extension of his backyard, and no one was keeping him out of his own backyard.

Kate came in then. Slim with pale blue eyes, a faint splash of freckles across her cheeks and nose, and a strong jawline. Her long blond hair, which she worked at keeping straight, had gone wavy in the humidity. Jack warmed at the sight of her. Eight years older and a natural nurturer, she'd practically raised him. She'd been his best friend growing up and had broken his heart when she left for college. Last year, when she'd spent her junior year abroad in France, had been the worst. He didn't know what went on over there, but it had changed her. Nothing he could put his finger on, but no denying the feeling that she'd come back just a tiny bit . . . different.

"Just got off the phone with Tim," she said.

Tom came in behind her, smirking. "Rekindling the old flame?"

He was ten years older with a bulging middle; his brown eyes and brown hair were the exact same shade as Jack's. They'd never got along well. Though Tom had never said it, Jack knew he saw him as a fifth wheel on the family car.

Kate gave Tom a tolerant smile. "Not likely. He's engaged. But he gave me what information he could on the body."

Jack was all ears. He licked his fingertips, red from opening the pistachios. He had seventeen of the little nuts piled before him—three more to go before gobbling time.

"Do they know who it is?"

She shook her head. "Not yet. They think it's maybe two years old."

"Aaaaw," Jack said as he popped open another shell. "There goes the Indian mummy idea."

Kate smiled. "Afraid so." Her smile faded as she glanced at Tom. "Tim says it was a murder."

Jack froze, feeling creeped out. The three of them stood silent around the counter. Even big-mouth Tom seemed to have lost his voice.

Finally Jack regained his. "R-really?"

She nodded. "Yeah, his skull is cracked. But more than that, he says it was some sort of ritual killing."

Jack's mouth felt a little dry. A ritual murder . . . images of an Aztec priest cutting out a still-beating heart flashed through his head. Definitely gross . . . but kind of cool.

"Did he say what *kind* of ritual?"

Kate shook her head. "I asked, but he said that's all he's heard."

Tom gave a low whistle and grinned at Jack. "And to think, this heinous crime would have remained undiscovered, maybe forever, if not for our own miracle boy."

Jack was about to say something when Dad popped his head through the door. He looked excited.

"Hey, kids. Come here. You've got to see this."

Jack left his pistachios behind as the three of them trooped into Dad's study. They found him seated before his brand-new home computer. It looked like little more than a beige electric typewriter with a couple of oblong boxes atop it, crowned with a six-inch black-and-white monitor. On the table next to it lay copies of a magazine called *inCider*.

Years ago Dad had built an Apple I from a kit, but it never worked right. This one he'd bought fully assembled. Unlike the Apple I, which used tape cassettes to store programs, this baby used things called disk drives.

Generally pretty quiet, Dad seemed fired up. He worked as a CPA, recently moving from Arthur Anderson in Philly—for some reason, he hadn't been getting along with them—to Price Waterhouse in Cherry Hill, which meant a shorter commute. His two loves, outside of his family, were tennis and this contraption, his Apple. Unlike Jack, Tom, and Mom, his eyes were blue, and he wore steel-rimmed glasses for reading. His formerly full head of hair had begun to thin on top.

"I just wrote this little program," he said, pointing to the screen. "Watch."

Jack caught a glimpse of a short column of text with lines like "N=N+1" and "Print N" and "GOTO" before Dad hit a key. Suddenly numbers began cascading down the left side of the screen:

1

2

3

4 . . .

And on and on, progressing from one-digit, to two-digit, and eventually three-digit numbers.

"Neat!" Jack said. "When will it stop?"

"Never—unless I tell it to."

"You mean it'll count to infinity?"

"If I let it."

"That's great, Dad," Tom said, his voice dripping sarcasm. "But what's it good for?"

"Nothing. I'm teaching myself BASIC, and this is a demonstration of a program called an infinite loop." He patted his Apple. "Here's the future, kids. I've got forty-eight K of RAM—could have gotten sixty-four, but I can't imagine ever needing *that* much memory."

Jack had some idea of what he was talking about—he'd been helping Steve Brussard build a Heathkit H-89 computer—but he had a lot to learn.

As Tom, Kate, and Jack returned to the kitchen, Tom whispered, "The future of *what*? Maybe if you're a math geek, but for us normal folks?" He shook his head. "Dad's gone off the deep end."

"Oh, yeah," Kate said. "Like you'd know a thing about it."

"Remember when he said Betamax would last and VHS would fade away? This is the same thing—a dead end."

The crossing topics of computers and VCRs brought to mind the tape Jack had rented last month: *Tron*. Much of the film took place inside a computer. The story was kind of boring but cool to watch.

"I think it's neat," he said.

Tom pointed to Jack. "Hear that? Miracle boy thinks it's neat. I guess I'll have to revise my opinion."

Then, with one swift motion, Tom swept Jack's shelled pistachios off the counter and popped them into his mouth.

"Hey!"

"What?" Tom said, chewing. "Were those yours?"

"You know they were!"

Jack raised a fist and started toward him—Tom was bigger but Jack didn't care. Anger had taken control.

Kate stepped between them. "That was pretty lame."

"What? They were just lying there." He grinned at Jack over Kate's shoulder. "Want 'em back?"

Jack started for him again, but Kate held him back. He could have pushed her aside but no way he'd do that to Kate.

As Tom sauntered out, Jack said, "Bastard."

"Don't let Mom hear that," Kate said.

"Well, he is."

"Immature is more like it." She ruffled Jack's hair. "You rocked his world when you were born. He was cock of the walk around here for ten years, and then Mom's 'miracle boy' arrived. I don't think he's ever gotten over it. A bad case of arrested development."

"How about you?"

She laughed. "Are you kidding? You were a baby, a real, live baby. Suddenly I didn't have to play make-believe with dolls anymore, I had the real thing to care for. I was in heaven." She hugged him. "I thought you were the best thing that ever happened to me. I still do, Jackie."

"Jack, Kate. *Jack.*"

6

Jack lay in bed reading a copy of *The Spider*, a 1939 magazine with yellowed, flaking pages. Mr. Rosen at USED, where Jack worked part-time, had stacks of old magazines and let Jack take home a couple at a time to read—"As long as you return them in the condition you received them."

Jack had already read the half-dozen copies of *The Shadow* in the stacks. Lately he'd moved on to *The Spider—Master of Men!*, obviously a Shadow rip-off, copying the slouch hat and the billowing black cape, but a different kind of guy. Jack had thought the Shadow was cool, but the Spider was even cooler. The Shadow fought mostly regular crooks while the Spider dealt with threats to the world. Like this issue: "King of the Fleshless Legion," with all sorts of skeletons on the cover and the Spider rushing in to save a woman locked alive in a coffin.

Neat.

He wished he could buy posters of these covers. Some of the posters he had now—especially the one of Devo in their flowerpot hats—were getting ratty. Besides, he hardly listened to Devo anymore. He certainly wasn't going to replace his Phillies pennant, not when they looked like they had a shot at the World Series this year.

His beloved Eagles, however . . .

After that stupid football players' strike last season they went a whopping three and six. Wasn't easy being an

Eagles' fan these days. Maybe with Vermeil out and that new coach—

He jumped as he heard a single knock on his door. He looked up and saw his father enter.

"How's it going, Jack?"

"Fine."

He sat on the edge of the bed. "You sure? Finding that . . . body today isn't bothering you?"

Jack realized this was a side Dad didn't show much. He tended to be the stiff-upper-lip sort: If you fall down you pick yourself up and keep going without whining or complaining.

"Really, I'm fine."

In fact, what the bad guys were doing to the Spider and what he was giving right back to them had pretty much wiped the body from his mind.

"You going to be able to sleep okay?"

"Think so. I'm not scared, if that's what you mean. It was gross, but I won't be dreaming about him coming for me or anything like that."

At least he didn't think so. He figured if anything kept him awake it would be questions about who was dead and who had done it and why he was killed and what sort of ritual was used. The last time he'd been too scared to sleep had been a couple of years ago, right after reading *'Salem's Lot*—afraid to look at his window for fear he'd see Eddie floating outside it.

Dad patted Jack's leg. "Good. But if you have any problems during the night, don't be afraid to give a holler." His gaze drifted to the magazine. "Good God, where'd you get that?"

Jack handed it to him. "Mister Rosen's got a bunch."

Dad stared at the cover, a smile hovering about his lips. "I used to read these as a kid."

Jack did a quick calculation: They'd celebrated Dad's fifty-third birthday last month, which meant he'd been born in 1930. So he would have been nine when this issue was printed. Nine might have been kind of young, but yeah, he could have read this very copy. Jack knew his father had been a kid once, but this made his child-hood . . . *real*. He suddenly saw Dad in a new light.

"Did you like them?"

"You kidding? Doc Savage, the Shadow, and this guy . . . I loved them." He flipped through the yellowed pages. "Can I borrow this?"

Jack was only halfway through the story and didn't want to give it up. He reached into his nightstand drawer and pulled out another issue he'd already finished.

"How about this one?"

Dad grinned at the cover: High atop the George Washington Bridge, the Spider battled with a guy in some sort of diving suit over a girl in a shredded red dress.

" 'Slaves of the Laughing Death.' I love it." He rose and slapped Jack on the leg. "Thanks. This'll bring back old memories. And I think you'll be just fine tonight."

Jack thought so too. But he was concerned about the magazine. Mr. Rosen would have his hide if it came back damaged.

"Just return it in the condition you got it."

1

"No matter what I do, I can't get it open."

Jack could sense Weezy's frustration. It filled her bedroom like a storm cloud.

He and Eddie knelt on the floor with the black cube from the mound between them. Weezy sat on the edge of her bed, rubbing her hands together. Jack had told them about the ritual murder story from the sheriff's office. Usually that kind of thing would grab Weezy's attention like one of those leg-hold traps they'd seen yesterday, but she seemed completely focused on the cube.

The Cure's *Pornography* was running in her eight-track player and, as usual, the whiny voice was grating on Jack's nerves.

"Can't you play something else?"

Her smile had no humor in it. "You'd like Siouxsie and the Banshees better? Or how about Bauhaus?" Her taste in music matched her taste in clothes and posters.

He found the black-and-white Bauhaus poster of some shirtless guy hanging by his hands a little too weird. Give Jack the Spider plugging hot lead into mad villains any day.

Jack winked at Eddie. "I know she's got *Flashdance* hidden around here somewhere."

Eddie picked up right away. "She must. I've heard it through the wall." He began to sing. Badly. " 'She's a maniac, maaaaaniac—' "

Weezy tossed a pillow at him. "You *lie*! And what have you been told about that?"

Eddie looked puzzled. "What?" Then a light seemed to go on. "Oh, hey, I wasn't thinking."

Weezy only glared at him.

Jack didn't know what was going on between these two, but doubted it had anything to do with *Flashdance*. He tried to bring the talk back to music.

"Bauhaus, then," he said. "Anything but this."

As she popped out the Cure cassette—thank you, God—he picked up the cube and turned it over in his hands.

"Can't open it, eh? What've you tried?"

Eddie said, "Anything toolacious. Knife, fork, screwdriver, razor blade, chisel—you name it. Even a hammer. I'm ready to get my dad's electric drill."

"Really?" The glossy black surface looked unmarred. "How come it's not all scratched up?"

"Because it doesn't scratch," Weezy said, returning to the edge of her bed. "No matter what we do to it."

"Bela Lugosi's Dead" began to play. Jack kind of liked this song.

"Maybe it doesn't open. Maybe it's just a solid cube of—what did you call it yesterday?"

"Onyx."

"What's onyx?" Eddie said.

"A kind of black stone."

Eddie snorted. "Black, huh? Figures you'd know about it."

Weezy gave him a gentle kick. But Eddie had a point. Weezy was into dark—dark clothes, dark music, dark books. She even kept her shades drawn to make her room dark. The bright morning sun outside had been locked out. At least she didn't have black sheets, although her bedspread was dark purple. Half a dozen gargoyles peered down at them from her shelves.

"It's not solid," she said. "Give it a shake."

Jack did just that—and felt something shift within. Not much. Just the slightest bit, but enough to tell it was hollow.

For no particular reason, he dug his thumbnails into the faint groove along one of the edges and—

The sides of the cube fell open and it tumbled to the floor where it flattened out in a crosslike configuration.

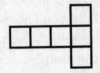

But what captured and held his attention in an icy grip was the black pyramid inside—but not like any pyramid Jack had ever seen.

Weezy was off the bed and on the thing like a cat on a mouse. She grabbed it and held it up, turning it over and over.

"I knew it—I *knew* it!" Then she looked at Jack, frowning. "How'd you get it open?"

He shrugged. "I just—"

"Doesn't matter. What's important is it's *open*."

But it mattered to Jack. He hadn't done anything special, just edged his thumbnails into the—

"Some kind of pyramid," Eddie said. "Maybe it's Egyptian."

"No, the Egyptian pyramids are four-sided. This has six. And it's engraved with these weird-looking symbols."

"Let's have a look," Jack said. When Weezy hesitated, he added, "What? Afraid I'll steal it?"

She flashed a nervous smile as she handed it over. "Don't be silly."

But Jack could tell she didn't want to let it go.

The pyramid felt cold against his skin, and Weezy was right: The symbols, a different one carved into each face, were kind of weird. Not exactly hieroglyphics, but not like any letters he'd ever seen either. He upended it and checked the base. Yep. Another symbol there too.

"Maybe there's something in this as well. Maybe it's like one of those Russian dolls, you know—"

"Matryoshka," Weezy said. "A nesting doll."

How did she *know* this stuff?

Jack searched the surface for a seam but came up empty.

"Looks like this is it."

"Check this out," Eddie said, pointing to the flattened box. "There's something carved on this too."

Jack looked and saw what he meant. Some sort of grid had been carved inside the crosspiece of the T.

Eddie echoed Jack's sentiments when he said, "What's all this mean?"

Jack looked at Weezy, who had retrieved the pyramid and was studying it like a jeweler grading a diamond. All she needed was that little magnifying eyepiece. What was it called? A loupe. Right.

"Ever see anything like this in any of your secret

histories?" He waved at her sagging bookshelf. "One of those books *has* to—"

She was shaking her head. "Nothing like this at all. Trust me. I know those books by heart."

"Then we've got to ask somebody."

"No-no-no!" She clutched the pyramid to her chest. "They'll say it's evidence and take it from us."

"We don't have to mention it's got anything to do with the body. We'll just say we found it somewhere in the Pines and leave it at that."

"Okaaaay," she said slowly. "Let's say we do that. Who can we show it to?"

A name popped into Jack's mind immediately. "Mister Rosen."

Weezy made a face. "He's just a junk dealer."

"Yeah, but it's *old* junk. He knows *everything* about old stuff. You even got some of your weirdo books from him, didn't you?"

"Yeah, but—"

"No buts. If he can't help us, he'll know someone who can."

"Okay. But first . . ."

She jumped up and hurried from the room, taking the pyramid with her.

"Hey, look," said Eddie, holding up a reassembled black cube. "I got her back together. The sides just clicked into place. Simplacious." He started prying at the edges. "But I can't seem to get her open again."

Jack showed him where to position his thumbnails but, try as he might, Eddie couldn't get it open.

"Here. Let me have that."

He took the cube, positioned his thumbnails the way he'd shown Eddie, and pried.

The box popped open.

"How do you *do* that?" Eddie said.

Jack had no idea.

2

Weezy returned carrying the family Polaroid camera.

"Before we do anything, I'm getting some photos."

She set the pyramid on her desk, knelt before it, and snapped a picture from about two feet away. The flash lit the room.

Probably more light than this room's seen in a long time, Jack thought.

The camera whirred and spit out the photo. As expected, it came out blank. Weezy put it aside to let it develop as she rotated the pyramid and—*flash, whir*—photographed the other side. Then she turned to Jack.

"Lay that on the floor, okay?" she said, pointing to the unfolded box in his hand.

He did, then watched as she snapped another picture.

"Okay," she said, stepping back to her desk. She picked up the first photo and frowned. "Damn."

Jack stepped closer and peered over her shoulder. "What's wrong?"

"I was too close."

Jack wasn't so sure. "Maybe. But funny how that pen lying right next to it is in perfect focus."

Weezy picked up the second photo: Same thing. And then the one of the unfolded box, where she hadn't been close at all. The box pieces were blurred but the rug around it was in perfect focus.

"All blurred."

Eddie came over and took a look.

"I don't know about you guys," he said, "but that's creepitacious."

Jack agreed, but didn't say so. There had to be an explanation.

"Let's try this," he said, grabbing the pyramid and stepping back. He held it waist-high before him. "Take a shot of me holding it."

Weezy did just that. The three of them clustered and watched as the image slowly took shape. There stood Jack, his head cut off by the top of the photo frame. The Phillies logo on his T-shirt was perfectly legible, but resting in his hand was a . . .

Blur.

He felt a chill run over his skin.

Beside him, Eddie said, "I don't like this. I don't like this one bit."

Jack couldn't have agreed more.

But Weezy . . . she looked like she'd just found the Holy Grail. Her eyes shone as she clutched the photo and stared at it.

"We've found one!" she whispered.

"One what?"

"A secret . . . a secret object."

Eddie groaned. "Your Secret History of the World again?"

She turned on him. "You like to make fun of me and that's okay. Why should you be different from anybody else? But there *is* a secret history. We think we know what's happened in the past but we don't. Most history books don't even get the *events* right, and they haven't a *clue* as to what was going on *behind* those events."

Eddie snorted. "Oh, and you do?"

"I wish I did. But I know *something's* been going on. Secret societies and mysterious forces are out there pulling strings and manipulating people and events and everyone wants to believe they're in charge of their lives but they're not because we're all being pushed this way and that for secret reasons and we don't even know it."

She was talking a hundred miles an hour, like she'd had a box of Cocoa Puffs and a couple of quarts of Mountain Dew for breakfast. She took a breath and continued.

"There's too many coincidences out there. Something's going on—*has* been going on throughout human history. And this—" She held up the pyramid. "We weren't supposed to find this. We're not supposed to have it. Because it's proof that not everything is as it seems. I mean, why can't we photograph it? Answer me that."

Eddie shrugged. He looked a little cowed by Weezy's outburst. "I dunno. Maybe the camera's broken."

Weezy tilted back her head and screeched at the ceiling. "Just because you can't see something doesn't mean it's not there. Look at those pictures! It's staring you in the face but you don't see it because you don't *want* to see what you can't explain because it will upset yours and everybody else's comfortable little worldview that we're in control. Well, we *aren't*!"

She stopped, breathing hard. Eddie didn't speak. Neither did Jack. He'd never seen Weezy like this. Sure, she got hyper at times and had all sorts of strange theories about everything from the Kennedy assassination to Charles Manson, but this was kind of scary. Someone had pushed her hyperdrive button.

She turned to him. "What about you, Jack? What do you say?" She held up the pyramid. "Something wrong with the camera or something wrong with this?"

He remembered how clearly he could read his T-shirt in the last photo, yet how blurred the pyramid was, even though he'd been holding it against his chest.

"The pyramid." He quickly held up his hand to cut off another speech. "I'm not saying it has anything to do with secret histories—could be it's made of something that does tricks with light—but I don't think it's the camera."

She sighed and fixed him with her big dark eyes. "Thank you, Jack. That means a lot."

Even though he'd witnessed her mood changes before, her sudden calm jarred him. She'd dropped from pedal-to-the-metal to cruising speed in the blink of an eye.

"I want to know what it is," he said.

She nodded. "I've *got* to know what it is."

"Well, we won't find out sitting here."

"Right," she said, her voice barely audible. "Let's go see Mister Rosen."

3

Eddie had decided that defending the Earth in *Missile Command* would be more interesting than listening to whatever Mr. Rosen might have to say. He talked of beating the world-champion score of eighty million points. Fat chance.

Jack and Weezy could have walked but figured bikes were faster. Neither wanted to wait any longer than necessary. Jack led the way as they pedaled west, the morning sun warm on their backs.

Funny, he thought as they rode, how he'd lead the way around town, but Weezy tended to take the point whenever they entered the Barrens. Almost as if something in Jack knew the Barrens were her turf and made him take a step back when the pines closed in.

As they headed for downtown, Jack noticed people in passing cars slowing to stare and point at them.

Those are the kids who found the body.

Calling it "downtown" was kind of a local joke. It consisted of eight stores clustered around the traffic signal at the intersection of Quakerton Road and Route 206, a rutted, patched stretch of two-lane blacktop running from Trenton to the Atlantic City Expressway. Johnson didn't rate a full traffic light, just a blinker.

As Jack had heard it, Quakerton was the town's name until 1868, when President Andrew Johnson, maybe trying to get away from the impeachment proceedings in Washington, spent three nights in the town's one and only inn, now long gone. Seemed no one had liked the name Quakerton—after all, not a single Quaker had ever lived there—so they changed the name to Johnsonville. By 1900 it had been shortened to Johnson.

The traffic-light cluster consisted of a Krauszer's convenience store, a used-car lot, and Joe Burdett's Esso station—the company had changed its name to Exxon better than ten years ago, but old Joe had never changed the sign. Back east along Quakerton sat Spurlin's Hardware, Hunningshake's pharmacy, gift, and sweet shoppe, the VFW post, and Mr. Rosen's place, USED. The sign used to say USED GOODS, but the nor'easter of 1962 ripped off the right side and Mr. Rosen never replaced it.

The store had two large display windows on either side of the front door. Mr. Rosen had told Jack they'd been peopled with naked mannequins when he'd bought it back in the 1950s from a wedding shop that had gone out of business. Now they were full of what some people called junk but Jack had come to see as treasures from the past. USED was his personal time machine.

A bell atop the screen door tinkled as they entered. One step inside and the odors hit him—old wood, old cushioned furniture, old paper, a little dry rot, a little rust, and a lot of dust. He loved the smell of this place.

"Mister Rosen?" he called. "Mister Rosen?"

A painfully thin, elderly man with a stooped posture, pale skin, and gray hair wandered into view from the rear.

"All right, already," he said with a thick accent that sometimes sounded German and sometimes didn't. "I'm coming, I'm—" He stopped when he saw Jack. "Well, if it isn't the Finder of Corpses."

"You've heard?"

"Heard? Who hasn't? Probably all over town before you got home." He studied Jack. "You okay? You want the day off maybe?"

"No, I'm fine."

"Good. They know who it is yet?"

"Not that I've heard."

The old man glanced at the gold-and-glass Jefferson mystery clock on a nearby shelf. "At noon you're due."

"I know." Jack stepped up to the counter and motioned Weezy forward. "But we've got something we'd like you to see."

Mr. Rosen slipped on a pair of glasses as he moved behind the counter. "Something maybe to sell?"

"No way," Weezy blurted. "I mean, we'd just like your expert opinion."

"Expert, shmexpert, I'll tell you what I know."

Before leaving Weezy's they'd reassembled the cube with the pyramid inside. Now she unfolded the bath towel she'd wrapped it in for transport, and placed the cube on the counter.

Mr. Rosen adjusted his glasses for a closer look. "You bring me a box, a black box, and want to know what it is? In my expert opinion, it's a black box. Anything inside?"

"Oh, yeah," she said. "That's what we really want to know about." She stepped aside. "But it'll open only for Jack."

Jack didn't understand why Weezy and Eddie couldn't do it. He'd shown them, they'd followed his directions perfectly, yet it refused to open for anyone but him.

Which only increased the thing's creep factor.

He did his thing to make it pop open, and then the three of them stood there at the counter, staring.

Finally Mr. Rosen reached for the pyramid. "May I?"

"Sure," Jack said as Weezy gave a barely perceptible nod.

Mr. Rosen lifted it, but instead of examining it he set it aside and picked up the unfolded cube. He wiggled it in the air and watched as the six panels flapped back and forth.

"Fascinating," he said.

Jack was baffled. "Why?"

"No hinges. The squares appear to be made of thin sheets of some sort of material I've never seen. That's strange enough, but they move back and forth without any sort of hinge. Just . . . creases. Odd. Very, very odd."

"Tell me about it," Jack said.

Mr. Rosen looked at them. "This I'd be willing to buy."

Weezy gave her head an emphatic shake. "Uh-uh. It's not for sale. Sorry."

Mr. Rosen nodded as he put it down and picked up the pyramid. He turned it over and over in his hands, making little humming and grunting noises as he held it up to the light and checked it with a magnifying glass. His sleeve slipped back revealing a string of numbers tattooed on his forearm. Jack had seen them before but had hesitated to ask about them.

"Let me tell you, I've seen many strange objects in my day—you wouldn't believe the things people bring in to try to sell me—but the likes of this I've never seen. I couldn't even guess what it is."

"Oh," Weezy said, her voice thick with frustration.

Jack hid his own disappointment. "Too bad." Mr. Rosen

had seemed to know a little bit about everything. "We were hoping—"

"But I know someone who might be able to help you."

"Who?"

Jack half expected him to say, *The Great and Powerful Oz!* But instead . . .

"Professor Nakamura. He's a maven of anthropology at the University of Pennsylvania."

Weezy looked at Jack. "U of P? How are we going to get to Philadelphia?"

"You don't have to. He lives right here in town."

Jack frowned. He thought he knew pretty much everyone in Johnson. "Never heard of him."

"Moved in about a year ago. Keeps to himself, I think, but he's been in here a few times. Interesting fellow. His grandfather ran a laundry in San Francisco but was driven out in the twenties by the Jap haters—all fired up by William Randolph Hearst who hated Jews as well—and fled back to Japan. Now his grandson has returned as an Ivy League professor. For all we know he might be teaching the great-grandchildren of the bigots who drove his ancestors out. What sweet irony that would be."

Jack didn't remember any Oriental customers.

"Have I—?"

Mr. Rosen shook his head. "Hasn't been in since you started. Collects Carnival Glass, of all things."

"What's Carnival Glass?"

"Iridescent kitsch is what it is. But he loves it. Bought every piece I had last spring."

That explained why Jack had never seen any—he hadn't started here until late June.

Mr. Rosen was fishing under the counter. "He left his number to call as soon as any new items came in." Finally he came up with a card. "Here it is. Let me give it a try. I got the impression his schedule at the university isn't too heavy, so who knows? You may get lucky."

4

They didn't. Professor Nakamura wasn't home but Mr. Rosen left a message to call him back. Jack and Weezy headed back to her place. He didn't have long before he was due at work.

"What do we do now?" he said as they coasted along Quakerton Road.

"Wait and see if this Professor Nakamura can help us, I guess."

"And if he can't?"

Weezy shrugged. "I don't know. Don't you wish the TV had a channel where you could, say, ask a question and it would search every library in the world and pop the answer onto the screen? Wouldn't that be great?"

"Yeah." Then he thought about it a little more. "Or maybe not so great. You'd have to make TVs two-way before that could happen. I mean, it's just one-way now—we can watch it and that's that. But if it became two-way . . . it might start watching us."

Weezy looked at him and smiled, something she didn't do often enough. "And you call *me* paranoid?"

"Hey, less than five months till Big Brother starts watching."

Nineteen Eighty-Four was on his high school summer reading list and he'd found it majorly disturbing.

"Yeah, but—" She braked and pointed. "Aw, no!"

Jack looked and saw two guys pushing around a third

near the rickety one-lane bridge over Quaker Lake. The pushers were Teddy Bishop and a blond guy Jack didn't recognize. Teddy, with long greasy hair and a blubbery body, was sort of the town bully. His father was a lawyer and that seemed to make Teddy feel he could get away with anything.

The beard and olive-drab fatigue jacket on the guy getting pushed around identified him as the town's only Vietnam vet, Walter Erskine—or, as he was more commonly known, Weird Walt. It looked like Teddy and his friend were trying to grab the brown paper grocery bag Walt had clutched against his chest.

Before Jack knew it, Weezy was pedaling toward the scene, yelling, "Hey! Stop that!"

Jack wasn't surprised. Though young enough to be his daughter, Weezy had a thing for Walt. If she met him on the street she'd walk with him; sometimes they'd sit on one of the benches down by the lake and talk—about what, Jack had no idea.

No use trying to stop her, so he followed. Couldn't let her face those two creeps alone. He watched her jump off her bike and quickly set the kickstand—Walt or no Walt, she wasn't going to let that cube fall. Then she ran over, stepped in front of Teddy, and pushed him back. Not that she had much effect. Teddy was an ox. But Weezy was fearless.

"Leave him alone!"

"Yeah, lay off!" Walt said, raising a gloved hand. He *always* wore gloves.

Walt had a hippieish look with a gray-streaked beard and long, dark hair. His voice sounded a little slurred. No surprise there. Jack didn't know of anyone who'd ever seen him completely sober.

Teddy laughed. "Look at this! Weird Weezy and Weird Walt together. How about that?"

Jack lay his bike on the grass and looked around. Last time Mom had taken him for a checkup he'd been five-five and one-hundred-two pounds. Teddy had two years, two inches, and maybe fifty lardy pounds over him. He'd need an equalizer. He looked for a weapon, a rock, maybe, but found nothing.

Swell.

He approached the group empty-handed.

"What do you *want* with him?" Weezy was saying. "He's not bothering you!"

"We just think he should share some of his hooch. We ain't greedy. We don't want it all, just a little. So get outta the way."

Teddy's friend's hands moved toward Weezy, as if to shove her aside.

"Don't touch her!" Jack shouted.

Teddy spun, looked surprised, then grinned. Jack saw now that he was wearing a Black Sabbath T-shirt.

"Well, look who it is. What is it with you two—you find a dead body and suddenly you're Guardians of the Universe?"

"Just let her take him home."

Teddy, his expression menacing, took a step closer. "And if I don't?"

Jack felt his heart racing, but with more anger than fear. And the anger was growing, quickly overtaking the fear, blotting it out.

"You lay one finger on her and I will kill you."

The cold way the words came out startled Jack. He sounded like he meant it. And at the moment, he did.

Teddy stopped and stared, then smiled. Jack wondered at that smile until he felt a pair of arms wrap around him, pinning his arms at his sides.

"Gotcha, squirt!" said Teddy's friend.

Jack had been so intent on Teddy and Weezy he'd forgotten the friend.

Teddy's grin widened as he cocked a fist back to his ear. "Let's see who's gonna kill who."

Jack lowered his head as he struggled wildly to get free. This was going to hurt. He heard Weezy scream, quickly followed by a cry of pain from Teddy, and another from the guy holding him. Suddenly he was free. He leaped to the side, raising his fist, ready to swing, but stopped.

Teddy and his friend were cowering and rubbing their heads. Between them stood a heavyset old woman brandishing a silver-headed cane. She wore a long black dress that reached the sidewalk and had a black scarf wrapped around her neck. Like Walt's gloves, she wore that scarf no matter what the weather. Beside her stood a three-legged dog.

Mrs. Elizabeth Clevenger.

But where had she come from? Jack was sure she hadn't been in sight when he'd come over here. How—?

"Damn you!" Teddy shouted.

He took a step toward her but stopped when the dog bared its teeth and growled. A thick-bodied, big-jawed, floppy-eared mutt—Jack thought he detected some Lab and some rottweiler along with miscellaneous other breeds—it seemed all muscle under its short, mud-brown coat. He'd seen it lots of times; the missing leg didn't slow it down at all.

"That dog bites me my dad'll sue you for every penny you've got."

"If I let him at you it won't be for a bite—he'll have you for lunch. All of you."

One look at the dog's cold eyes and big jaws and Jack believed her. So did Teddy, apparently, because he backed off.

Jack felt his heartbeat slowing but his hands felt cold, sweaty, shaky. He'd been awful close to getting his face rearranged. Too close.

"Bitch!" Teddy said.

"Don't you dare speak to your mother like that!"

"You ain't my mother!"

"Sadly, I am. But only because I cannot pick and choose my children. Now be gone." She brandished her cane. "Off before I cast a spell on you!"

That seemed to do it. Teddy jammed his hands into his jeans pockets and started to move away.

"C'mon, Joey. Let's go," Teddy said to his friend.

"Wait," Joey said, his eyes wide with disbelief. "'Cast a spell on you'? Is she kidding?"

"Shut up, Joey. You don't know nothin'."

The two of them walked off, arguing, Teddy looking over his shoulder from time to time.

Clearly Joey wasn't from Johnson. Otherwise he'd have known that old Mrs. Clevenger was a witch.

"Are you all right, Walter?" Mrs. Clevenger said, rubbing her hand along his upper arm.

He nodded. "Yeah. They just pushed me around some. I've been through worse."

"I know," she said. "Much worse." Then she turned to Weezy. "That was a brave thing you did, child."

"Not so brave." She seemed to have trouble meeting Mrs. Clevenger's eyes. "I was scared half to death."

"The brave are always scared." She turned to Jack. "I know why she helped Walter—he's her friend. But why did you?"

Jack figured the reason was obvious. "Because she's *my* friend."

The old woman gave him a long stare, her green eyes boring into his, then nodded. "Friendship . . . there is nothing better, is there?"

"Nothing," Weezy said, beaming at Jack.

The lady said, "Walter is *my* friend. I'm going to walk him home now, but first . . ." She looked past them to Weezy's bike. "That box . . . put it back in the ground where you found it."

Jack spun and stared at Weezy's bike. Only a little bit of the towel wrapping the box was visible in the basket, nothing more.

Weezy's mouth dropped open. "H-how do you know about that?" Her brow furrowed. "Did Mister Rosen—?"

Mrs. Clevenger smiled, which added more lines to her already wrinkled face. "I know more than I should and less than I'd like to." The smile disappeared. "But hear me well. That thing is an ill wind that will blow nobody good. It was hidden from the light of day for good reason. Return it to its resting place." With that she started to turn away. "Besides, you will never get it open."

"But we did," Weezy said.

Mrs. Clevenger's turn came to an abrupt halt, then she swiveled back to fix Weezy with her stare.

"*We*? Who is *we*?"

Weezy looked flustered. "Well, not 'we,' really. Just Jack. He's the only one who can do it."

She turned her gaze on him. "Not such a surprise, I suppose. But that does not change anything. Put it back where it belongs."

Jack wanted to ask her why that wasn't a surprise but she'd turned away again. She took Walter's arm and the two of them began walking, her dog close behind. Jack heard bottles clinking in Walter's paper bag.

"Now, Walter," Jack heard her say, "you're overdoing the drinking. You must learn to pace yourself, otherwise you won't survive to complete your mission."

Walter shook his shaggy head. "Not surviving . . . that doesn't sound so bad. I hate this . . ." He glanced back at Jack. "Do you think he might be the one?"

"I can understand why you might feel that way. But no, he's not the one you seek . . ."

And then their voices faded.

What were they talking about? Why was Walt seeking someone, and why could Mrs. Clevenger understand why he might think Jack was the one? Jack wanted to trail after them and hear more, then realized that they were both sort of crazy. He couldn't expect to make sense out of a conversation between those two.

Weezy too was watching them go, but she had her own questions.

"How could she know about the box?"

Jack shrugged. "And where did she come from? Did you see?"

Weezy shook her head. "No. All of a sudden she was there, swinging her cane."

Jack looked at the Old Town bridge that spanned the narrow midsection of the figure-eight-shaped lake. On the far side of that creaky one-lane span lay the easternmost end of Johnson, where it backed up to the Pine Barrens. The area included the six square blocks of the original Quakerton settlement, called Old Town for as long as anyone could remember. Nobody knew for sure when it had first been settled. Most said before the revolutionary war—*long* before the war.

Mrs. Clevenger lived in Old Town. She must have come from there.

Jack reconstructed the chain of events: Johnson didn't have a liquor store, so Walt must have been stocking up in Old Town. Some of the Pineys had stills, but instead of using corn they made their moonshine from apples. Every Wednesday and Saturday one or two of them would come in from the woods; they'd park their pickups at the end of Quakerton Road where it dead-ended at the edge of the Pines and sell their applejack. They transported it in big jugs and customers had to bring their own bottle—or in Walt's case, bottles—to be filled.

Nearly everybody in Johnson had at least one bottle of applejack in the house, and it was an ongoing argument as to who made the best—Gus Sooy or Lester Appleton.

Walt must have gone over to get his bottles filled and run into Teddy and Joey on the way back. Mrs. Clevenger must have been close behind him.

Well, wherever she came from, Jack was glad she'd arrived when she did.

He looked back and saw the pair turning the corner onto the block where Walt lived with his sister and brother-in-law.

"There goes an odd couple," he said.

Weezy nodded. "Way odder than Oscar and Felix. She wears that same scarf day in and day out, and he wears gloves no matter how hot it gets."

"You believe she's a witch?" Jack said as they headed back to their bikes, and immediately realized Weezy was probably the wrong person to ask.

"Could be. She's hard to explain. I mean, how did she know about the box?"

Remembering that caused a trickle of uneasiness to go down Jack's spine.

"I don't know, but should we follow her advice?"

Weezy looked at him as if he'd suddenly grown a second nose and a third eye. "Are you kidding me? Go back and bury it? No way! Even if she *is* a witch."

Obviously he'd struck a nerve. No surprise, though.

"Well, I don't believe in witches, but did you hear her threaten Teddy with a spell?"

"So? I can threaten *you* with a spell, Jack. Doesn't mean I can cast one."

"Yeah, well, maybe she just pretends to be a witch. She's already got the Clevenger name. Maybe letting the more superstitious folks around here think she's the Witch of the Pines come back from the dead works for her somehow."

She and her dog had moved into Old Town a dozen or so years ago. Her mysterious ways—disappearing for months at a time and then suddenly around every day, wandering through the Pines at night—had started some folks whispering that she was really Peggy Clevenger, the famous Witch of the Pines. But how could that be? Everybody knew how the real Peggy Clevenger's decapitated body had been found in her burned-out cabin back in the 1800s.

Weezy shrugged. "Could be." She gave Jack a sidelong look. "You know they say Peggy's body wanders the Barrens at night looking for her head. But I'm just wondering . . ."

"Wondering what?"

"What if she found it and put it back on?"

Jack laughed. "Come on! Even you don't believe that."

"Maybe I do, maybe I don't. But how do you explain Mrs. Clevenger's ever-present scarf? Why would she wear it on a hot day like this?" Weezy dropped into her *ooh-spooky* voice. "Unless she's hiding the seam where she reattached her head."

Jack picked up his bike and waited for Weezy to knock back her kickstand.

"You gotta be kidding me."

She looked at him with those big, dark, black-rimmed

eyes. "Okay, fine. Your turn then: Give me another explanation for the scarf."

Jack couldn't come up with one. Not for lack of trying. He really wanted another explanation. Because he didn't like Weezy's one bit.

6

Jack spent the afternoon at USED.

The best thing about the job was he hardly ever did the same thing two days in a row. One day he'd spend dusting all the antiques and just plain junk; the next he'd supply a third or fourth hand to help Mr. Rosen fix an old clock; another he'd wind all the clocks and watches—not too far—and make sure they were set to the right time. Today he was helping Mr. Rosen pretty up some antique oak furniture he'd just bought—a rolltop desk and a round table with cool lion paws at the ends of its legs.

The old man's fingers weren't as steady as he'd have liked, so he oversaw Jack as he used a stain-soaked Q-tip to darken scratches in the old wood. After the stain dried, Jack would polish the surface.

For his time and effort he was paid $3.50 an hour—not a princely sum, but fifteen cents above minimum wage. Mr. Rosen had offered him the extra if Jack would save him all the government paperwork by taking cash. Fine with Jack, because that in turn saved him the trouble of finding his birth certificate and applying for a Social Security number.

He supplemented the USED money by mowing lawns, but that was always subject to the whims of weather—not enough rain and the grass didn't grow, which meant no mowing; too much rain and the wet grass clogged the mower. He liked the reliability of the weekly cash from USED.

Not that he had much in the way of expenses. He'd go

to the movies—he planned on seeing *Return of the Jedi* for a fourth time this weekend—or rent sci-fi or horror films on videocassette. He liked to keep up with certain comics like *Cerebus* and *Ronin* and *Swamp Thing*, but he'd lost interest in most of the titles he used to love—especially ones with characters in tights. Occasionally he'd buy a record album if he liked it enough. His latest had been Prince's *1999*; he'd probably buy *Synchronicity* by the Police next.

Dad had insisted he find a part-time job that would, in his words, "allow you enough time to enjoy the summer but help you learn the value of a dollar."

Well, fine. But Jack would have found one anyway because he wasn't comfortable with an allowance—*given* money didn't feel like it was really his. But the money he earned—that belonged to him and him alone.

The phone rang and Jack hustled over to pick it up.

"USED."

"Yes, hello," said an accented voice. "This is Professor Nakamura. May I speak to Mister Rosen, please?"

He handed over the phone and listened while Mr. Rosen talked about Carnival Glass, then moved the conversation to the "artifact" he and Weezy had found.

"You say you'll be around tomorrow morning?" he said into the phone, then pointed to Jack, who nodded vigorously.

Yeah, they could make it.

"Fine. I'll send them over around ten o'clock."

Yes! Now they'd get some answers.

He hoped.

7

Jack kept a careful watch for his brother as he sat at the kitchen counter and shelled his pistachios. He had a pile of sixteen. Four to go. No sign of Tom, but he had this strange sensation of being watched. He looked around and saw no one. Was he getting paranoid?

Mom had *My Fair Lady* playing on the stereo. Of all the soundtracks, that was probably his favorite. He loved the melodies, but the lyrics were outstanding.

He was thinking about the meeting with this professor tomorrow, and about what he might say, when he knocked half a dozen unshelled pistachios off the counter. As he squatted to gather them up he saw a shadow swoop by. Before he could react, Tom had scooped up the shelled pistachios and tossed them into his mouth. Without breaking stride or even looking around, he hit the back door and was outside before Jack could get over his shock and react.

Rage blazed. He looked at the cutlery drawer and imagined himself grabbing one of the Ginsu knives his father had bought from the TV last year and chasing after Tom. But what would he do when he caught him—cut off his hands?

Nice fantasy, but . . .

Calming himself, Jack sat and stared at the spot where his pistachios had sat. How'd that expression go? *Fool me once, shame on you . . . fool me twice, shame on me.*

Yeah, he thought. Shame on me for leaving those out

there. But that didn't mean Tom wasn't due a little payback.

He was calm now, calm enough to remember another
old saying: *Revenge is a dish best served cold.*

Cold . . . he'd have to think on this.

Relax, Tom. Enjoy the moment. Rest easy that you're
home free. But your time is coming. Soon you're going to
regret messing with me.

Kate rushed into the room then, with Mom and Dad
close behind.

"Jack, they've identified the body you found!"

He held his breath.

Dad said, "Anyone we know?"

Mom's hands folded under her chin. "It's not that Kurek
girl, is it?"

"No. Dental records identified him as Anton Boruff, a
jeweler from Mount Holly who disappeared two years ago.
It'll be in the papers tomorrow." She lowered her voice.
"But what won't be in the papers is that the police have
suspected him of being a fugitive."

"Really?" Jack said. This was getting better and better.
"From the law?"

Kate nodded. "Seemed he'd been ripping people off, sell-
ing fake diamonds as investment grade. The police thought
he'd absconded with the money, but I guess one of his victims got to him before he made his getaway."

"At least he's not a local," Mom said. "I mean, it's a
shame he's dead, of course, rest his soul. Just that I was afraid
it was someone we knew. The thought of having a killer
among us . . ." She shuddered. "But if he's from Mount
Holly—"

"Well," Kate said, "he must have been in and out of here a lot because he was some sort of pooh-bah in the Lodge."

"Oh, dear," Mom said. "I've never liked those people. They're so sneaky. I wish they'd find someplace else to meet."

Everybody called it simply "the Lodge" but Jack had heard it was a branch of something called the Ancient Septimus Fraternal Order. The Lodge building had been in Old Town forever. The Order was secretive about its activities and purposes and membership. One thing everybody knew: It was *very* selective about who it accepted. Every once in a while a newcomer to town would try to join, only to learn that membership was by invitation only—you had to be *asked*. Nobody knew what the qualifications were. Rumor had it the membership included some of the state's most influential and powerful people.

"How do they know he was with the Lodge?" Jack said.

"Because he had some unrotted skin left on his back and the Septimus Lodge's seal had been branded into it."

Mom gasped, Dad winced.

Everyone knew that seal: an intricate starlike design that made you a little dizzy if you looked too close. A huge model of it hung above the Lodge's front door.

Smiling, Kate raised a hand before Jack could speak.

"I know how your mind works, Jack, and the answer is no: He wasn't tortured with the brand or anything like that. The medical examiner said it was many years old. Probably some sort of rite they go through."

Jack hesitated to ask his next question. He didn't want to seem too morbid, but he had to know.

Finally he cleared his throat and said, "What about the ritual?"

Kate shook her head. "I asked Tim about that and he says they're holding the details back for now." She smiled. "But don't worry. I'll find out. Jenny Styles from Cherry Hill—you've met her, Mom. She's a year ahead of me at med school, but guess where she's externing."

Jack and his mother shrugged.

"The ME's office. She's been assisting with the autopsies. I know I'll be able to get it out of her. She *loves* to talk."

"Cool." Jack could always depend on Kate. "I wonder if they stuffed his mouth with the fake diamonds."

Mom said, "Jack!"

"Well, the Mafia stuffs a dead bird in a stoolie's mouth, so I just thought—"

"That's not exactly a ritual," Kate said.

A ritual . . . Jack figured the possibilities would haunt his dreams tonight.

"Any other news?"

She laughed. "Isn't that enough? Don't worry, I'm on the case." She lowered her voice to a mock announcer's tone, like Walter Cronkite's. "News bulletins will be reported as soon as they're received."

"Great."

He scooped up the unshelled pistachios and dropped them back into the bag. Tom's theft had stolen his appetite for them.

"I'm heading over to Steve's."

Steve had been calling all day, saying Jack had to come over tonight because his father had something to show him.

Dad said, "How's that computer coming along?"

"Okay, I guess. The instructions aren't very clear."

"Well, my hat's off to you for trying. I know what I went through with that Apple One."

Jack wondered if they'd ever get finished, what with Steve Brussard getting half smashed every night.

8

"So you saw only the head?" Mr. Brussard said.

He and Jack and Steve sat around the kitchen table—the boys drinking Pepsi, Steve's father sipping some sort of mixed drink. He'd started quizzing Jack the instant he arrived.

Steve's expression was avid. "Was it gross?"

"Majorly."

Steve was a reduced Xerox copy of his father—same round face, same hazel eyes, same thick, curly reddish hair that clung to the scalp like a bad toupee.

"So that was it?" Mr. Brussard said, leaning closer. "You didn't see the rest of the body?"

"No, and maybe I'm glad I didn't. I mean, what with it being a ritual murder and all."

Steve slammed his palm on the table. "*What*? No way! You're putting me on!"

His father had his eyes squeezed shut and was rubbing them with a thumb and forefinger. "What sort of ritual?"

Me and my big mouth, Jack thought.

He'd forgotten that no one was supposed to know about that. At least not yet.

"I don't know. They're . . . they're keeping that secret."

"Have they identified him yet?"

With a start Jack wondered how Mr. Brussard knew it was a *him*, and then realized he'd been thinking of the corpse as a "him" as well.

"Maybe it's Marcie Kurek," Steve said.

Marcie again. Well, no surprise. For a while last year her disappearance had been all anyone talked about.

Jack figured he could tell them the identity since it would be in tomorrow's papers. But he couldn't remember the man's name.

"A jeweler from Mount Holly."

"Anton Boruff," Mr. B said in a low voice.

Steve's eyes were wide. "Dad, you *knew* him?"

His father said, "Heard of him. It was in all the papers a few years ago. Vanished without a trace. Some people thought he'd left his wife and run off with another woman, but . . ." He shrugged.

Jack couldn't mention the diamonds, and anyway he was tired of talking about the body. Looking for a way off it, he remembered Steve's calls.

"Steve said you had something you wanted to show me, Mister Brussard."

The man looked confused for a couple of seconds. "What? Oh, right. But it's not something to see. More like hear. We'll have to go into the living room."

They rose and followed him until he turned and pointed to the middle of the family den floor.

"All right, boys, sit yourselves down right there—that's what we call the sweet spot."

Jack had no idea what was going on, but complied. Sipping from their Pepsis, he and Steve situated themselves cross-legged on the shag carpet while Mr. Brussard fiddled with a bunch of electronic components racked on a shelf at the far end of the room.

"Now I know you've heard parts, or maybe even all of this before, but you've never heard it like this."

He seemed to be trying to sound cheerful when he really wasn't. If that was the case, he was doing a lousy job.

"Heard what?" Steve said.

"Tchaikovsky's *1812 Overture.*"

Steve groaned. "Aw, man! Classical music?"

Jack was no fan himself. The only thing he liked less was opera. Listening to some of those fat ladies' wailing voices was like fingernails on a blackboard.

"Wait. Just wait. It's a long piece, but I'm going to get you to the good part. This was digitally recorded and they used *real cannons* for the finale. You've got to hear it to believe it."

Jack didn't know what "digitally recorded" meant, but real cannons . . . that might be cool.

Mr. B fiddled with some buttons. "Let me advance it to the sixteen-minute mark so as not to strain your short attention spans. There. Now . . . listen."

With a flourish he hit a button and instantly the living room filled with an orchestra playing a familiar tune Jack had heard a million times on commercials and TV shows. But *loud.* And so clear. No hiss, no static, no pops . . . just pure music.

And then the cannons started blasting. Jack jumped and almost dropped his Pepsi can. He looked at Steve who was looking back all wide-eyed and amazed. The explosions were so real and so loud Jack could feel them vibrating through the floor into his butt. He started laughing with the pure excess of the sound.

When the cannons stopped, Steve's father turned off the music and hit a button that popped a little drawer out of one of the components. Then he turned to them.

"Ever hear anything like that? You've just experienced

state-of-the-art tweeters and mid-range speaks plus a sixteen-inch subwoofer." He held up a silvery plastic disk. "All playing this."

"What's that?" Steve said.

"It's called a compact disc, or CD, for short. It's the latest thing in music."

Steve's father was known as a gadget freak. As soon as anything new came out, especially in electronics, he'd be on it.

Jack had never heard of a CD, but he wanted to hear more. The sound quality, the bone-rattling bass . . . the possibilities . . .

"Do any of these CDs have real music—I mean, rock music?" He looked at Steve. "Just think what Def Leppard would sound like."

Steve grinned. " 'Foolin'!' Yeah. That would be awesome!"

"Sorry, guys. Not much available yet, and it's mostly classical. But in the future . . . who knows?"

"Can you play that again, Dad?"

He popped the disc back in the tray, slid it closed, and did his thing with the buttons.

"You listen. I'll be right back."

As soon as his father left the room, Steve hopped up and rushed to the nearby liquor cabinet. While the cannons boomed and shook the room, he pulled an unlabeled bottle from within and poured a long shot into his Pepsi. He replaced the bottle, closed the door, and was back at Jack's side just as the music began to wind down.

From upstairs he heard Mrs. Brussard yelling, "Would you *please* turn that noise *down*?"

"Okay, guys," Mr. B said as he hurried back into the

room. "I've got some calls to make, so why don't you two hit the basement and get to work on that computer."

Steve jumped up. "Okay. Let's do it."

As Jack followed Steve toward the basement door he glanced back and saw Mr. Brussard standing by his rack of stereo equipment, staring off into space with a worried expression.

Though the music had been awesome, he wondered if Mr. Brussard had used this new CD player as an excuse to get him over so he could quiz him about the body.

"Are you *trying* to get caught?" Jack said when they reached the finished basement.

Steve grinned at him. "Don't worry about it. Besides, that just makes it more fun." He offered his Pepsi to Jack. "Sip?"

Jack hesitated, then took the can and swigged.

Awful.

"You do know how to ruin a good Pepsi," he said, handing it back. "What's in there this time?"

Steve tended to grab whatever was available from the liquor cabinet. He didn't seem to care.

"Applejack."

Jack shook his head. Dad had given him a taste once—"To take the mystery out of it," he'd said—and he'd hated it. Burned his tongue and nose and made him cough. Same with Scotch, although that tasted more mediciney. And beer . . . he didn't know about other brands, but Dad's Carling Black Label was bitter. He couldn't imagine ever liking beer.

Give him Pepsi any day.

"Let's get to work."

They had all the pieces to the Heathkit H-89 laid out on a card table. The company had been bought and had stopped making the kits, but Steve's father had picked up this 1979 model for a bargain price. Jack couldn't wait to get it assembled and up and running. It looked so much cooler than Dad's Apple because it was all one piece: keyboard, monitor, and floppy drive all in the same casing.

According to the instructions they were almost halfway there. They'd have been further along if Steve had been more help. But he'd developed this thing for liquor.

He hadn't always been like this. In fact he'd never been like this before he went away to that Pennsylvania soccer camp last month. He was a great soccer player, and because of that he tended to get teamed up with older players. Jack had a feeling some of those older players had introduced Steve to hard liquor and it had flipped some sort of switch in his head.

"Why don't you put off your cocktail or whatever until we've got the CPU installed."

The Heathkit came with a Z-80 processor, whatever that was, which was the heart and brain of the computer. If they didn't install it correctly, nothing would work.

"Okay, okay."

He took a long swig before placing the can on the far corner of the table, then he moved up beside Jack to study the diagram. Jack was a little worried about him.

"Still don't know why you want to ruin the taste of a Pepsi."

"Well, the booze tastes too bad to drink straight."

"Then why—?"

"Because maybe I like the way it makes me feel, okay?" he said with an edge in his voice.

Obviously Steve didn't like talking about it. Maybe he knew he had a problem. Jack tried warning him off another way.

"Sooner or later your dad's going to notice his bottles

getting empty, and since they can't be emptying themselves . . ."

Steve gave a dismissive wave. "My dad's too busy at the Lodge to notice."

Jack couldn't hide his surprise. "The Lodge? Your father's a member of the *Lodge*?"

Steve shrugged. "Yeah. Like forever. Why?"

"Nothing."

But Jack's mind whirled. Just a little while ago when Steve had asked if his father had known the dead man, Mr. Brussard had said he'd "heard of him." But if they were both members of the Lodge, wouldn't he have more than heard of him?

1

Professor Nakamura lived on the other side of Route 206 in the well-to-do area of Johnson—the most recently developed section, where they had real sidewalks and curbs and where homes tended to be bigger and more lavish than regular folks'. Since it occupied the westernmost end of town, as far as possible from Old Town on the east, its residents had started calling their neighborhood "New Town." The name never caught on with anyone else.

A little after nine-thirty, Weezy swung by Jack's place with the cube and the two of them biked down Quakerton Road. They had plenty of time so they rode slowly, weaving back and forth as they talked.

Jack told her what Kate had said about the identity of the corpse and how he had the Lodge's seal branded on his back.

"The Ancient Septimus Fraternal Order," Weezy said, shaking her head. "Should have known."

"Why should you have known?"

"All right, I should have *guessed* when you said ritual murder."

Jack's stomach did a flip. "They kill people?"

Weezy shrugged. "Who knows what they do? They're

rumored to have all sorts of rituals. I've tried to read up on the order but there's almost no hard facts. Lots of theories, but it's so secretive no one seems to know much for sure. One thing that's certain is the Ancient Septimus Order is really and truly *ancient*. Lots older than the Masons."

"The masons? You mean bricklayers?"

Weezy rolled her eyes. "No, another secret society. The order has lodges all over the world and they call the shots in many places. Like New Jersey, for instance. It's said nothing gets done in this state unless the Lodge approves. Everybody chalks it up to corruption, but it's the Lodge."

Jack had to laugh. "C'mon, Weez! We're talking about Johnson, New Jersey, here. The butt end of nowhere. If this order is oh-so-powerful, don't you think it'd set up in Trenton or Newark? I mean, anywhere but Johnson."

Weezy gave him that tolerant smile she used when she was about to tell someone what she thought everyone should already know.

"The Lodge wasn't built in Johnson . . . Johnson—or Quakerton, as it was called back then—was built around the Lodge."

"What are you talking about?"

"The Lodge was here first. Some say it was here even before Columbus came to the Americas, but no one can prove that."

"How can that be? Look at the building. It can't be that old."

Another eye roll. "Ever hear of rebuilding and remodeling? Anyway, some accounts—and I can't say how reliable they are—say that members had settled themselves around

the Lodge in what they called Quakerton—what *we* now
call Old Town—long before the Pilgrims arrived."

"How is that possible?"

"Well, it's pretty well accepted that the Norse and even
Irish had settlements in North America in the eleventh cen-
tury. Who's to say who else was around? But here's what's
really interesting: If the Lodge's settlement was already here
when the Pilgrims arrived in 1620, how could they have
called it Quakerton when the first Quakers didn't even exist
until 1647?"

Jack said, "I don't know about you, but that sounds like
pretty good proof that somebody"—his turn to give a
look—"has her dates screwed up."

"Maybe it meant something else. Maybe their idea of
a Quaker wasn't our idea of a Quaker."

Jack found that unsettling, but couldn't say why.

"And another thing—" She stopped and pointed.
"Look!"

They'd reached the light at the highway, and Jack saw
what had caught her attention. The flashing lights of a pair
of cop cars and an ambulance were spinning like mad at
Sumter's used cars across 206.

He looked at Weezy, she at him, and they both nodded.

Jack led the way across the highway and into the car
lot where they stopped behind two deputies. Both were
watching a guy and a woman from the volunteer
first-aid squad work on an unconscious man who lay
spread-eagled on the pavement. They'd torn open his shirt
and slipped some kind of plastic board under his back.
The first-aid guy was on his knees, thumping on the man's

chest while the woman held a face mask over his nose and mouth and squeezed a football-shaped bag to pump air into his lungs.

Jack wondered who it could be. He noticed one of the deputies was Tim but didn't dare ask him. He'd shoo them away for sure.

The first-aid guy was bathed in sweat. He stopped thumping and listened to the chest while pressing two fingers against the man's throat. Then he leaned back and looked at his watch.

"Twenty minutes of CPR and nothing. He's a goner." Another look at his watch. "I'm pronouncing him at nine-forty-seven."

The deputies pulled out pads and pens and made notes as the woman first-aider removed the mask. The dead man's face was white, his mouth hung open, and his glassy eyes stared at nothing.

Jack and Weezy gasped in unison when they recognized Mr. Sumter.

Tim must have heard, because he turned and saw them.

"Okay, you two. Move on. Nothing to see here."

Jack said, "What happened?"

"Looks like a heart attack." He waved them off. "Come on, now. Get going. Clear the area. Haven't you two seen enough dead bodies this week?"

That startled Jack. It hadn't occurred to him. Come to think of it, he and Weezy had seen two dead people in less than forty-eight hours.

Wow.

As they were wheeling away he glanced back just as the first-aiders were rolling Mr. Sumter onto his side to remove the plastic board from under him. His shirt had ridden up, revealing a symbol scarred into his back.

The seal of the Ancient Septimus Fraternal Order.

Two dead men . . . both Lodgers. But they couldn't possibly be connected.

Could they?

2

Jack led the way to Professor Nakamura's place.

He lived on Emerson Lane, home to Johnson's biggest houses, and the only street in town that ended in a cul-de-sac. The so-called New Town used to be Eppinger's sod farm, and so it had no native trees. Any oaks and maples in sight had been trucked in and planted by the homeowners. A cornfield stretched to the north, the leaves on the green stalks waving gently in the breeze. To the south lay an orchard, its trees sagging with fruit.

The professor answered the door and welcomed them in. A chubby little man with a round face, gold-rimmed glasses, short black hair graying at the temples, he led them to a library. All sorts of stone heads and statuettes vied for space with the books crammed on the shelves. A big window overlooked a sand garden in his backyard. Three big lava stones of varying sizes had been set at odd intervals, and the sand had been raked into curving patterns around them. Jack liked the effect. Very peaceful.

"Now, what have you brought me?" the professor said in a soft, accented voice as he seated himself behind a mahogany desk. Jack recognized it as mahogany because Mr. Rosen had been teaching him about the different kinds of wood that went into the old furniture in his store. "Mister Rosen says I will find it very interesting."

Weezy handed Jack the cube. He placed it on the desk blotter and opened it.

The professor stared at the pyramid for a moment, then ran his hands over its surface. He removed a magnifying glass from a drawer and gave it a quick once-over.

"You found this in the woods?" He spoke without looking up.

"Yes." Weezy glanced at Jack. "We dug it out of something that might be a burial mound."

He grunted and continued his examination. "Really. And you think it is . . . what? Some sort of ancient artifact?"

"We don't know," Jack said. "That's why we brought it to you."

Professor Nakamura grunted again, then put down the pyramid, took off his glasses, and looked at them. His lips were pursed like he'd just bitten into a lemon.

"Are you trying to hoax me?"

The question took Jack by surprise. "Hoax? No way! We really dug that up and—"

"If that is true, then someone is hoaxing you."

"Impossible!" Weezy said. She looked majorly upset. "Nobody knew where we'd be digging, not even us!"

The professor raised a hand and smiled. "No-no. Not you purposely. Anyone. Hoaxers like to find a mound—burial or otherwise—and plant phony artifacts in them, then wait until they're found."

"But—"

"A tablet with Phoenician writing 'discovered' in Grave Creek mound in West Virginia in eighteen hundreds—*fake*. Piltdown man—*fake*. Ica stones from Peru—*fake*."

"I don't know about that stuff," Jack said. "But I can tell you, if someone buried that cube and hoped someone else would find it, he must have been ready to wait a long, long time. Because it was buried in an area of the Barrens where hardly anyone goes."

Professor Nakamura frowned. "But you said it was a mound. Someone must have told you about it."

"Uh-uh." Jack jerked his thumb at Weezy. "*She* found it."

The professor stared at her. "This is true?"

She nodded.

He picked up the pyramid again, tracing his pinkie finger along the symbols.

"These symbols look pre-Sumerian, which would make them six or seven thousand years old. But on this pyramid . . . notice how cleanly they have been etched into its surface? Back then, scratching quills on wet clay tablets was state of the art. So it is obviously a hoax."

"It's not a hoax," Weezy said. "Can't you feel it? It feels *old*."

The professor offered half a smile. "Archaeology and anthropology cannot operate on feelings, young miss."

Weezy looked ready to explode, so Jack jumped in. "Isn't there some carbon-dating test you can do to see how old it is?"

His smile broadened. "Carbon-fourteen dating is not a test one does in one's basement. And besides, carbon-fourteen can date only organic material, like wood or bone." He tapped the pyramid. "This is not organic."

"There must be *some* way," Jack said.

The professor sat silent, as if thinking. Finally he said, "I suppose we can try potassium argon dating. It can date nonorganic material—"

"Great! Let's do it."

"I must take this to the university then—"

"No!" Weezy cried. "You can't take it away!"

He spread his hands. "Then I cannot help you."

Jack touched her arm. "Come on, Weez. Otherwise we'll never know."

"I'll never see it again. I just know it."

She looked at him with glistening eyes—were those tears? He hoped she wasn't going to cry. He'd never seen Weezy cry and didn't want to now.

"Look—"

"I finally found one, Jack," she said, her voice barely above a whisper. "I finally got my hands on one of the secrets. I can't just let it go."

He had a sudden idea.

"Hey, why don't we compromise? Keep the box and let the professor take the pyramid."

She opened her mouth as if to say no without even thinking, but stopped. After a moment's thought she said, "Look, if we've got to give him something, let him take the box. I want the pyramid."

"The pyramid will work out better," the professor said. "Its engravings might be the easiest to date most accurately."

Weezy chewed her lip, her gaze locked on the pyramid. Finally she said, "Okay. But you promise I'll get it back? You *promise*?"

"I promise," the professor said. "My department handles artifacts and specimens all the time. We are experts. You have nothing to fear."

"I hope not. But there's something I've got to do before you take it." She looked around. "Can I have a pencil and a piece of paper?"

"Of course."

The professor produced them immediately from the top drawer of his desk. Weezy grabbed the pyramid and laid the paper over one of its sides. Then she began rubbing the pencil over it. The engraved symbol appeared. She did this with all six sides.

"Don't forget the bottom," Jack said.

Weezy nodded and finished up with that. She put down the pyramid and held up the paper to look over her work.

"Got it."

Jack peered over her shoulder at the strange symbols. What could they mean?

$$\lambda \xi \eth \lambda f \eta \hbar$$

He gathered up the flattened panels and snapped them back into a cube while the professor lifted a hard-sided briefcase from the floor. He laid it on the desk, opened it, and placed the pyramid inside.

As he snapped it closed, Jack glanced at Weezy. She looked like some of those mothers he'd see at the bus stop every fall when they sent their child off to school for the first time.

3

Moments later they were standing outside, blinking in the bright summer sunshine. Weezy looked downhearted.

"It'll be all right, Weez," he said as they got back on their bikes.

She looked at him. "Will it? What if they lose it?"

"Come on. He's an archaeologist. He does this sort of thing all the time."

She sighed. "I know, but . . ." She let the word hang.

"At least we'll know how old it is. That's important, don't you think?"

She shrugged. "I guess so. But on the other hand, I don't care how old they say it is, I *know* it's old and I *know* it's important."

Jack felt a growing impatience. "But that's just it, Weez—you *don't* know. You feel, you wish, you believe, you hope, but that's not knowing. To *know* you've got to have some facts."

She looked at him and shook her head. "You just don't get it, Jack. I don't think you'll ever get it."

He was about to ask her just what she meant by that when he heard a car horn *toot-toot*. He looked around to see a new, light blue Mustang GLX convertible with the top down. They were still in the professor's driveway and the car had pulled to the curb a few feet away. He instantly recognized the driver.

Carson Toliver.

Everybody knew Carson Toliver. Son of Edward Toliver, the rich, big-shot real estate developer who lived in the biggest house in town at the far end of the cul-de-sac. Local boy hero who'd enter his senior year as captain and quarterback of the Burlington Badgers, the high school football team. Probably wind up captain of the basketball team too. He had the tanned skin, long blond hair, and good looks of a California surfer dude.

And he was looking at Weezy.

"You're Weezy Connell, aren't you."

Weezy nodded but said nothing. She looked like a deer in headlights.

"Yeah, I've seen you around. Heard you found a body in the Pines."

She may have found a body but she hadn't found her voice yet.

"We both did," Jack said.

He looked at Jack for the first time. "And you are?"

"Just Jack," Weezy said, her voice sounding thick. "He's a friend. Just a friend. He's going to be starting as a freshman next month."

Carson had already lost interest in Jack and was refocused on Weezy.

"So . . . this body. Was finding it gross or cool?"

"A little bit of both, I guess."

"I'll bet it was. I'd offer you a ride but I see you've got your bike. Maybe we can get together sometime and talk about it."

"W-with me?" Weezy said.

"Sure. I'd love to hear all about it." He put the car in gear and waved. "Later, Weezy."

She waved, then stood with her jaw hanging open as she watched him go.

"Close your mouth before you start catching flies."

She turned to him, mouth still open. "Do you believe that? He spoke to me. He actually stopped and spoke to *me*." She closed her eyes and tilted her head back. "I can't *believe* it!"

"Am I missing something here?"

"Carson Toliver wants to get together with me!" She was talking to the air. Jack could have been miles away.

"So?"

Finally she came back to Earth—or at least into shallow orbit—and looked at Jack as if he'd just told her he was from the Crab Nebula.

" '*So*'? He's a *hunk*! He's more than a hunk, he's *the* hunk! And he . . . he asked me out. Well, kind of. How cool is that?"

"Too cool for words," Jack said, letting the sarcasm drip. "Let's ride."

She didn't seem to hear him. She was tugging on her ponytail. "Look at my hair! And how I'm dressed! *Lame*! And I'm on a bike! A *bike*! I must look like a total dweeb!"

"Well, it's not as if you can drive yet. You're only fourteen."

"I'll be fifteen next month!"

"Still . . ."

"If I'd been walking he'd have given me a ride."

Jack had about all he could take. He started riding back toward 206. If Weezy wanted to come that was up to her, but he wasn't going to stand there and listen to any more of her burbling babble.

He didn't know why he was feeling ticked off. Okay, maybe he did. To see Weezy go all gaga just because some guy stopped and said hello . . . it shouldn't bother him, but it did. That wasn't his Weezy—or rather, not the Weezy Jack knew. His Weezy wasn't like other girls. She was different. Special. Carson Toliver should be gaga because she'd spoken to *him*.

"Hey, Jack!" he heard her call behind him. "Wait up!"

He was tempted to say, *Don't you mean, 'just Jack'?* but didn't want to let her know how that had bothered him, or that he'd even noticed. Talk about getting dropped like a hot potato.

She'd probably wanted to let Carson know they weren't going out or anything like that. And . . . well . . . they weren't. So why had it bothered him?

He didn't know.

He slowed to let her catch up.

"What's the hurry?" she said.

"Got an errand to run."

"Oh. Want me to come along?"

"That's okay."

No traffic in sight when they came to 206 so they buzzed straight across.

"Is something wrong?" she said when they reached the other side.

"No, why?"

"You're acting weird."

Yeah, he probably was. He needed a cover.

"My brother's been hassling me. I want to teach him a lesson and I need a special ingredient for that."

"And that's the errand?"

He nodded.

She said, "Anything I can do to help?"

He glanced at her. "This is gonna be pretty much a one-man show, but if I need a hand, I'll let you know."

She smiled. "If you need me, I'm there."

Jack didn't know why, but suddenly he felt a change. Like a weight had lifted from his shoulders.

Weird.

4

Mr. Vito Canelli lived on a corner up the street from Jack and was known for having the best lawn in town. An older, retired, white-haired widower, he wouldn't let anyone else touch his lawn. He cut it twice a week, watered it by hand every other day, and trimmed its edges so neatly it looked like he'd used scissors.

Although his lawn was off-limits, he would hire Jack to shovel his walks and driveway in winter.

His front yard was open but he kept his back fenced in to protect his vegetable gardens from rabbits and the Pinelands deer that wandered through town. Except for the paths between the beds, almost every square inch of his backyard was planted with tomatoes, zucchini, asparagus, and half a dozen varieties of peppers.

Toward the end of summer—like now—he'd set up a table in the shade and sell the excess from his garden. Jack's mom was a regular customer for his huge Jersey beefsteak tomatoes.

But Jack wasn't in the market for tomatoes.

He leaned his bike against a tree and waved to where Mr. Canelli sat in the middle of his lawn pulling crabgrass by hand.

Jack inspected the peppers on the table. He saw green, red, and yellow bells, and pale green frying peppers. Not what he was looking for.

"Do you have any hot peppers?" he said, walking up to the old man.

Mr. Canelli looked up from under a broad-brimmed straw hat.

"Of course," he said in his Italian accent. "But I keep for myself. They much too hot for people around here."

"I'd like to buy the hottest you've got."

He shook his head. "You won't be able to eat. I can eat habañeros like they candy, but my hottest—no-no-no. I use a tiny, tiny amount in soup or gravy."

"It's not for me. This person will eat them."

He gave Jack a long stare, then raised his hand. "Help me up and I show you what I got."

Jack helped pull him to his feet, then followed him into the backyard.

"These are jalapeños," he said, pointing at some dark green oblong peppers maybe two inches long. "They hot." He moved on and pointed to a shorter orange pepper. "Even more hot habañeros." And then he stopped at a bushy plant with little berry-size peppers. "And here the king. The smallest of the lot, but the most hot. A special breed of tepin I cross with habañero."

"Tay-peen?" Jack had never heard of it. But then, what did he know about peppers? "How much apiece?"

Mr. Canelli shook his head. "I don't sell. Too hot."

"Please? Just a couple?"

The old man stared at him, smiling. "You up to no good, eh?"

Jack fought to keep his expression innocent. How did he know?

"What do you mean?"

"You know exactly what I mean. But you a good kid. I see you with the lawn mower, I watch you shovel snow. You work hard. I give you some."

"I can pay."

"I have dried one inside. You wait."

While Mr. Canelli went inside, Jack wandered through the garden, marveling at the size of the tomatoes and zucchinis. The old guy definitely had a green thumb.

When he returned a few minutes later he handed Jack a small white envelope.

"You take."

Jack peeked inside and saw half a dozen little red peppers.

"Hey, thanks."

"You be careful. You wash you hands after you touch. Never rub you eyes. If you burn you mouth, take milk. Or maybe butter. Water only make worse."

"Got it," Jack said. "Thanks a million."

He hopped on his bike and stifled himself until he was well down the street. Then he did the *mwah-ha-ha-ha* laugh the rest of the way home.

5

As Jack was biking to USED at midday, he heard someone call his name. He looked around and saw a long-haired, bearded man waving to him from the front porch of the Bainbridge house.

Weird Walt.

"Hey, Jack! Got a minute?"

Jack had a few. He swung the bike around and coasted into the driveway. Walt was rocking in the shade of the porch. He pointed a gloved hand at an empty rocker beside him.

"C'mon up and set a spell."

"I gotta get to work."

"Just a coupla minutes."

Jack shrugged. "Okay."

He laid his bike down on the dry lawn that badly needed watering. Walt lived here with his sister and her husband. He took care of the yard, but wasn't very good at it.

As Jack hopped up the steps to the porch, Walt patted the seat of the rocker again.

"Here. Sit."

He noticed his gloves were leather. His hands had to be majorly hot and sweaty in those. As Jack seated himself, Walt leaned close and stared, his gaze boring into him. It made Jack uncomfortable.

"What?"

"Just checking."

"Checking what?"

"I thought you might be him, but you're not."

"What made you think—?"

"Don't worry. I'll know him when I meet him."

With that Walt scooted his rocker a foot farther away, as if afraid to stay too close.

Well, he wasn't called Weird Walt for nothing.

Jack leaned back and started rocking. Not a bad way to spend a summer afternoon.

"What's up, Mister Erskine?"

He laughed. "They called my father 'Mister Erskine.' Call me Walt. I wanna thang you for comin' to my aid yesterday."

Jack gave him a closer look. Barely lunchtime and already he had red eyes and slurred words. Jack felt a mixture of sorrow and distaste. And worry . . . Steve Brussard could end up like this if he didn't get a grip.

"I didn't do anything," Jack said. "Mrs. Clevenger did all the work."

"Yeah, but you were there and you were on my side. Would've been just as easy for you and Weezy to join the crowd against me. But you two aren't herd members."

"Yeah, well . . ."

"Don't minimize it, Jack. Look, I know what people think of me. I know I'm the town weirdo and the town drunk—I know I'm 'Weird Walt.' I'm a lot of things, Jack, but I ain't stupid."

"I . . . I never thought you were." Where was this going?

"An' I'm not crazy. I know I act crazy, but I have very good reasons for what I do. Like these gloves." He held up his hands. "I wear them so's I don't touch anyone."

"Yeah. Okay." This was getting weird.

"An' I don't drink 'cause I want to, I drink 'cause I have to. I drink to survive."

Jack couldn't help saying, "I don't understand."

"You wouldn't. You couldn't. Nobody can. Not even my buddies in 'Nam."

"Is it something that happened in the war?"

Walt stared at him with a strange look in his eyes. Jack tried to identify it. The only word he could come up with was . . . lost.

"Yeah."

"What?"

"I don't talk about it. I used to, but I don't anymore. It landed me in a mental hospital once. I don't want to go back again."

"My dad was in the Korean War. He won't talk about that either."

Walt looked away. "Lotta people like that. War changes you. Sometimes it's something you did, sometimes it's something that was done to you. Either way, you don't come back the same."

Jack was thinking his dad seemed pretty normal—except for never talking about it. Jack would have loved to hear some war stories.

He thought of something he needed to know.

"You know, um, Walt. If you were a soldier and all, why'd you let a couple of punks like Teddy and his friend push you around?"

He shrugged. "I'm nonviolent."

"But—"

"When I got drafted I said I wouldn't fight but I'd be a medic."

"So you spent the war fixing people up instead of shooting them down?"

"I don't know about the fixing-up part. Mostly I just shot 'em up with morphine so they could stand the pain and maybe stop screaming until dust-off."

"Dust-off?"

"That was what we called a medevac mission—when a chopper would come in and carry off the wounded." He shook his head. "The things I saw . . . the things I saw . . ." His voice became choked. "Maybe I shouldn't have been a medic. If I'd been just a grunt back in sixty-eight, my life would be different now. But it got ruined."

All this was making Jack a little uncomfortable. He wished he'd worn a watch so he could look at it.

"Um, I gotta run."

Walt swallowed and smiled. "I know you do. Thanks for stoppin' and listenin' to me ramble. I just needed to talk to you. You did the right thing yesterday and I wanted you to know that you didn't do it for some useless, drunken lump of human protoplasm. That the guy you see on the outside is not the same as the guy on the inside. Did I get that across?"

"Yeah, Walt," he said, going down the porch steps. "Yeah, you did."

He smiled through his beard. "Good. Because I owe you one, man. And don't you forget it. Because I won't."

Jack hoped he'd never need to collect.

6

After putting in his hours at USED, Jack stopped at the Connell house on the way home. He and Eddie were battling for high score in *Donkey Kong*. Weezy came in just as Jack was handing the joystick back to Eddie.

"Hey, Weez. I need to borrow the cube tonight."

She stopped in midstride and frowned. "Why?"

"Want to show Steve. He's handy with gadgets. I want to see if he can open it. I can't be the *only* one."

"Gee . . . I don't know."

Jack felt a flash of irritation. "Don't know what? You think I'm going to lose it or something?"

"No, I mean I don't know if it's a good idea to let it get around too much that we have it."

"If that pyramid is as special as you think it is, I'll bet word of it is all around U of P by now."

She sighed. "Yeah, I guess you're right." She looked deep into his eyes. "You'll take good care of it, right?"

Jack put his hand over his heart. "Guard it with my life."

"And you won't tell anybody we found it with the body, right? 'Cause they'll take it away."

He held up three fingers. "Scout's honor."

"I'm serious, Jack."

"So am I. You'll have it back tomorrow."

"Promise?"

"Promise."

"Okay, come upstairs. I need you to open it for me first."

He followed her up to her room where he opened the cube and laid it on her desk. He watched her pull out a sheet of paper and trace the design on the inside of the panels.

"Why are you doing that?"

"Just in case."

"You're acting like you might not get it back."

"You think so?" she said without looking up.

When she was finished she snapped the cube back together, then wrapped it in a towel and put it in a shopping bag. She handed it to him.

"Don't let it out of your sight."

Jack shook his head as walked back downstairs. You'd think he was borrowing her first-born child.

7

After dinner, Jack took the bag of pistachios to his room but didn't bother shelling them right away. He needed to do something else first.

He put on Journey's *Escape*—loud—and played a few runs of air bass to "Don't Stop Believing." Nodding his head in time, he placed the dried tepin peppers in a cereal bowl and crushed them into flakes. Then, making sure no one was in sight, he crossed to the hall bathroom and added an ounce or two of tap water.

Back in his room he mixed everything well, then set it aside and started shelling the pistachios. He'd done about ten when he heard a knock. Knowing it wasn't Tom—he never knocked—Jack placed the latest issue of *Cerebus* over the pepper bowl and left the pistachios on his desk.

"C'mon in."

He turned down the music as Kate stepped through the door. Her gaze flicked to his desk where she spotted the pistachios.

She smiled. "Figure it's safer to eat them in here, huh?"

"At least tonight. What's up?"

Kate's smile faded and she bit her lip. "I know I promised to find out for you, but I'm not sure I should tell you."

"You mean about the murder ritual?" Jack felt his heart rate kick up. He'd been dying to hear this. "Go ahead. You can tell me."

"It's really bizarre."

Even better.

"Tell-me-tell-me-tell-me!"

"Okay. Well . . . Jenny told me that it seems whoever killed the man cut off his forearms at the elbows and crudely sewed them into his armpits."

"*What?*"

Kate nodded. "Truth, I swear."

Jack tried to envision it but had trouble. "Oh man, that's so *weird*. Was he . . . ?"

"Alive when they did it?" Kate smiled as she gave him a gentle slap on the back of his head. "Mister Morbid . . . I knew you'd ask."

"Well?"

"Was he alive when they cut off his forearms? No."

That was a relief—in a way.

"But what does the arm thing mean?" He snapped his fingers as an idea hit. "Maybe it has something to do with stealing."

"Traditionally thieves lose their right hand—and it's not sewn into their armpit. I asked Jenny about it and she says the medical examiner's going to make some calls, but he's never heard of anything like it."

"Maybe it had nothing to do with the diamond scam." Jack lowered his voice into an imitation of Weezy's *ooh-spooky* tone: "Maybe it's an ancient, secret cult, living unseen in the Pinelands for thousands of years, killing and mutilating unwary victims who cross their path! Mwah-ha-ha-ha!"

She laughed and ruffled his brown hair. "Stop it. You read too many of the wrong books and watch too many crummy movies."

The crummy part was sure true. He'd seen *Jaws 3-D* last

month and what a waste of money—crummy 3-D and crummier story.

Kate pointed to the pistachios. "May I have one?"

He cupped his palm around the pile and pushed it toward her. "*You* can have them all."

And he meant it. Anything Kate wanted she could have, no questions asked.

She took just one, picking it up between a dainty thumb and forefinger. "This'll do." She popped it into her mouth and stepped to the door. "You want this closed?"

He nodded. "Definitely."

"You're not going to have nightmares tonight about being chased by short-armed men, are you?"

He laughed. "As if."

On the other hand, that might be kind of cool—as long as it was only a dream.

As soon as the door closed he went to work shelling another half dozen pistachios. When he was done he dropped the whole pile into the tepin bowl and swirled the mixture around and over them. Satisfied they were all nicely coated, he picked them out one by one and lined them up on his windowsill to dry.

When he was finished, without thinking, he licked his two wet fingertips and instantly his tongue and lips were on fire. *Fire!* Like he'd licked the sun.

He jumped up and dashed across the hall to the bathroom for water, but remembered Mr. Canelli's words just in time: *Water only make worse.*

His mouth was killing him, making his eyes tear. What had the old guy said to use instead? *If you burn you mouth, take milk. Or maybe butter.*

Jack dashed for the kitchen, yanked open the refrigerator. On the door he spotted an open stick of Land O'Lakes butter. He gouged a piece off the end and shoved it into his mouth, running it all over the burning area. Slowly, the heat eased—didn't leave entirely but at least became bearable.

He hurried back to his room and stared at the drying pistachios. He'd touched just a drop—less than a drop—to his tongue and look what happened. If Tom ate that whole pile . . .

Jack didn't want to think about how that would feel. Might be *too* much payback, even for Tom.

But on the other hand, Jack wasn't handing them to his brother. Tom would have to steal them to taste them.

The decision would be Tom's, the outcome entirely up to him.

8

Steve couldn't open the cube either.

They'd been sitting at the Brussards' kitchen table where Jack had demonstrated the technique at least a dozen times.

He wondered if Steve had already been drinking. His fingers seemed kind of clumsy.

"Hey, Dad!" Steve called. "Come check this out!"

Mr. Brussard strolled in from the living room where Jack could hear some sort of classical music playing.

"What's—?" He froze in the doorway like he'd been hit with a paralyzer ray. His eyes were locked on the cube. "Where did you get *that*?"

Remembering Weezy's warning, Jack told a vague story of the two of them digging it up in the Barrens a while back.

He concluded with, "I'm not even sure I could find my way back there."

Not true, of course, but his promise to Weezy overrode Mr. Brussard's nosiness.

"Get this, Dad. It's impossible to open—at least for me."

Mr. Brussard frowned. "What makes you think it opens?"

"Jack showed me how but I can't do it."

Mr. Brussard stared at Jack. "You can open it?"

Jack wondered why he looked so surprised. "Yeah. Kind of weird that I'm the only one."

"Yes . . . yes, it is."

Jack picked it up. "You ever seen anything like it before?"

He shook his head. "No. It's very strange looking, isn't it."

Jack wasn't sure, but he had a feeling Steve's father wasn't being totally honest.

"Yeah, I guess."

"Open it for me," Mr. Brussard said. "Let me see you do it."

Jack showed where he placed his thumbnails, then popped it open. Mr. Brussard's eyes popped too.

"But it's empty!"

Obviously. But he was acting as if he'd expected to see something.

Jack told him about the pyramid. No point in keeping that a secret. Mr. Rosen and Professor Nakamura already knew about it, along with a bunch of people at U of P, no doubt. So why not?

When Jack finished, Mr. Brussard looked like he had an upset stomach. "It's at U of P? For dating?"

"Yeah. Can't wait for the results."

"Neither can I," he said in a flat tone. "Be sure to tell me."

"Hey, Dad," Steve said, clicking the cube back together and handing it to him. "See if you can open it."

Jack showed him, placing the man's thumbnails in the seam as he'd done for everyone else who'd tried.

"Now . . . pull them apart."

Mr. B did just that—

And the box popped open.

"You did it!" Steve cried.

Mr. B didn't seem surprised, but Jack certainly was. He didn't know if he felt relieved or disappointed that he was no longer the only one. He'd belonged to an exclusive club, with a membership of one. Now . . .

"Cool!" Steve said, snapping it back together again. "Let me give it another shot."

Just then the doorbell rang. When Mr. B opened it, Jack saw a worried looking man who seemed vaguely familiar. They shook hands in a funny sort of way, then Jack heard the newcomer say, "Gordon, we've *got* to talk. Sumter—"

Mr. Brussard shushed him. "Wait here." He returned to he kitchen and said, "Okay, boys. Got some business to discuss. Why don't you two get back to work on the computer?"

"Okay," Steve said. "We're almost done."

His father pointed to the cube. "You can leave that here."

Jack remembered Weezy's warning: *Don't let it out of your sight.* But he didn't have to say anything. Steve did it for him.

"Uh-uh," he said, still fiddling with it. "I'm gonna get this yet."

Jack took another look at the nervous man and suddenly knew why he was familiar: Every few years he plastered his face all over the county during the freeholder elections. The freeholders ran the county, and Winston Haskins was one of them.

The funny handshake, Steve's remark about how his father was so involved in the Lodge . . . did this have anything to do with the Lodge? Or the corpse? The freeholder had mentioned Mr. Sumter.

Jack burned with curiosity. He didn't know what was going on, but things were connecting in the strangest ways, and Steve's dad seemed to be in the middle of it all.

He even could open the cube.

9

When they reached the basement, Steve put down the cube and produced two little bottles from his pocket.

"Look what I found." He grinned as he waggled them in the air. "Airline bottles. My dad's got a drawer full of them."

Jack took a closer look. Booze. The labels said one was Jack Daniel's and the other Dewar's Scotch.

Swell.

"Which one you want?"

Jack shook his head. "Maybe later. Hey, your father know Mister Sumter, the guy who died?"

"Sure. Didn't everybody? Matter of fact, he was here last night, right after you left."

"Here? What for?"

Steve shrugged and Jack realized he probably hadn't been very alert at the time.

He could contain his curiosity no longer.

"Hey, I gotta go tap a kidney. Be right back."

"Hurry up." He twisted off the cap on the Jack Daniel's and started pouring it into a Pepsi. "You'll miss all the fun."

Jack padded up the basement stairs and paused at the top. The kitchen looked empty so he stepped out and peeked down the hall. He heard voices coming from the den. The guest bathroom lay halfway between the kitchen and the den. Holding his breath, he made it to the bathroom and closed the door behind him without latching it. Leaving the light off, he stood with his ear to the opening and listened.

Mr. Haskins was talking.

"Damn it, Gordon, it wasn't supposed to be like this. This wasn't supposed to happen."

"Well, it is and it did. So we deal with it."

Jack wished he'd arrived sooner. Then he might know what "it" was.

Mr. Haskins sighed. "Poor Sumter. Why now? What lousy timing."

"Timing had nothing to do with it," Mr. Brussard said. "He was brought down."

"Brought down by whom? No . . . the High Council can't know."

"They don't have to. I'm certain they've sent out a klazen."

A klazen? Jack thought as he heard Mr. Haskins gasp. What's that?

"That's a myth," the freeholder said. "An old wives' tale. There's no such thing."

"You're so sure? I'm the Lodge lore master, remember, and I'm telling you a klazen can sniff out those responsible. And when it finds them . . . well, Sumter was healthy as a horse but now where is he?"

Responsible? For what?

"B-but he had a heart attack."

"Did he? Maybe his heart simply stopped. That's not a heart attack, but it's the way a klazen works."

"Oh, God!" Haskins moaned. "What do we do?"

"The *Compendium* offers protection."

"The *Compendium*? But that's a myth too."

Mr. B sounded ticked off. "This is getting tiring, Winston. We have partial transcripts in the vault."

"What do they say?"

"To use this. Not now . . . tomorrow at dawn, face your back to the sun, and use it."

" 'Back to the sun'? Oh, come on!"

Jack could imagine Mr. Brussard shrugging. "It's up to you, Winston. I did it. I'm protected. If you want to risk going without it, be my guest. I've discharged my responsibility. What happens now is on your own head."

"All right, all right. God, I'm scared. This had better work."

"It will. A klazen can run for only a week. At the end of that time, it will vanish and the Council will assume it's done what needed to be done. We'll be home free."

"Five more days . . . if we can just last . . ."

"The key to doing that rests in your palm."

"What about Challis?"

"Out in L.A.—some insurance brokers' convention, his wife said. But who knows? I don't know about you, but Bert Challis worries me."

Bert Challis? Jack thought. The insurance guy?

He had his office up in Marlton but insured most of the houses and people in Johnson. Jack remembered him coming to the house last year with a life insurance policy for Dad to sign.

Mr. Haskins nodded. "I know what you mean. He's a loose cannon. No telling what he'll do."

"Well, if you see Bert or hear from him, tell him to get in touch will me immediately. His life will depend on it. Same with Vasquez."

"Yes. Sure. Of course."

Jack heard footsteps enter the hallway and felt a flicker

of panic. What if they caught him in here? If he'd put the light on it would look like he'd simply been using the bathroom. But standing here with the light off . . . how would he explain that?

He didn't see much choice but to stay hidden and hope neither of them needed a bathroom break.

He peeked through the slit opening and saw Mr. Haskins standing by the front door. In his left hand he held a funny-shaped red box, maybe two inches across. Mr. B stood there holding something that looked like a cross between a cookie jar and a cigar humidor. Since Jack had never seen a black ceramic cookie jar, he assumed it was a humidor.

"Good luck to us both, Gordon."

Mr. B nodded. "We'll need it."

They shared that strange handshake again, and then the freeholder left.

Mr. Brussard looked unhappy as he closed the door. With a sigh he returned to his den.

As soon as he was out of sight, Jack darted from the bathroom and headed back to the basement.

His mind whirled as he descended the stairs. What was this "klazen" they'd been talking about? From what he'd just heard, it killed people. But not just any people . . . "those responsible."

Responsible for what?

It sounded crazy, but here were two grown men, one of them a freeholder, both frightened by this thing Jack had never heard of.

Despite previous worries about *Nineteen Eighty-Four*'s Big Brother, Weezy's idea about a two-way TV that could search all the libraries in the world was starting to sound pretty good to Jack.

No one in his family had heard of a "klazen" and, try as he might, he couldn't find a word about it anywhere. The big problem was not knowing how to spell it. So he'd tried every variation he could think of: *clazen, klazen, clayzen, klazin,* and on and on, but found nothing in the family's *Encyclopedia Britannica* or its unabridged dictionary.

So he called up the source of all weird knowledge—at least in his world.

"Please tell me the cube's all right," Weezy said as soon as she came on the phone. "It is, isn't it? You didn't lose it or anything, did you?"

"And a good morning to you too," he said.

"Please, Jack. I'm serious. You're not calling me to tell me—"

"Everything's fine, Weez. I've got it right here. And guess what? Mister Brussard can open it too. But Steve can't. Isn't that weird?"

A pause, then, "Yeah, I guess so. Is that what you called to tell me?"

"No. I heard a strange word last night: klazen. Ring a bell?"

"No. How do you spell it?"

He read off all the variations he'd written down.

"Nope," she said. "Never heard of it. What's it supposed to be?"

"I'll tell you later. I'm going to ask Mister Rosen if he's ever heard of it. Want to come along? I can explain on the way."

"Okay. But stop here first. And bring the cube."

He laughed. "You sound like Linus and his blanket."

"Ja-ack!" She made it a two-syllable word.

"Okay, okay. Will do."

Before leaving he returned to his room and checked the tepin-treated pistachios on the windowsill. Nice and dry. Great. He opened the envelope Mr. Canelli had used for the peppers and scooped them into it, then placed that in the top drawer of his desk.

He rubbed his hands together. Later today, if Tom stayed true to form, big brother would get his. Oh, yes. In spades.

Mwah-ha-ha-ha!

2

On the way from Weezy's to USED, Jack noticed that she looked different. Her hair was down and her clothes were a little dressier than usual. Still all black, though.

He explained what he'd overheard about the klazen.

Weezy shook her head. "I don't get it. What's it supposed to do? Kill you?"

Jack remembered Mr. Brussard's words: *Maybe his heart simply stopped . . . it's the way a klazen works.*

"I think so. He said it can 'sniff out those responsible.'"

Weezy looked at him. "Responsible for what?"

"That's what I'd like to know. I'm pretty sure it's a Lodge thing."

"Which means it could have something to do with that body we found."

That would be cool, but too coincidental.

"Oh, that reminds me," he said, realizing he should have told her earlier. "Kate learned something about how he was killed."

He told her about the arms being cut off at the elbows and sewn into the armpits.

Weezy looked shocked, then annoyed. "And when were you going to tell me about this?"

Jack gave a sheepish shrug. "This klazen thing sort of knocked it out of my head."

"Forearms cut off . . . sewn into his armpits . . ." She

visibly shuddered. "I've never heard of anything like that. It's gross." Then she smiled at him. "But kind of cool that we found it."

Jack hesitated, then decided to go ahead. "There's something I need to talk to you about."

"Something *else* you haven't told me?"

"It's about Steve."

"Brussard? What's up?"

"He's drinking. Like every night."

"You mean alcohol?"

"No, Gatorade." When she looked puzzled, he said, "Yes, alcohol. I'm afraid he's going to wind up like Weird Walt. But I don't know what to do. Any ideas?"

"Tell his folks."

Was she kidding?

"I can't do that."

"Why not? He's your friend, isn't he?"

"Yeah, sort of."

"So what are you going to do, stand by and watch him go down the tubes?"

"No, but I can't rat him out. He'll never speak to me again."

"At least he'll still be able to speak."

"Yeah, but—"

"Then make an anonymous call to his dad. Disguise your voice—"

"He'll know it's me."

"Well, if he's your friend, then you've got to do *something*." She threw up her hands. "I don't believe this. You ask me what to do, and then you shoot down every suggestion I make."

Jack shook his head. "Probably shouldn't have said anything. Girls just don't understand."

"Well, I've given you my solution." She sounded annoyed. "You don't like it, come up with your own."

"I will."

But just what that would be, he didn't know.

They arrived at USED then. Jack led the way inside and found Mr. Rosen behind the counter. He looked up with a surprised expression.

"You're clairvoyant, maybe?"

Jack stopped and felt Weezy bump into his back. "What do you mean?"

"I was just looking up your number to call you. I heard from Professor Nakamura and he wants to tell you something about that pyramid you brought him."

Weezy grabbed Jack's upper arm and squeezed. "He's found out something?"

Mr. Rosen shrugged. "He didn't say, just that he needed to talk to you."

In a blink Weezy was out the door, heading for the bikes. "Let's go!"

"Be right there," Jack said as he stepped closer to the counter. "Mister Rosen? You ever heard of something called a klazen?"

"A klazen?" The old man shook his head. "Never. What is it?"

Jack hid his disappointment. "That's what I'm trying to find out. Okay, see you later."

When he stepped outside, Weezy was already on her bike, wheeling in tight circles.

"Come on, Jack! What are we waiting for? He's found out what it is!"

"Don't get all worked up. Mister Rosen said he just wants to tell us something. That something could be anything—like it was made in Japan two weeks ago."

She gave him a hard look. "Why are you always trying to rain on my parade?"

Jack couldn't help but hear Barbra Streisand belting out those lyrics from Mom's *Funny Girl* album. Not his favorite.

"I'm not, Weez. You know better that that."

She sighed. "Yeah, I guess I do. Sorry."

"I just don't want you disappointed. I mean, you know, sometimes your parades march right off a cliff. And then you know how you get."

She tended to get herself so worked up in anticipation, only to crash and burn when it fell through. He'd seen an up mood change to down in a heartbeat. It wasn't pretty.

"I'll be fine. Because I *know* he's found all sorts of strange things about it, keys to a secret. Who knows? It might open the door to the hidden truths of all history!"

There she goes, Jack thought as she headed toward the highway—off on her bike and off on a bubble of expectation. He hoped the professor wouldn't burst it, but he sensed it coming. He didn't want to be there when she fell, but someone had to catch her.

3

The professor took them to the library and pulled up an extra chair so both Jack and Weezy could sit, then seated himself behind the desk.

"What is it?" Weezy said, squirming in her seat. She couldn't seem to sit still. Looked like she was going to vibrate herself into another dimension. "What did you find?"

"Nothing useful, I am afraid. Most sorry. Almost everything points to your artifact as of modern origin."

Uh-oh, Jack thought, glancing at Weezy. Here it comes.

"That can't be," she said softly—too softly. "Your tests are wrong. They've got to be."

He shook his head slowly. "I fear not. We did electron-micro scanning of the symbols and found they have the fineness and sharp edges that only a laser can do. Actually, sharper than most lasers."

" 'Sharper than most lasers,' " she said, her voice rising. "Doesn't that tell you something right there?"

"It tells me it is a hoax. Those engraved characters are meant to lead us to believe your object is pre-Sumerian, but no pre-Sumerian culture had such technology. As I told you yesterday, they scraped their writings, their pictograms and ideograms, onto clay tablets."

"But what if there was an advanced civilization before Sumer? One that was wiped out by the Great Flood?"

The professor smiled. "That is the stuff of fantasy. No record of such a culture or civilization exists."

"All right then," she said. "What's the pyramid made of? Did you figure that out?"

He shook his head—a bit uncertainly, Jack thought. "No. But we know it is some kind of alloy."

Weezy leaned back. "An alloy that can't be scratched—or at least I couldn't scratch it. Could you?"

Professor Nakamura looked even less certain. "We did not try. It is not our property—it is yours."

"That's right. And I'd like it back now."

Jack said, "We're forgetting about the most important test. What about that argon dating you mentioned?"

"Yes-yes. Potassium argon. We did that."

Jack waited to hear the results but the professor did not go on.

"And?" Weezy said.

Now the professor looked *really* uncomfortable. "The results were . . . how shall I say it? . . . inconclusive."

Weezy shook her head, "I don't understand what you mean. I understand what 'inconclusive' means, but what kind of inconclusive results are you talking about?"

"You couldn't date it?" Jack said.

"Oh, yes, we got a date, but an impossible date."

Jack felt a fleeting tingle up his spine. *Impossible?* What kind of date would be impossible? He glanced over at Weezy and saw her sitting rigid in her chair.

"W-what was the date?" she said.

The professor waved his hands. "I hesitate to tell you because it will only fuel groundless speculation."

Weezy looked ready to explode. She spoke through her teeth. "What . . . was . . . the . . . date?"

Professor Nakamura folded his hands on his desk and stared at them. He spoke in a low voice.

"Fourteen thousand years."

In a flash Weezy was out of her seat and on her feet, leaning over the desk.

"Did I hear you right? Fourteen thousand years? *Fourteen?*"

"Yes." The professor looked up at her. "And if you know anything about human history, you will know that is impossible."

"I know there's a lot we *don't* know about human history."

The professor nodded. "This is true, and there are arguments about which human civilization was first. It appears to be Sumer, but that can be traced back only to five thousand B.C.—seven thousand years ago. The test says your pyramid is twice as old. Clearly that is impossible."

"Not if it belonged to an advanced civilization that was wiped out by the Great Flood."

Jack glanced at her, not sure if she was kidding or not. But she looked dead serious.

"You mean like in the Bible?" he said. "Noah's flood?"

Weezy kept her eyes on the professor. "The Sumerians had exactly the same legend, long before the Bible was written. All the ancient civilizations of that region had a story about a great flood that cleansed the land. Am I right, professor?"

He stared at her. "How old are you?"

"I'll be fifteen next month."

"Fifteen . . . you know much for fifteen."

"I read a lot. But back to the Great Flood. Maybe a flood was only part of it. Maybe it was much more severe. Maybe it wiped out the civilization that made that little pyramid and forced human beings to start all over again from scratch."

The professor rolled his eyes. "Next you will be quoting Immanuel Velikovsky."

"I know the name," she said, "but I've never read him. I've heard he's a kook." She smiled. "But then, some people think *I'm* a kook, so maybe I should look him up." She held out her hand. "May I have my fourteen-thousand-year-old 'hoax' back now?"

"I am afraid I do not have it with me."

Weezy frowned. "You're going to run more tests?"

"Yes, but not me, personally. I took the liberty of sending it to the Smithsonian Institution for dating."

"You *what*? Without asking me?" She glanced quickly at Jack. "I mean, us?"

Jack didn't care all that much that she'd added the "us." He too was ticked that the professor had taken it upon himself to send their pyramid all the way to Washington, D.C.

"Now just a minute, young lady. You gave that over to me for investigation and that is precisely what I am doing. The Smithsonian Institution has access to equipment I do not. They will find an accurate date of origin. Is that not what you wanted from me?"

Jack thought about that. He'd been to the Smithsonian on his eighth-grade trip just this past spring and had been wowed by the sheer size of the place—all the buildings, all the exhibits. Too many to see on just one trip.

Weezy's lower lip showed just a trace of a quiver. "But you should have asked first."

The professor nodded. "Yes, I suppose I should have. But I thought you would be happy to know that some of the greatest experts in the field will be studying your artifact."

"Well," she said slowly, "I guess I am. But what if something happens to it along the way? Or what if it gets lost? Things get lost in the mail, you know."

"Oh, no. I did not send it by mail. I used overnight delivery. Federal Express. And I packed it very carefully in a box. It will be fine. The Smithsonian Institution handles valuable artifacts all the time. They will take good care of it."

"They'd better," she said.

Jack didn't see much point in hanging around here any longer so he rose and stood next to Weezy.

"Will you call us as soon as you hear anything?"

The professor slid a sheet of paper and a pencil across the desk.

"Leave me your phone numbers. As soon as I hear from the Smithsonian, you will hear from me."

As Weezy wrote down their numbers, Jack said, "Professor, have you ever heard of a klazen?"

Weezy stopped writing but did not look up.

The professor frowned. "An unfamiliar term. What does it refer to?"

"I'm not sure. A creature, maybe? A spirit?"

"No. Most sorry. I have never heard of such a thing."

Swell, Jack thought. I'm batting zero today.

4

"Well," he said, squinting at Weezy outside Professor Nakamura's house, "what do you think?"

Her expression was grim. "I think I wish I had the pyramid back. I've got a bad feeling . . ."

Jack tried to look on the bright side. "Yeah, but you've got to admit, if anyone can find out what that thing is, it's the Smithsonian."

"I suppose." Suddenly she perked up and looked at him with bright eyes. "What if they come back with the same age? Fourteen thousand years! Do you know what that means?"

"It means Professor Nakamura will have to eat a big plate of fricasseed crow."

She gave his arm a gentle slap. "Who cares about that. It means we'll have to start rewriting human history!"

Jack thought about that and found it kind of scary.

"Yeah, I guess we will."

Just then a blue Mustang convertible pulled up with a grinning Carson Toliver behind the wheel. He pointed to Weezy.

"Hey, you following me?"

She reddened. "No, I, no, I mean, no, we were just visiting Professor Nakamura."

This guy had just turned the smartest girl Jack knew into a babbling boob.

"Aw, too bad," he said, dramatically snapping his fingers.

"I was hoping you were. A guy likes to have a pretty girl following him."

Weezy said nothing, just stared.

"Hey," Carson added, "I bet you like the Sex Pistols."

Weezy hesitated, then said, "Yeah. They're cool."

"Knew it! I could tell by the way you dress. I love to blast them as I tool down the road."

You *are* a tool, Jack thought.

"Want to try that sometime?"

"Yeah." She swallowed. "Sure."

"Great. I'll call you up sometime and we'll go for a spin."

He waved and roared off. Weezy watched him go, then grabbed Jack's arm.

"Did you hear that? Carson Toliver just asked me out."

"Yeah, to listen to the Sex Pistols—which you hate by the way. Or did you forget?"

"I didn't forget. They're awful."

"Then why'd you tell him they were cool?"

"I couldn't insult him."

"If you ask me, *he's* following *you*."

"Don't be silly. He lives right on this street." She beamed. "And he thinks I'm pretty."

Weezy had said she had a bad feeling about the pyramid going to the Smithsonian. Well, Jack had the same sort of feeling about Weezy getting into Carson Toliver's car.

5

Jack sat by the living room window, pretending to read but really watching the driveway.

Mom had the annoying *Oklahoma!* score playing, and he was forced to listen to "The Surry with the Fringe on Top" as he stood watch. Stupid, lame-o song.

She was in the kitchen fixing dinner and Kate was helping. Dad wouldn't be home from work for another half hour or so. Only Tom was unaccounted for. He'd been gone most of the day but Mom said she expected him for dinner.

Jack wanted to know when he arrived so he'd have time to set up his sting.

When he saw Tom's '79 Malibu pulling into the driveway, he jumped up and hurried to the kitchen. He pulled out the bag of pistachios and, while Kate and Mom weren't looking, emptied the envelope with the tepin-treated nuts on the counter. He'd just tucked the envelope into his back pocket when Kate turned and saw the pile.

She frowned. "I'd eat those right now, Jack. You-know-who just arrived."

Good old Kate, always looking out for him.

Jack shrugged. "They'll be okay."

She shook her head. "You're a glutton for punishment, aren't you."

"Trust me, Kate," he said with a smile. "I'm anything but a glutton for punishment."

But, he thought, I've arranged some punishment for the glutton.

He started shelling pistachios but ate them instead of adding them to the pile. He tensed as he heard the front-door screen slam. This was it. Tom still had a chance. He could turn Jack's plan into wasted effort by walking past and leaving the pistachios where they were. His fate was in his own hands.

Jack pretended to be looking the other way as his big brother breezed into the kitchen. Without breaking stride and without the slightest hesitation, Tom swept the nuts off the counter and into his hand, then popped them all into his mouth.

Jack yelled, "Hey!"

Kate said, "Tom!"

Mom hadn't noticed and Tom said nothing as he opened the refrigerator and reached for a beer. He never made it. He froze in mid-reach, then coughed and spat the nuts into his palm.

"What the—?" As he turned toward Jack, his face started to redden. "What did you—?" Then the redness darkened. "Oh, my *God!*"

As Tom dove for the sink, Jack remembered what Mr. Canelli had said about water making the burning worse. He felt it only fair to warn Tom, but he lowered his voice, Willy Wonka style.

"Stop. Don't. Come back."

"Dear Lord!" Mom cried as Tom dumped the partially chewed nuts in the sink and turned on the water.

He didn't wait to get a glass, simply tilted his head under the faucet and let the water run into his mouth.

"Tom?" Kate said. "What on Earth are you doing?"

Tom lifted his head—his face was almost purple now—and pointed to Jack. "That little bastard—!"

Mom whipped him with her dish towel. "Thomas! I will not have that kind of language in this house. Now you—"

Tom wailed and stuck his mouth under the faucet again.

"The burning!" he croaked between gulps. "I can't stop the burning!"

Jack watched him, trying to keep from smiling. He felt like going over there and dancing around him, chanting, *Gotcha-gotcha-gotcha!*

Kate turned to Jack. "What did you do?"

Jack raised his hands, palms up, and shrugged. "Nothing much. Just spiced them up a little."

She smiled. "With what? Pepper?"

Jack nodded.

"What kind? Jalapeño? Habañero?"

"Hotter."

She began to laugh. "Oh, this is rich—this is too rich!"

"It's not funny!" Tom yelled, his voice echoing from down in the sink.

Mom was clueless. "What's the matter? What's wrong with him?"

"He poisoned me!" Tom cried, then went back to drinking.

Mom obviously knew that wasn't true, because she was half smiling as she turned to Jack.

"Why did you poison your brother, Jackie?"

Kate was still laughing. "Tom stole his pistachios, but they had pepper on them!"

Mom hit Tom again with the towel. "*Now* are you going to stop stealing from him? Have you learned your lesson?"

"I'm going to kill him!"

"You'll do no such thing. And drink some milk. Water makes it worse."

Tom lifted his dripping face. "What?"

Kate grinned at him. "The stuff that burns is an oil. Water spreads it around."

"Oh, no!" Tom leaped for the fridge.

"And don't you dare drink from the carton!" Mom told him.

6

Jack stood by while Kate told Dad what had happened.

"Serves him right." He laughed, then settled down to watch the evening news before dinner.

Though the burning from the tepin juice had been intense, it hadn't lasted long. Tom recovered and had retreated to his room in embarrassment. Jack was heading back to the kitchen when he heard a knock. He reversed direction and arrived in time to see his dad opening the front door for Mr. Bainbridge.

They shook hands, then Mr. Bainbridge pointed at Jack and smiled.

"There's the man I want to see."

Jack looked around. Man? Me? Was he in trouble?

"Jack?" Dad said. "What for?"

"Seems he stood up for my brother-in-law the other day when that Bishop punk was hassling him."

Dad tilted his head down and looked at Jack over the top of his reading glasses.

"That so?"

Embarrassed, Jack shrugged. "Not really. Weezy's the one who—"

"Yeah. Walt's not always reliable in what he says, but he told me you and the Connell girl took his back against two guys a lot bigger." Mr. Bainbridge looked at Dad. "Sound like your boy's not afraid of anything—just like his old man."

Dad gave him a sharp look, then turned to Jack. "Grab us a couple of beers, will you?"

"Sure."

As he left the room he heard Dad say, "No Korea talk, Kurt. You know how I feel about that. Save it for the VFW."

Yeah, Dad never wanted to talk about the war. He and Mr. Bainbridge had met in Korea. Then, seven years ago, when his company transferred him from Kansas City to Trenton, he looked up Dad. He loved to fish, and when he learned how plentiful the trout and bass were in these parts, he decided Johnson was the ideal place to live. So he moved in with his wife, Evelyn, and her brother, Weird Walt.

Jack pulled out a couple of Carlings, red cans with a black label, and brought them back to the living room. On the way in, he heard Mr. Bainbridge speaking in a low voice.

"Yeah, Walt's all right. Keeps to himself. Mostly we don't know he's there. But the drinking . . . man, the guy's always half lit. He says it's because of 'Nam, but come on—he couldn't have seen any worse than we did above the thirty-eighth. We—"

He cut off when Jack arrived with the beers.

"Ah, here's the man we've been waiting for." He laughed as he took the can from Jack. "'Mabel! Black Label!' I see you're still stocking the Canuck stuff, Tom."

"They know their beer."

They popped their tops, clinked cans, and drank.

Jack hesitated, then had to ask: "What did you mean by 'above the thirty-eighth'?"

Dad shot Mr. Bainbridge an annoyed look, then said, "North Korea and South Korea are divided along the line of

latitude thirty-eight degrees north of the equator. It's called
the thirty-eighth parallel. When the commies in North Korea
tried to take over the south, we were sent in to kick their
butts back above the thirty-eighth."

Mr. Bainbridge wiped his mouth. "Which we did pretty
easily, and that should have been that. But some REMF
ordered us above the thirty-eighth, and that's when it got
ugly. I remember—"

"Hold on there, Kurt," Dad said, raising a hand. Then
he turned to Jack. "What you've just heard is a history
lesson. Let's leave it at that."

Before Jack could protest, or ask what a REMF was, Mr.
Bainbridge said, "Hey, you hear what happened at Al
Sumter's wake?"

With no prospect of war stories, Jack had been about
to retreat to his room. But now he was all ears.

"I thought that was tonight," Dad said.

"They had a viewing this afternoon. That freeholder,
what's his name?" He snapped his fingers. "God, you see
his name everywhere—"

Jack's mouth felt as dry as pine needles. Finally he
managed to say, "Mister Haskins?"

He pointed to Jack. "You nailed it!" He smiled at Dad.
"Good citizen you've got there. Knows his civics."

Jack decided to let him go on thinking that. No way
could he tell him about eavesdropping on Haskins and
Steve's father.

"But tell me," Mr. Bainbridge went on, grinning. "Do
you have any idea what the hell a freeholder does?"

Jack shook his head. "Not really."

Mr. Bainbridge laughed. "Neither does anybody else!"

Jack wasn't interested in what freeholders did. Who cared? He was interested in the fate of just one of them. He had a premonition he needed confirmed.

"What happened to him?"

"Keeled over dead, just like Sumter. Couldn't bring him back. Seems like his heart just stopped cold."

Stopped cold . . . that was how Jack felt. Could it have been the klazen? Was there really such a thing?

"Wonder who'll be next?" Mr. Bainbridge said.

"What do you mean?" Jack asked.

"They say deaths come in threes. We've had Sumter, and now Haskins. Who's going to be the third?"

Jack must have looked as upset as he felt because his dad reached out and gave his shoulder a gentle squeeze.

"That's just an old wives' tale, Jack. And don't worry, if there's a third, it won't be anyone from this house."

Jack hadn't been worrying about that—the idea of anyone in his family dying was, well, unthinkable. He'd been worrying about Mr. Brussard. He didn't want Steve to lose his father. But he couldn't say that to Dad. How could he explain something he didn't understand himself?

He turned to Mr. Bainbridge. "Can I ask you something?"

Both Dad and Mr. Bainbridge looked at him expectantly.

"Go ahead," Mr. Bainbridge said.

"Have you ever heard of a klazen?"

Both frowned. Dad shook his head. "You asked me about that this morning." He glanced at Mr. Bainbridge. "Kurt?"

Mr. Bainbridge shrugged. "Doesn't ring a bell. What is it?"

"Well . . . I heard the word and just wanted to know—"

"Hey, wait," Mr. Bainbridge added. "I knew a Hans Kla-zen back in Mizzoo. Dutchman. But that's the only time I've heard the word." He glanced at his watch. "Oops. Ev'll have dinner ready. Gotta go."

He polished off his beer and handed Jack the empty. "Thanks for the brew, sport." Turning to Dad, he said, "You coming down to the VFW tonight for the smoker?"

Jack knew that was a code word for the one night each month the VFW showed dirty movies.

Dad shook his head. "Not my thing."

Mr. Bainbridge laughed. "Deadeye, you amaze me. After all we went through, how can you still be a prude?"

Dad didn't smile. "Just the way it is, I guess."

Jack barely heard him. Deadeye? Mr. Bainbridge called him *Deadeye*. Wasn't that what they called marksmen?

7

After their guest was gone, Dad headed upstairs to change out of his suit into something cooler. Jack followed.

"Why'd he call you 'Deadeye'?" he asked as his father unbuttoned his shirt.

"Did he?"

"Yeah. Does that mean you were a good shot in the army?"

He slipped out of his suit pants and hung them on a hanger. He was wearing light blue boxer shorts beneath.

"We don't discuss the army or the war, remember?"

"Yes, but—"

"No buts."

"Walt told me he was in a mental hospital once."

Dad gave him a sharp look. "When?"

"After the war."

"No, I mean, when did he tell you?"

"Yesterday afternoon. Why was he in?"

"From what Kurt tells me, he came home from 'Nam saying he could heal people with a touch. The VA hospital in Northport diagnosed him as a paranoid schizophrenic, but harmless. He joined a faith-healing tent show in the South, and Kurt was told some wild story about him really curing people until his drinking got him kicked off the tour. They say he's harmless, but still . . . keep your distance."

Heal with a touch . . . was that why he wore gloves all the time?

As Jack watched his father hang up his pants, he spotted the metal box on the top shelf of the closet. He'd seen it a million times but now it took on special significance.

"What's in the box?" He'd asked before but it never hurt to try again.

"Nothing important."

"You always say that."

He pulled off his undershirt and Jack spotted the scar where he'd had his appendix removed.

"That's because the contents don't change."

Jack was sure now that Dad kept his marksman medals and other cool army stuff hidden there.

First chance he got, he was going to sneak a peek.

8

After dinner, Jack turned on the living room television and started switching through the channels. Cable TV had arrived in Johnson during the winter, and Jack's family had signed up the instant their street was wired. For as long as he could remember, Dad had been complaining about the poor reception from their aerial. At last he had a cure.

The really neat thing about cable TV was the remote that came with the box. Their living room set was an older model where you had to get up and cross the room if you wanted to change the channel. All he had to do now was stand back and press a button. He loved it.

An all-news channel called CNN was on, showing some comments by President Reagan followed by a story on Hurricane Alicia. Tom stopped to watch on his way out the door. Jack kept an eye on him in case he had some sort of vengeance in mind for the pistachio episode.

After a few minutes his brother said, "An all-news channel? Whose stupid idea was that? Won't last a year—I guarantee it." Then he turned to Jack. "And don't think you're home free, numbnuts. I never forget. Reprisal is on the way. It'll hit when Miracle Boy least expects it."

Jack waggled his hand. "Ooooh, I'm shaking."

Tom's mouth tightened into a thin line. He looked like he wanted to throw a punch. Jack readied himself for evasive maneuvers.

But Tom only pointed a finger and said, "It's coming. Get ready."

As he slammed out the front door, Jack resumed switching channels. He'd decided to skip Steve's tonight and catch some TV—maybe *Cheers* and *Taxi*. They were always good for a laugh.

"Hold it," Dad said.

Jack jumped and looked around. He hadn't heard him come in.

His father pointed to the set. "Go back one."

Jack did and saw a man in a blue blazer, a light blue shirt, and a patterned yellow tie sitting at a desk and talking to the camera. His hair looked funny: He'd parted it just above his right ear and combed it all the way across the top of his balding scalp to end above his left year.

"Who's that?"

"Ed Toliver," Dad said, snorting. "Mister Big Shot, telling everyone the surefire way to get rich in real estate."

Carson's father . . . that was why he looked familiar.

"Is that a bad thing?"

"According to him, the only sure way is to give him your money and have him invest it for you—and then let him take a hefty cut of the profits."

Jack stared at the screen. "Well, he must do pretty well if they've got him on TV."

Another snort from Dad. "That's a public access channel run by the local cable company. Toliver gets a weekly slot because he claims his show is educational. My eye."

"You want to listen?" Jack prayed his father would say no.

"You kidding? See what else is on."

As Jack's thumb moved toward the channel button, he heard Mr. Toliver say, *"I'd like to close tonight's installment a little differently than usual—with a few important remarks about the Septimus Lodge."*

He paused to listen.

"I know this will sound strange coming from a broadcast about real estate, but I feel it my duty to speak out. This week has presented us with three dead members of the Septimus Lodge. One was murdered years ago, and the past two days have witnessed the sudden deaths of two more."

Jack spun to face his father. "Was Mister Haskins in the Lodge?"

When his dad nodded, Jack turned back to the screen. Haskins was a member too! And he'd visited another Lodger last night—Mr. Brussard.

"I think we're long overdue for answers from the Septimus Lodge. Did it or any of its members have anything to do with the murder of Anton Boruff? Although the cause of death of members Sumter and Haskins appears natural, it seems odd that they coincide so closely with the discovery of Anton Boruff's corpse. I don't know about you, but I have questions—questions that will not be answered if I alone ask them. That is why I am calling for a public inquiry into the Septimus Lodge."

"He should know better than that," Dad muttered.

"Why?" Jack asked.

"Because he's not going to get anywhere."

"In this day and age of a free and open society, there is no place for exclusive and elitist secret brotherhoods like the Septimus Lodge. Haven't we learned any lessons from Watergate? Or are we doomed forever to go on repeating the same mistakes? That is why I am calling on the Septimus Lodge to open its

records to the public. And if they will not do so voluntarily, then I am calling on the Burlington County DA and the state attorney general to initiate legal action to force them to do so. What have they got to hide?"

Jack turned to his father. "Do you really think the Lodge has anything to do with—?"

Dad shrugged. "How can I answer that? Nobody except its members knows anything about the Lodge—and there, I believe, lies the crux of Toliver's little tirade."

"He doesn't like secrecy?"

"No. I think he'd love the Lodge's secrecy if he was in on it, but he's not. They gave him a thumbs-down when he tried to join and I don't think he's ever forgiven them."

That surprised Jack. "But, like you said, he's a big-shot real estate guy. I'd think they'd *want* him."

Dad shrugged again. "Everything about that Lodge crew is odd. Membership is by invitation only. But they're not like some exclusive country club that admits only folks of a certain religion and a certain color with a bank account of a certain size. They've got whites, blacks, yellows, Jews, Catholics—you name it. Rich, poor, and everything between."

"Then what was wrong with Mister Toliver?"

"Who knows?" Dad smiled. "Maybe they don't like his comb-over."

Jack wasn't sure if asking might embarrass his dad, but he needed to know.

"Did you ever try to join?"

"Me? Nah! They tried to rope me in back in the early seventies—used a full-court press—but I wasn't interested."

Jack stared at his father in shock. "They asked *you?*"

Dad laughed. "What? You say that like you think there's something wrong with me."

"No . . . I just . . . I don't know . . . you never said anything."

"What for? We went 'round and 'round for about a year, them asking, giving me tours of the Lodge—"

"You've been inside? What's it like?"

"A lot of old furniture, odd paintings, and that strange sigil everywhere you look."

"What's a sigil?"

"Their seal—the thing over their front door. They must love it because it's on everything."

Jack shuddered. "Yeah, even its members."

"Oh, so you heard about that."

"Yeah. That dead body we found had one, and I saw it on Mister Sumter's back after they gave up trying to revive him. Burned into their backs—ugh!"

"If that's part of being a Lodge member, they didn't mention it to me. But let me tell you, even if I'd wanted in, that would have changed my mind. That would have been a deal-breaker."

"I can't believe you turned them down. They say anybody who's somebody is a member."

Dad smiled. "Well, maybe I'm as much a somebody as I want to be. Besides, it's easy to say anybody who's somebody is a Lodger because no one knows their membership. They're secretive as all hell about that and everything else. I mean, if an individual member wants it known that he belongs, he's free to tell anybody who'll listen. But if not, it remains a secret guarded like Fort Knox."

Jack shook his head. "But I still don't see why you didn't join."

Dad shrugged and headed back toward the kitchen.

"It's a secret society. Too many secrets can wear you down."

Wear you down? Jack thought after he was gone. Did that mean *he* had secrets? How many?

9

"That's gotta be the suckiest game ever made," Steve said as they walked through the growing darkness.

"I thought the *Pac-Man* I got last year was bad," Jack said, shaking his head, "but this was even worse."

He and Steve had spent the last couple of hours on Eddie's Atari trying to make sense of his *ET: The Extra-Terrestrial* game.

Steve waved his arms. "How do you take such a great movie and make a boring game out of it. Boooooring!"

This was the Steve Brussard Jack had grown to like over the past few years—funny, kind of loud, and very opinionated.

"And who designed ET? He looked like a pile of green Legos."

Steve shook his head. "Enough to drive you to drink."

Uh-oh.

Jack landed a friendly punch on his shoulder. "Come on. We had laughs without any of that."

"Yeah, but we'd've had more with a toot or two. But it turns out you were right."

"About what?"

"The booze. My old man asked me today if I'd been 'sampling' any of it."

"What'd you tell him?"

He grinned. " 'Who, *me*?' "

"Which means you need to stay away from it—unless you're looking to get busted."

Jack hated sounding like Steve's conscience, but he didn't mean it that way. He was talking common sense here. When you see someone heading for the edge of a cliff, you warn him.

"I *am* staying away. Got no choice. He locked the liquor cabinet."

"But what if he hadn't?"

Steve grinned. "Well then—different story."

"Well, then, maybe it's a good thing it's locked."

"Wait," Steve said, stopping and looking at him. "You think I've got some kind of drinking problem?"

Jack hesitated, then went ahead. "Well, you've been hitting it pretty hard."

"There's no problem, Jack. I just like it, is all. I can stop anytime I want."

Jack decided to back off. He wasn't getting through anyway.

They resumed their journey toward Steve's house—maybe tonight they'd make some real progress on the Heathkit—and were just crossing Quakerton Road when Steve pointed off to their left.

"You see that?"

Jack followed his point but saw nothing.

"What?"

"A guy walking toward the lake. Looked like my dad."

Really . . . ?

Jack looked again. Streetlights were few and far between in Johnson so it might be a while before whoever it was passed under another.

"Does he go out for walks much?"

"Hardly ever."

"Probably not him then. But just for the heck of it, why don't we follow and see?"

Because if it was Mr. Brussard, Jack wanted to know what he was up to.

His stomach tingled as they hung a left and hurried along. Tracking an unsuspecting man . . . kind of cool.

Then a strolling figure passed under a light ahead.

"Yeah, that's him," Steve said. "Let's catch up."

Jack spotted a light in Steve's eyes. He seemed to really like his dad.

Jack felt a growing sense of disappointment. Mr. B wasn't doing anything other than walking. Looked like he was heading for Old Town, most likely to the Lodge.

They were getting closer as he came to the Old Town bridge, but instead of crossing over he veered right.

Interesting.

Quaker Lake was really a pond, but "lake" sounded better with Quaker. It had a sort of dumbbell shape with the bridge crossing the narrow point. Mr. Brussard stood on the bank of the south section, staring across at the Lodge on the far side.

As they approached Jack saw him reach into a pants pocket, pull something out, and throw it into the lake.

Whoa! What was that all about?

Jack mentally marked the location of the splash. He might want to come back sometime.

After another moment or two of staring—watching the ripples fade?—Mr. B turned and looked around and spotted them. He looked surprised and concerned, but his tone was pleasant.

"Hey! What are you two doing here?"

"We were on our way home and saw you," Steve said.

Before Mr. B could answer, a stocky man with longish black hair strolled up. They shook hands and Mr. B introduced him as Assemblyman Vasquez.

Vasquez . . . Mr. B had mentioned him last night. Jack had the impression this was a prearranged meeting because neither seemed surprised to see the other.

"Mr. Vasquez and I have things to discuss back at the house. What are you boys up to?"

"We're gonna work on the computer," Steve said.

"I think I'll take a rain check on that," Jack blurted. "I've got a couple of lawns to do early tomorrow."

True, but not why he was begging off.

"Later," he said, and trotted away.

But instead of heading home he began running through the shadows. Sure as night follows day they'd be walking back along Quakerton Road. To avoid it he cut through backyards, setting more than one family dog to barking. Jack wanted to reach the Brussard house first.

10

Now I *am* acting like a boy detective, he thought as he crouched in the shadows of the Brussards' yard. How lame is this?

But so what? He had nothing better to do. TV offered only summer reruns anyway.

The man he'd seen with Mr. Brussard last night had dropped dead, and now this Vasquez guy they'd mentioned shows up. He sensed something going on, but couldn't say what.

No way he could talk to his folks about it—they'd think he was crazy.

Hey, Dad, there's this thing called a klazen that's killing members of the Lodge and Mister Brussard thinks he can protect people against it but he's not doing too well.

Right. That would fly—right out the window. They'd be rubberizing his bedroom.

He knew he should mind his own business, but he couldn't. He told himself he wasn't out to solve a crime or anything—wasn't trying to be the Hardy Boys—he simply wanted to *know*.

He had a good view of the front of the house from here. He'd watched the three of them enter, and now he saw the two men step into the den. After a moment or two of hesitation—what if he got caught?—he steeled himself and crept forward to peek through the open window.

Mr. B and Vasquez stood facing each other. Steve's father

cradled an open humidor in one arm and was placing a little red box in Vasquez's hand.

He heard Mr. B saying, "Well, here it is, Julio. I tried to help Sumter and Haskins, but I don't think they believed the klazen was such a real threat. Don't you make the same mistake."

Some of what followed was garbled as they turned away from the window—then he heard him say, ". . . tomorrow at dawn, face your back to the sun, and use it."

Use what? Was the "it" in one of those little red boxes? Jack was dying to know.

The rest was garbled as well. Next thing he knew, Mr. Brussard was leading the assemblyman out of the room. Jack darted back into the shadows and watched the front door. He saw that strange handshake followed by good-luck wishes, and then they parted.

When Vasquez was gone, Jack crept back to the window and stared at the humidor.

What was in it? More little red boxes? And what was in *them*?

Not knowing was making him crazy.

11

When Jack got home he found his folks sitting side by side on the couch watching *Hill Street Blues*. After a little small talk, he pretended to head to the kitchen for a snack, but instead he sneaked upstairs to their bedroom. He went straight to his father's closet, stood on tiptoe, and grabbed the box. As he pulled it down he heard things clink and thunk within.

Marksmanship medals and what else? Maybe some bullets or other souvenirs from Korea. He reached for the latch, but stopped.

This didn't feel right.

Since when was he so nosy, he wondered, feeling the cool metal against his palms. He'd gone from eavesdropping on Mr. Brussard to poking through his father's private belongings.

No . . . the reason this didn't feel right was because it *wasn't* right.

But something inside was pushing him, egging him on to pop the lid and take a look. Just one look—how much could it hurt? He pressed the lid release and—

Nothing happened.

He pressed again but the lid wouldn't budge. He fingered the tiny keyhole: locked.

Just his luck.

But the key had to be somewhere. He went to Dad's dresser and searched the top. No luck. He pulled open the top drawer, the sock drawer, where Dad kept a shallow bowl for odds and ends. Jack found spare change and rubber bands and paper clips, but no key.

And then an idea hit—he knew exactly what to do.

Replacing the box on the shelf, he closed the closet door and padded downstairs to the kitchen. He went straight to the cutlery drawer and pulled out one of the black-handled steak knives. It had a slim blade and a sharp point.

Perfect.

He slipped it into his pocket and sneaked upstairs again. Kneeling by the closet with the box cradled in his lap, he worked the knife point into the keyhole, twisting it this way and that. He did it gently to avoid scratching the metal, but no matter how he angled or wiggled or twisted the blade, the lock refused to turn. He fought the temptation to give a quick, hard twist—that might bend the blade or, even worse, break the lock. How would he explain that?

Disappointed, he stared at the knife, then at the lock. They made it look so easy on TV.

Well, no use in sitting here like he was waiting to get caught.

Quickly he replaced the box, angling it just the way he'd found it, then made his way back downstairs as quietly as possible.

Two boxes—Mr. Brussard's and his father's—and no idea of what they held. Maybe he'd never know.

Bummer.

12

He didn't feel like watching *Hill Street Blues*—for a cop show it was mostly talk—so he headed for his bedroom. He still had that issue of *The Spider* to finish. He passed Kate's room—empty. Same with Tom's. Both were out. He didn't know where they'd gone, but he knew it had to be far from Johnson. Nothing happening here. Ever.

He stopped when he came to his room and noticed the closed door. He always closed it when he was in it, but left it open when he was out. Could have blown shut, but it was a heavy old hunk of wood and he hadn't noticed much of a breeze tonight, if any.

Only one possibility: Tom.

And don't think you're home free, numbnuts. I never forget. Reprisal is on the way. It'll hit when Miracle Boy least expects it.

Well, Jack hadn't been expecting anything tonight. Was this it? Had Tom left a booby trap of some sort before going out?

Jack inspected the doorknob. Nothing on it. He turned it and eased the door open an inch or so. He checked the space above the inside of the door just in case Tom had set that corny old bucket-of-water-over-the-door trick. He couldn't see Tom coming up with anything original.

But no—no bucket poised above. He pushed the door open the rest of the way and stood on the threshold, examining his room from a distance. Finding nothing obvious, he stepped in and looked around.

At first everything seemed fine, but then a strange sensation began to creep over him, a feeling that something was *wrong*. He couldn't put his finger on exactly why or how, but he was sure someone had been in here, poking through his stuff.

Things weren't quite as he'd left them. At first glance *The Spider* magazine looked right, but then he noticed how its back cover was partially bent under it. He'd never leave it like that—not after Mr. Rosen's warning. He picked it up and smoothed it out. A least it hadn't left a crease.

He took another look around. He was sure it hadn't been his mom. Because if she'd messed with *The Spider* she'd have left it in a nice neat pile with his comic books. She was a neatnik. When she came into his room—or any room, for that matter—she couldn't help straightening and neatening things up. Nothing here had been straightened. Touched, yes, but not straightened.

That left Tom.

Carefully, Jack opened his closet door. No problem. He pulled the string to light the bulb in the ceiling. He was wearing his Vans today, and his black Converse All-Stars lay where he'd kicked them off Monday. Or did they? He couldn't be sure. He picked them up and looked inside to see if Tom had left him a little surprise. They were still damp from Monday's rain, and didn't smell all that great, but he found nothing hidden inside. The clothes on the hangers looked pretty much the same, but the top shelf . . .

Someone definitely had been messing around up there.

He stepped out and dragged his desk chair over for a better look. His comic book collection was arranged in the usual way, but he could swear he'd left his *Hulk*s stacked against the left wall. They angled out now. He checked for his jar of leftover pepper juice. Yep. Still sealed and as red as he'd left it. If Tom had been up here he'd have taken it for sure and tried to figure out a way to use it on Jack.

But if it hadn't been Tom, then who?

No. Had to be Tom.

He jumped down and pulled the chair back. But why hadn't he taken anything, or left anything?

Maybe whatever he was up to was still in the planning stage.

As Jack pushed his chair into the desk's knee hole he noticed how the screen in the window to the right wasn't seated square in the frame. Never noticed that before.

Why not?

Because I'm paranoid now, that's why.

Maybe that was what Tom was up to. What did they call it? *Gaslighting*. Right. Do weird little things to someone to make them think they're crazy, like in that movie.

But that wasn't Tom's style. A bucket of water over the door was more his speed.

Well then, what was the story with the screen?

Jack stepped over to it and saw that the old-fashioned hook-and-eye latch had popped free. He grabbed the hook, pulled the screen all the way in, then latched it.

He looked out into the darkened yard. Their property lay on the north flank of Johnson and backed up to a neighboring cornfield. He couldn't see the moon itself, but its light played off the stalks.

Had somebody come in through the window? That somebody could be out there now, watching him. In fact he almost felt as if someone was.

He shook off a chill. Nah. Nothing like that. He was just reading too many weird books and magazines. Why on Earth would any stranger want to sneak into his room? Not as if he kept a fortune in his desk.

Desk—his money from USED and mowing.

He pulled open his middle drawer and found his neat stack of bills.

Whew!

Get a grip, Jack.

13

A little later he flopped back on his bed and stared at the ceiling.

Somebody—a somebody named Tom—had been in his closet tonight. And the only reason for that would be that he was planning something.

Since the best defense was a good offense, Jack figured it might be smart to do some planning of his own. But not something completely different. He didn't want to waste a second idea on Tom. Besides, he had all that pepper juice left.

He lay there thinking, scheming, and after a while he felt a smile stretching his lips: the exact same trick, only this time with a new wrinkle.

He went to the kitchen and searched through Mom's junk drawer—where she kept everything she had no other place for—and found an old eyedropper he'd seen some time ago. He grabbed that and the pistachios and headed back to his room.

He set up at his desk with the pepper juice and the eyedropper. This time he wouldn't shell the nuts. Instead, he'd dose them while they were still inside. He picked out fifteen good-size nuts with wide-open shells. Using the dropper, he added a generous amount of juice into each opening. When he was finished, he placed the nuts on the windowsill to dry—and couldn't resist taking a quick look outside to make sure no one was there.

Back in the kitchen he replaced the bag of pistachios in the cabinet. Then he wrapped a paper towel around the eyedropper, crushed it under his heel, and threw the pieces into the trash. No way he wanted anyone—not even Tom—to use that on their eyes.

He returned to his room and dropped back on his bed, thinking about Tom sneaking through his room, just as he'd been in Dad's. He didn't like the idea, just as Dad wouldn't.

Maybe he should just forget about that box. He couldn't get it open anyway.

Then he remembered something he'd seen at USED and suddenly the world seemed a little brighter.

1

"Hi, Mister Rosen!" he called as he strolled into USED. "It's me, Jack."

"I can hear you," the old man said as he ambled from the rear. "In China they can hear you." He glanced at the clock. "And it's just after nine. What are you doing here three hours early?"

Jack held up the issue of *The Spider* he'd finished last night. "I wanted to bring this back." He gently and reverently laid it on the counter. "See? The same condition as when I took it."

"So it is," he said as he inspected it, turning it over and back again. "And this couldn't wait until noon?"

Jack had thought he could wait but found it impossible. He'd been so anxious to get here he'd had trouble concentrating on the Spider's exploits last night.

"I want to buy something."

Mr. Rosen stared at him over his reading glasses. "Again—it couldn't wait till later?"

"I suppose it could've but I wasn't sure you still had it."

"And what might that be?"

"Let me get it and show you."

Jack hurried all the way to the very rear of the store to

where a beat-up old dresser sat in a corner. He'd been dusting it off last month when he'd pulled open the top drawer and found a folded piece of felt containing an assortment of metal doohickeys of varying shapes, all odd. Some of them reminded him of the picks his dentist used when he was looking for cavities, others were half cylinders made of thin metal and flanged along the top.

Folded within was a small booklet titled *Lock Picking Made Easy*.

He remembered thinking at the time how cool it would be to know how to pick a lock, but a quick look through the booklet had convinced him it was too complicated to learn without spending more time than he cared to.

Last night had changed his mind.

He pulled the kit from the drawer and brought it to the front where he slapped it on the counter in front of Mr. Rosen.

"How much?"

The old man picked it up, looked it over, then shook his head.

"Not for sale."

Jack stiffened. "But—"

"If it was for sale it would be in one of the display cases already. You did not find this in a display case, did you."

"Well, no—"

"Then it's not for sale. Put it back."

Jack had trouble hiding his disappointment. "Then why do you keep it around?"

"Because often—too often, if you ask me, and even though you didn't, I'm telling you anyway—I get locked trunks and furniture and the owners have lost the key.

Now, if the piece is old enough to have a warded lock, no problem—I have a set of skeleton keys that will take care of those."

Skeleton key . . . Jack liked the sound of that.

"But," Mr. Rosen went on, "if it has a pin-tumbler lock—like that curved-glass china cabinet I've got sitting back there—I have to call a locksmith." He frowned. "After a while, that runs into money, so I decided I'd learn how to pick locks myself."

Jack's spirits leaped. "You know how?"

Mr. Rosen shrugged. "It took a while, but I learned. Lot of good it does me now." He raised his hand and held it palm side down. Jack noticed how the fingers trembled. "A steady hand, you need, and I haven't got that any longer."

Jack's mind shifted into high gear.

"Can you teach me?"

"Why should I do that?"

"So I can open locks for you."

Mr. Rosen stared at him. "Am I detecting possibly another reason for wanting to be so helpful?"

Jack wasn't about to admit to that.

"I just think it would be cool to be able to say I know how to pick a lock."

True—every word.

"I don't know." Mr. Rosen put his hand on Jack's shoulder as he continued to stare. It made him a little uncomfortable, as if the old guy was trying to do a Vulcan mind meld. "Teaching a teenager to pick locks . . . that doesn't strike me as the wisest thing."

Jack didn't have to fake feeling offended.

"If you think I'm going to rob somebody, then forget it. You can call a locksmith instead."

Jack gathered up the kit and started back toward the rear of the store.

"Wait-wait-wait. You shouldn't get yourself in a dither already. I didn't mean that. I meant . . ." He paused, obviously searching for something to say. "I'm not sure what I meant. I know you're a good boy."

Jack wasn't so sure he liked the "good boy" bit. He tended to think of himself as kind of cool and detached. He didn't know if he really was, but that was how he wanted to be. At times he feared he was a nerd and didn't know it. Nerds never knew they were nerdy. Not knowing was a major component of nerdiness.

Mr. Rosen added, "And I know you're honest too."

That puzzled Jack. "How? I could be a master thief."

He smiled. "I doubt that."

And then Jack knew, or at least thought he did.

"The money I found!"

Mr. Rosen was nodding. "I may be many things, but careless with my cash I'm not."

On three separate occasions since he'd started working here, Jack had found bills lying around. First a single, then a five, and just last week a tenner.

"You were testing me?"

"Of course. Who knows when I might have to leave you in charge? When I return I'd like to find at least the same amount in the till as when I left."

"You don't trust me?"

"I do now. I didn't know you when I hired you. This is

your first real job, so it's not like I could ask for references. So I tested you and you passed. Others before you have failed."

"Didn't Teddy Bishop work here a few years ago?"

Mr. Rosen's expression never changed. "Not for long. And don't ask me any more because that's all I'll say."

Jack had found the bills, known they weren't his, and given them to Mr. Rosen. That was a test? He hadn't given it a second thought: They didn't belong to him.

He'd learned that lesson back when he was eight.

He'd been out on a trip with his folks—couldn't remember where—and they'd come to an unattended tollbooth on an off-ramp from the Parkway. The toll was twenty-five cents at the time and drivers were supposed to drop the exact change into a basket, which then funneled it down into the coin machine. Whether by accident or someone's design, the coin slot had become blocked, allowing the basket to fill with change.

Jack remembered his excitement when he'd seen the overflowing coins and how he'd starting rolling down the rear window, yelling, *Free money! Let me grab some!* But his excitement had died when his father turned to stare back at him with a disgusted expression. Jack couldn't recall what he'd said—something like, *Are you kidding? That's not yours . . .* or maybe, *You'd take something that doesn't belong to you?* But that withering look . . . he'd never forgotten that look.

Jack smiled up at Mr. Rosen. "So, I guess that means you'll teach me, right?"

2

"Keep tension on the wrench, Jack. Not too hard, but keep it steady."

After almost half an hour of coaching, with Mr. Rosen hovering over his shoulder, Jack wondered if he'd ever learn this.

Good thing it was a weekday morning, because they tended to be pretty slow at USED. Weekday afternoons were slightly busier, but things started moving Friday afternoon and stayed pretty busy through the weekends. That was when the "tourists"—really just folks from Philly and Trenton and thereabouts—went out for a ride in the country.

As a result, the lesson wasn't rushed or interrupted.

Since the curved-glass china cabinet was pretty much worthless if it couldn't be opened, Mr. Rosen had said it would be as good a place as any to start.

Uh-uh. The lock seemed so small.

He'd inserted the end of the thin little bar with the right angle at each end—called a tension wrench—into the bottom of the keyhole. Jack was supposed to keep pressure on it in the direction he wanted the lock's cylinder to turn. Then he'd inserted one of the slim little instruments that looked like a dentist's probe into the opening and gently pulled and pushed it forward and backward inside—Mr. Rosen called this "raking"—to move the pins and make them line up with the edge of the cylinder. Once they were all in line, the tension wrench would be able to turn the cylinder and open the lock.

The tension wrench seemed to be the key—too much pressure on it and the pins wouldn't move; too little and they wouldn't stay lined up.

It wasn't hard work, but Jack could feel the sweat collecting in his armpits.

Mr. Rosen sighed and said, "We maybe should try a bigger lock. I thought this might be better because it has fewer pins, but they're small and sometimes harder to—"

"Hey!" Jack cried as the tension bar suddenly rotated.

A strange, indescribable elation surged through him as he heard the latch slide back with a click. He grabbed the knob and pulled open the door.

"I did it!"

Mr. Rosen clapped him on the shoulder. "Good for you, my boy. Once you get that first success under your belt, the next will be easier, and the one after that even easier."

Jack stared down at the pick and tension wrench in his hands. He'd simply unlocked a china cabinet, but he felt as if he'd opened the door to a world of infinite possibilities.

He glanced up and found Mr. Rosen staring at him.

"What?"

The old man shook his head. "I hope I haven't created a problem."

Jack had a pretty good idea what he meant. He lowered his voice into *Super Friends* mode.

"I promise to never use my newfound power for evil."

Mr. Rosen's stare widened. " 'Newfound power'?"

Jack laughed. "I remember reading something like that in a comic book once."

"This isn't a comic book. This is life. Do I have your word you will not use what you've learned here today for anything illegal?"

Jack held up three fingers. "Scout's honor."

"You're a Boy Scout?" Mr. Rosen said with a frown. "I had no idea."

"Only kidding." Jack laughed. "About the Boy Scout part, I mean. But I won't do anything illegal. I promise."

And he meant it . . . at the time.

3

For the next hour or so, Jack worked on various locks around the store. Mr. Rosen had keys to all of those, so it wouldn't matter if Jack couldn't pick them.

As he worked he heard classical music waft from the front. Somehow Mr. Rosen had found an FM station out of Philly that played only classical. Jack wished he had one of those new Walkmans so he could listen to his own music, but his dad had refused to buy him one.

Turned out Mr. Rosen hadn't been quite right: Each new lock did not become easier than the last. But as each fell victim to Jack's array of picks and tension wrenches, he felt a growing sense of knowing what he was doing. He learned to refine his raking technique and how to use the finer picks to nudge the more stubborn pins into line.

He felt a rush every time one clicked open.

He was sitting on an old ladderback chair near the front of the store, working on a padlock, when an announcer interrupted Mr. Rosen's music to say something about someone's "sudden collapse." He dropped the lock when he heard him mention the name "Vasquez."

He leaped to his feet. "What was that?"

Mr. Rosen looked up from his newspaper. "One of the state legislators collapsed at some ribbon-cutting ceremony today." He stared at Jack. "You're all right? Like a ghost you look."

"I-I think I might have seen him last night."

Mr. Bainbridge's words echoed through his head: *They say deaths come in threes. We've had Sumter, and now Haskins. Who's going to be the third?*

Well, now he knew. He'd been worried that Mr. Brussard would be next, but it hadn't turned out that way.

What was happening? The most obvious explanation tied Jack's innards into knots.

According to Steve, Mr. Sumter had visited his father Monday night. Tuesday morning he was dead.

On Tuesday night Mr. Haskins had visited Mr. B. Wednesday morning, Haskins dropped dead.

Last night, Assemblyman Vasquez . . . and now he was dead.

Jack knew that at least two of the three men who'd visited Mr. Brussard had left with a little red box. They'd been told it held something that would protect them from the so-called klazen.

Jack could come to only one conclusion. The klazen didn't exist. He didn't know why or how, but he had an awful suspicion that whatever was in the boxes Steve's father had given these men had killed them.

And that would make Mr. Brussard a cold-blooded murderer.

4

"Steve's father?" Weezy said, her voice hushed. "Ohmygod, I can't believe it."

Jack shrugged. "Neither can I, but can you come up with any other explanation?"

"Could be coincidence."

Jack couldn't believe what he was hearing. "Whoa! The girl who finds conspiracies everywhere says 'coincidence'? Three visits, three days, three deaths?"

She shook her head. "But we're not talking about some mysterious stranger. This is Steve's father."

He'd needed someone to talk to, someone who'd understand, someone who wouldn't laugh at him. Only one person had fit that bill, though he'd had to wait until she returned from her weekly trip to Medford with her mother.

They'd biked into the Pines, taking the easy way by finding a semipaved road running through the Wharton State Forest preserve. This was one of the more civilized parts of the Pine Barrens, with canoeing and fishing areas, and even the restored Batsto Village. This time of year it was full of tourists. They'd parked their bikes and claimed an isolated park bench just off the roadway.

"You've got to tell somebody."

Jack nodded. "I know. But who? And tell them what? What can I say without everybody thinking I'm crazy?"

"How about that deputy?" Weezy said.

She wore her usual black jeans, black sneakers, and a

too-large black T-shirt with *Choose Death* in red letters across the back. As they talked she used a long stick to draw patterns in the sand at their feet.

"Tim Davis?" He thought about that and decided it wasn't a good idea. "Nah. He'd just think I was kidding him."

"Then it's gotta be your dad. I don't think your sister or brother—"

"Tom? Puh-*lease!*"

"Well, whatever, I don't think they've got the gravitas to make the right people listen."

" 'Gravitas'?"

She smiled. "My new word. It means substance, serious-ness. I've been waiting for days to use it." She patted the back of his hand. "Thanks."

Jack's hand tingled where she'd touched it. He felt some-thing stir inside. He liked the feeling and wished she hadn't taken her hand away.

He laughed to ease his inner turmoil. "You're amazing."

She smiled back at him. "And you're very perceptive."

They shared brief, soft laughter over that, then Jack sighed.

"I guess that leaves my dad."

She looked at him. "You can't talk to your dad?"

"Yeah, I can talk. But he doesn't take me seriously. I'm fourteen but in his head I can tell he still thinks I'm six."

"At least you can talk to him. My dad . . ." She shook her head. "He doesn't get me."

Jack nudged her. "What's not to get? You're just a typi-cal teenage girl all done up in frilly dresses and shiny little black shoes."

He'd been joking but his chest tightened when he saw her eyes puddle up.

"That's what he'd like me to be. But I just can't be a bowhead. It makes me sick." She blinked and glanced at him. "No, I mean really sick. If I had to knot a paint-splatter shirt at my hip, or wear floral-pattern jeans and Peter Pan boots, I really think I'd throw up."

"Only kidding."

"I know, but my dad's not. He wants me to look like everybody else. And he lets me know it."

Weezy's father was a pipefitter. Like everyone else in town, it seemed, he'd been in Korea. But he hadn't fought. He'd been in the construction crew that built Camp Casey. More than once Jack had heard his father say that instead of going to college after the war, he should have enrolled in a trade school and become a pipefitter like Patrick Connell. If he had he'd be less stressed and making more money.

"He just doesn't get me." She glanced at Jack again. "Do you?"

Jack hesitated. He wasn't about to lie to her, but knew he needed to put this just right.

"Truth?"

"Of course."

He took a breath. "I don't get you either."

She gave him a sharp look. "Oh, great. *Et tu, Brute?* Just great!"

He held up a hand. "Let me finish. I don't get you, but I don't need to. I don't get the black clothes or the downer music—it's like you've joined some club where I'll never be a member—but so what? We've known each other forever, Weez. You are who you are. You're Weezy Connell, the smartest and also the strangest person I know. Yeah, I don't get you, but I wouldn't have you any other way."

She dropped the stick, hopped off the bench, and walked maybe a dozen feet away. She kept her back to him but he noticed her chest heaving, as if she was sobbing, or maybe holding sobs back.

What'd I say? he thought.

He'd been trying to make her feel good but he guessed he'd screwed that up. Would he ever learn how to talk to a girl?

Watching her made him uncomfortable so he stared at the ground where she'd been doodling with the stick. He noticed with a start that they weren't random scratchings—they looked an awful lot like the pattern etched on the inside of the mystery cube. The longer he looked, the more convinced he became. Had she memorized it? But then he remembered how Weezy had told him she had a photographic memory.

Suddenly two black-sneakered feet stepped into view. Jack looked up to find Weezy's face only inches from his. She kissed him on the lips. Not a long kiss. Barely a second. But her lips were soft and their touch sent a shock through him.

And then it was over. She straightened and looked down at him. She was smiling but her face was blotchy and her eyes red.

"You're the best friend anyone could have. I don't deserve you."

She stepped over to where her Schwinn leaned against the side of the bench. She swung her leg over the banana seat and looked at him.

"Come on, Jack. Don't sit there like a lump. We've got to get you back to civilization."

But Jack did sit there, totally confused. He'd upset her, but then she'd kissed him. Weezy Connell had kissed him. Not that he hadn't kissed a girl before—sometimes hanging out turned into making out—but this was Weezy.

Of course, it hadn't been a make-out kiss, but still . . . she'd kissed him. And the feel of her lips lingered against his.

Unable to sort out the strange mix of feelings bubbling within, he pushed himself off the bench and grabbed his bike.

5

They took a different way home. Weezy, who seemed to have this entire end of the Pine Barrens laid out in her head, led him along deer trails and firebreaks he'd never seen before.

All along the way he watched her butt.

Well, what else was there to look at? As far as size went, it wasn't much. Hard to tell what her baggy clothes hid. She was thin, he knew that, but curvy thin or straight-up-and-down thin he couldn't say. Either way, he found he liked watching her from the rear as she pedaled along.

Her shortcut back to Johnson led through Old Man Foster's land and now things were starting to look familiar. When they came to the clearing with the spong where they'd found the leg-hold traps, she skidded to a stop, turned to give him a surprised look, and pointed.

There in the clearing stood a lady in a long black dress and a scarf around her neck. She carried a bundle of sticks in one arm and was moving from trap to trap, springing them with the sticks. Her three-legged dog stood by, watching.

Mrs. Clevenger.

Without hesitating, Weezy hopped off her bike and walked into the clearing. She seemed to believe in just about every kind of weirdness, but maybe she didn't believe in witches—or maybe she didn't believe Mrs. Clevenger was one. Jack wasn't so sure about that, but he followed anyway. The dog watched their approach but made no move toward them.

"Hi," he heard Weezy say as she neared.

Mrs. Clevenger looked up. She didn't seem surprised to see them. Jack had a strange feeling this old lady didn't surprise easily.

"Hi, yourself, Weezy Connell."

She took a stick from the bundle in her arm and jammed it into a nearby trap. It snapped shut, breaking off the end. She used the broken tip on a neighboring trap. When this one snapped closed, it trapped the stick. She abandoned it and grabbed another.

"Looks like fun," Weezy said. "Can I try?"

Mrs. Clevenger gave her a long look, then handed her a stick.

"I like you, young lady. But be careful where you step. Nasty things, these."

Jack grabbed one of the already sprung traps and worked its anchor free from the ground. Then he tossed it into the spong where it splashed and sank.

"You threw them in there a few days ago," Mrs. Clevenger said. It didn't sound like a question—she seemed to know. "A good thing, but in the end, only a temporary solution, as temporary as springing the traps. The trapper simply fishes them out and resets them. All we accomplish by what we do here is a respite for the animals and an inconvenience for the trapper."

Jack said, "That'll have to do, I guess."

Her eyes narrowed. "For now, yes. But someday he may do harm to creatures that must not be touched. Should that happen, he will pay dearly."

Her tone chilled Jack. For some reason he found himself very glad he wasn't that trapper.

"Oh, and we anger and frustrate him as well," she added, "so don't let him catch you at this."

Weezy looked up. "What do you think he'd do?"

Her expression was grim. "A man who sets these traps for unsuspecting animals coming to the spong to ease their thirst? What *wouldn't* he do?"

Jack looked over at her dog who hadn't moved from where it sat. He feared it might be a touchy subject but he had to ask.

"Did he . . ." He pointed to the dog. "Did a trap do that to him?"

Mrs. Clevenger looked at him and smiled. "No, he chose to have only three legs. Perhaps in sympathy for the animals hurt in the traps, perhaps for another reason. He's never said."

Jack could only stare at her. What on Earth was she talking about? It made no sense.

"What's his name?" Weezy said.

She turned toward Weezy, and as she did, Jack craned his neck to see if he could catch a glimpse of a scar beneath her scarf, but it was wrapped too tightly.

"He's had many names, and he has none. He simply is."

More weirdness. Mrs. Clevenger seemed to like to speak in riddles.

Weezy took a step toward the dog. "Can I pet him?"

"He would rather you didn't. He prefers not to be touched."

Jack looked around for a car or even another bike, but found none.

"How'd you get here?" he said.

She smiled at him. "The usual way."

Jack realized then that he might never get a straight answer from this old woman, so he bent to the task of ripping the traps from the ground and tossing them into the spong.

After springing the last trap, Weezy joined him. Mrs. Clevenger and her dog watched until the last trap was in the drink.

Jack was panting a little from the effort, as was Weezy. A sweat sheened her face and arms.

"Good," the old woman said. "I am proud of you both. But it's time for you to go."

"Why?"

"Because I hear the trapper coming."

Jack listened but heard only the incessant bug buzz of the Barrens.

"You sure?"

The old woman nodded. "Clear as day. He'll be very, very angry when he finds what we've done. So go now. Quickly."

"Are you staying?" Weezy said.

She shook her head. "No. Though I don't fear him, it's best he doesn't see me. I'll follow soon."

"It's an awful long walk."

"I'll return the way I arrived." She made shooing motions with her knobby, veiny hands. "Now get. Get!"

They got.

6

They rode side by side along the firebreak trails, talking about Steve's father and Mrs. Clevenger and this and that until they connected with the end of Quakerton Road in Old Town. They crossed the bridge, cut right onto North Franklin, then stopped at Adams Drive. Here they'd part ways. Weezy lived on Adams and Jack up at the end of Franklin on Jefferson.

"I've got something for you," she said in a low voice as she moved up close beside him.

Another kiss?

"What?"

She reached into her bike basket and pulled out two folded sheets of paper. She looked around, then thrust them at Jack.

"Here. Put these in your pocket."

He started to unfold them. "What—?"

"Look at them later! Just get them out of sight!"

Spurred by her urgent tone, he shoved them into a back pocket.

"What's going on?"

Weezy looked around again, then whispered, "I think someone was out in my backyard last night."

Jack felt a chill as he remembered his unlatched screen and the feeling that someone had been in his room. But that had been Tom, right?

Right?

"You see anyone?"

"I saw a shadow that moved."

"Could have been a deer."

"Yeah, could have been. I hope so. But just in case, when I was in Medford this morning, I had my mother drop me off at the library so I could Xerox copies of the symbols on the pyramid and the pattern inside the cube."

Weezy and her mother had been driving to Medford every Friday morning all summer long. Shopping, Jack guessed.

"Copies? Why?"

"In case someone steals mine."

Jack couldn't help rolling his eyes. "Weez . . ."

"It's part of the Secret History of the World, Jack. We're not supposed to have it. Doesn't it make sense that the people who want that history kept secret will try to get it back?"

Jack didn't like the way this was going.

"But who are these 'people'?"

She shrugged. "How should I know? They're *secret*, remember?"

Secret . . . the word brought back his father's comment about the Septimus Lodge: *It's a secret society.*

Could the Lodge be involved? After all, Weezy had found the cube next to a dead member.

But why would whoever it was search his room? After all, Weezy was the one who kept it and—

His stomach clenched when he remembered that Mr. Brussard was a member—no, more than just a member. He'd called himself "Lodge lore master." And Jack had showed him the cube. If the Lodge was involved, they'd assume Jack had it. And when they found out he didn't, they'd move on to the next person involved.

Weezy.

He shook it off. Crazy to think like this. Come on. This was lame-o Johnson, New Jersey. Nothing of any interest went on here. Especially not things like that.

"Okay, I'll hide them in a safe place."

She smiled. "Thanks. An ounce of prevention . . . you know the rest."

Jack did. And he'd do what he'd promised, even if it meant getting involved in one of her weird theories. If she'd rest easier knowing he had copies, that was reason enough.

He glanced at the sun. Almost noon. Enough time to get home, grab a shower, and rush over to USED.

7

Tonight was another of those rare evenings when everyone was home for dinner. Mom and Dad sat at the ends of the oblong dining room table, with Kate and Jack on one side, and Tom by himself on the other. Mom had made her Friday night meat loaf. She always mixed an envelope of Lipton's Onion Soup into the meat and Jack loved it. Add local corn on the cob and creamed spinach and he had heaven on a plate.

As Jack ate he looked for a way to bring up the latest death. Finally he found an opening.

"Remember what Mister Bainbridge said about never two deaths without three?"

Dad swallowed. "And like *I* said—an old wives' tale."

"But the death of that Assemblyman Vasquez makes three, right?"

"I suppose so." Dad shrugged. "Every so often old wives' tales work out, that's why they never go away." He looked thoughtful. "And this time not just three random people, but three Lodgers."

Jack almost dropped his fork. He'd half guessed the connection, but hearing it confirmed at his own dinner table came as a shock.

"He was in the Lodge too?"

Dad nodded. "Saw him there when they were trying to get me to join. Guess they thought it would impress me. It didn't."

Tom spoke around a mouthful. "You should've joined while you had the chance, Dad. They ever ask me, I'll join in a heartbeat."

"I'm sure you will." Dad shook his head, then smiled. "I wonder what Ed Toliver will have to say about another Lodger's death?"

Tom forked a big piece of meat loaf into his mouth before replying—a habit that drove Jack up the wall. Most people swallowed their food, then spoke. Tom rarely spoke *without* his mouth full. Made him sound like a tard.

"Not much, I'd guess. He's learning the hard way that you don't mess with the Septimus Lodge."

Kate looked up. "Oh?"

More meat loaf, then, "Toliver received notice today that his state income tax is being audited. And if that wasn't bad enough, his requests for variances and permits on that Mount Holly shopping center he's been working on have been sent back. He's got to resubmit."

"What's that got to do with the Lodge?" Jack said.

Tom picked up an ear of corn and began chewing on it left to right like a machine-gun typewriter. *Chomp-chomp-chomp.*

"Everything," he said between finishing the first row and attacking the second. "He called the lodge out." Another row—*chomp-chomp-chomp*. "He demanded an investigation." *Chomp-chomp-chomp.* "He drew attention to them." *Chomp-chomp-chomp.* "Lodge no like attention." *Chomp-chomp-chomp.* "Lodge is connected." *Chomp-chomp-chomp.* "Lodge lower the boom on Mister Edward Toliver."

"They've got that kind of power?" Jack said.

Tom nodded. "Ohhhhh, yeah."

Dad narrowed his eyes. "Where'd you get all this information?"

A huge forkful of creamed spinach went in, then, "The legal grapevine, Dad. Word gets around fast: Judges talk to their clerks, the clerks talk to lawyers and law students they know. In no time it's all over the place."

Mom shook her head. "What kind of a country has this become where you can't speak your mind?"

"The real world," Tom said. "The way it's always been. You push, you should expect a push back. The secret is to make sure you're on the side with the most muscle."

"How about being on the side that's right?" Kate said.

Tom grinned, showing a piece of spinach stuck to one of his front teeth.

"Wake up, Kate. Might makes right."

As Jack watched Kate shake her head sadly and go back to eating, he decided it was time for a little public pistachio shelling.

8

After dinner, Jack followed his father upstairs to his folks' bedroom.

"Dad, can I ask you something?"

"Of course—as long as it's not about that box."

"It's not. It's about Mister Brussard."

His dad looked at him. "What about him?"

Jack told him about the meetings, the little red boxes, the warnings about the klazen, the lies, and the three deaths.

Dad was staring at him. "You shouldn't be snooping on people. This is what happens with half-heard conversations. It's called taking things out of context."

"But they're dead, Dad. Three visits, three red boxes, three dead people."

He couldn't know if Mr. Sumter had been given a box, but he assumed so.

"And you suspect Gordie Brussard of killing them?"

"Don't you think it looks that way?"

A smile played around his dad's lips. "Since when did you become one of the Hardy Boys?"

Angry, Jack clenched his jaw. He'd known someone would think that. He'd even thought it himself. But this wasn't a novel. This was really happening, right here in Johnson, New Jersey.

"Call me a Hardy Boy, call me Nancy Drew, but there's something going on."

Dad sighed. "Remember that discussion we had about jumping to conclusions? Remember the trouble *post hoc, ergo propter hoc* can get you in?"

Jack nodded. "Yeah."

Dad had explained that the Latin phrase meant *after this, therefore because of this*, and how it led to wrong conclusions and superstition. His favorite example was, *It rained after I danced around a fire, therefore dancing around a fire causes rain.*

"Well, this is most likely a good example of that kind of thinking. Step back and look at it: What would Brussard's motive be?"

Jack shrugged. "I don't know."

"Right. And I can't think of one either. Those three dead men are his Lodge brothers. They're a very tight group."

"But he said the klazen would find the ones 'responsible.'"

"Responsible for what?"

Jack shrugged. "Murdering that man I found? I mean, that's when people started dying."

"There you go again, Jack. That's a *post-hoc* conclusion: The deaths began after you found the body, therefore finding the body is causing the deaths. Do you believe that?"

"Well, it could be. The man was a Lodger that nobody even knew was dead until I found him, and then three Lodge members die in the week after his body is identified. You think that's just coincidence?"

Dad was silent a moment, then, "Odds are it is, but I have to admit it's one hell of a coincidence."

Yes! Dad was beginning to see the light.

"But," Dad went on, "it's also one hell of a leap to accuse

Gordon Brussard of doing the killing. I'd almost prefer to blame this mysterious klazen."

That shocked Jack. His dad was the least superstitious person on Earth.

"But no one's ever heard of it. It doesn't exist."

"It doesn't have to, Jack. All it needs is for some people to believe it exists. Like voodoo. People who believe in voodoo and learn that it's being used against them will often sicken, and some have even died. Because they *believe* someone with magic is trying to kill them. Septimus Lodgers believe all sort of crazy crap—"

"Like what?"

"I don't know. They keep it to themselves. But when I was being courted they made veiled references to all the secret knowledge I would be privy to once I joined. So maybe if they believe a killer klazen is after them, they work themselves up into a heart attack. Don't forget, they all died of cardiac arrest in public places. Nothing came and tore their throats out."

Jack wasn't giving up. "But what's in those little red boxes? What if it's some sort of amulet with a spring-loaded poison needle?"

Dad laughed. "That's it! No more. Any more pulp fiction talk like that and I'll send those old magazines straight back to Mister Rosen."

Well, okay, Jack thought as he took the stairs down, maybe an amulet with a poison needle was taking it too far, but something was going on. Had to be.

9

After checking to make sure Tom was still around, Jack retrieved his doctored pistachios from his room. Back in the kitchen, he made a show of pouring a few dozen nuts onto the counter from the untreated bag. Keeping the spicy ones separate, he shelled five of those first.

From the corner of his eye he saw Tom walk past the doorway, slowing as he looked into the kitchen.

Perfect.

He shelled two of the regular nuts and ate them.

Kate finished loading the dishwasher and leaned against the counter.

"Mind if I snag a couple?" she said, pointing to the pile.

"Not those," Jack whispered without moving his lips.

Her eyes widened. "You mean . . . ?"

Nodding, he quickly shelled a couple of regular nuts and slid them toward her. As Tom passed again, Jack pretended to take them from the pile and hand them to her.

"Here you go," he said in a louder voice.

Kate popped them into her mouth and smiled. "I was going to go read, but maybe I'll hang around awhile."

She opened the paper and began to flip through it.

"Oh, look," she said. "Here's a picture of that assemblyman just minutes before he died. What a shame."

Jack resisted snatching the paper from her. Instead he hurried around the counter and stared over her shoulder.

The grainy photo showed a grinning Assemblyman

Vasquez holding a large pair of scissors poised to cut a wide ribbon outside a shopping mall. Yeah, he was the guy in Steve's house last night.

"Well, I'll be," Kate said. She tapped a figure in the small crowd behind Vasquez. "Look who's there: Bert Challis, our trusty insurance man."

Jack stifled a gasp as he recognized him. Hadn't Mr. B said he was in L.A. at some convention? A strange comment came back to him:

I don't know about you, but Bert Challis worries me.

Worried him how?

Had he been there to warn Vasquez . . . or was he the problem?

Just then Jack spotted Tom peeking around the edge of the doorframe. He lowered his voice again.

"I think the show's about to start."

As Jack resumed his seat on the far side of the counter, Kate wandered back to the sink and pretended to be busy.

With Tom watching, Jack shelled five more hot ones, all of which he added to the pile. That done, he made a show of opening one untreated nut and popping it in his mouth. Then a second. Then he quickly shelled the rest of the doctored nuts and added them to the pile.

Tom, apparently unable to hold out any longer, glided into the kitchen and slid the nuts off the counter into his palm.

"Gotcha!"

"Hey!" Jack cried. "Better not. Those are hot."

"Not this time. I saw you and Kate eating them."

"I'm warning you," Jack said.

Kate chimed in. "Better think twice, Tom."

"Oh, right," he said with a laugh. "Like you don't back up Miracle Boy every chance you get."

Kate shrugged. "Your funeral."

Tom waved and headed for the back door. "These'll taste great on the way to Philly."

Jack lowered his voice and did his Willy Wonka thing again. "Stop. Don't. Come back."

But Tom didn't—at least not right away. As the screen door slammed behind him, Kate grinned at Jack and began a countdown.

"Five . . . four . . ."

Jack joined her.

"Three . . . two . . ."

They heard a faint, *"Oh, no!"* from outside, then the screen crashed open and Tom rushed back in, holding his mouth. He ran for the refrigerator, yanked open the door, and started guzzling milk from the carton. Kate was hysterical, so weak with laughter she was down on her knees, clutching the counter so she wouldn't fall over.

But Jack wasn't laughing. Served Tom right for being in his room last night.

At least he hoped it had been Tom.

10

Following the old saying about discretion being the better part of valor, Jack had skedaddled before Tom recovered from the pistachios. He didn't want to deal with him tonight.

Was it okay to dislike your brother? Really, really dislike? He thought of another old saying: You can choose your friends but you can't choose your family. They had that right. No way in a million years would he have chosen Tom for a brother.

He reached Steve's front door and knocked.

"Hi, Mrs. Brussard," he said as she appeared. "Steve around?"

He was glad Steve's mom had answered instead of his dad. Maybe he wasn't a killer. Maybe he'd really been trying to protect his three Lodge brothers from the mysterious and dreaded klazen. Maybe they'd died of natural causes or, as Dad thought, scared themselves to death. But Jack had trouble buying that. And he feared that Mr. Brussard would take one look at him and realize that Jack suspected the truth.

Mrs. B smiled as she pushed open the door for him. She was short and pudgy with straight brown hair. Steve looked nothing like her.

"He's down in the basement with that computer. I swear, if he devoted that much time to his homework during the school year he'd be a straight-A student."

Jack doubted that. Not with the condition Steve was too often in by the end of the night. But he said nothing about that as he headed for the basement stairs, hoping he'd find Steve sober for a second night in a row.

No such luck. Steve was slumped on the couch watching that sappy *Knots Landing*. He looked looped.

"I never noticed before," he slurred with a silly grin, "but Michele Lee is cooooool."

She *was* pretty good-looking, but . . .

"I thought you were locked out of the liquor cabinet."

"I am."

"Could've fooled me."

Steve raised an amber plastic vial and rattled its contents. "I was forced to improvise."

"Pills? Whose?"

"My mom's." He tossed Jack the bottle. "Check it out."

Jack caught it and examined the label. Under Steve's mother's name it read: *Valium 5 mg #30*.

"What's this stuff?"

Steve grinned again. "A tranquilizer. My mother's had them around forever. Hardly ever uses them."

"You're taking a *tranquilizer*? Are you crazy?"

"Better believe it." He crossed his eyes and stuck his tongue out the side of his mouth. "Completely nuts."

Jack tossed the vial back. Steve tried to catch it but was too slow. It sailed right past his hand.

"Don't you want one? They take the edge off everything and make you feel sooooooo mellowwwwww."

Jack didn't get it. Life was too cool to spend in a fog. He didn't want to miss a thing.

"Maybe I prefer edgy to mellow."

Steve's gaze drifted back to the TV. "Isn't she beauuuu-tiful?"

"She's old enough to be your mother!"

"I wish she was. I'd sit and look at her aaaaaall day."

"I thought we were finally gonna get some work done on the computer."

Steve looked up at him with bleary eyes. "Let's do it."

"Yeah. Like you could be trusted with a soldering iron right now."

"Hey, I'm fine." He held up a hand. "Look. Rock steady."

It did look steady, but steadiness wasn't all that mattered.

"Yeah, but touch your pointer to your nose."

Jack demonstrated.

"Easy." But when Steve tried he missed by half an inch. "Aw, who cares anyway? I ain't soldering my nose."

Jack was losing respect for Steve. He'd been a smart, funny kid until he'd returned from soccer camp. Since then he'd been sprinting down the road to Loserville. Maybe he couldn't help it, maybe something had gone wrong in his brain. Nothing Jack could do about that.

Weezy's words from this morning echoed back to him: *So what are you going to do, stand by and watch him go down the tubes?*

No, Miss Know-it-all, he thought, I'm not.

But right now, other than ratting him out, Jack didn't see that he had much choice.

No, that wasn't true. There were always choices. Steve could choose whether or not to take one of his mother's pills, and Jack could choose *yes* or *no* as to getting him some help. He decided on *yes*. Easy to make a choice. The real problem was figuring out *how* to help without Steve feeling he'd been ratted out by a friend.

Jack needed to give this some serious thought. He was sure he'd find a way.

As Steve's eyelids started to drift closed, Jack shook his head.

Well now, *this* was exciting. He'd be better off watching TV at home.

He headed for the stairs.

"Later, man."

Steve mumbled something that sounded like, "Yeah."

Upstairs, as he was passing the den, he spotted the black humidor. Mr. Brussard had been holding it when he'd said good-bye to Vasquez. Why? They hadn't been smoking.

Did he dare?

No. Too risky.

But he hurried into the den anyway. Quickly he lifted the top and found an oddly shaped little red container about the size of a jewelry box for a ring; it had six—no, seven sides.

What was in them? What was the "it" that had to be "used" at dawn with your back to the sun?

He had to know.

As he was reaching for it he heard footsteps hurrying down the stairs. Too heavy for Mrs. B—had to be Steve's dad. With panic tightening his chest, Jack snatched his hand out of the humidor, replaced the lid, and leaped behind a high-backed upholstered chair.

Immediately he realized what a stupid move he'd made. If Mr. B came in and spotted him, what could he say? That he and Steve were playing hide and seek?

Yeah, right. That would fly—like a penguin.

Looking around he spotted Mr. Brussard's stack of stereo electronics. He jumped up and stepped over to it. With his hands behind his back, he stood before it and pretended to be studying all the neat-looking equipment.

He heard Mr. B come in behind him and stop.

"Jack?"

He turned. "Oh, hi, Mister Brussard. Just looking at your disc player here. I'd love to get my father to buy one, but he's not all that into music."

"Really liked the sound, did you?" His smile looked forced, like he had something else on his mind

"Awesome."

He picked up the humidor and looked inside.

"Well, I'd play some for you now, but I've got a little work to do. Why don't you get cracking on that computer. I'm really looking forward to seeing it in action."

"I've got to get home." Jack started for the hall. "We've still got a ways to go."

"Uh-huh." He seemed to be only half listening.

"See ya," he said and headed for the door.

When he reached the hallway he looked back and saw Mr. B pull a key ring from his pocket and lock the humidor in the liquor cabinet.

What was in that little box that needed to be locked up?

11

He suspects something, Jack thought as he trotted toward home.

He'd have to be careful.

He was a block away when he realized he'd just missed a perfect opportunity to expose Steve's problem. He could have said something to his father, something like, *I don't think Steve's feeling so hot.* That would have sent Mr. B down to check on him. Or at least he thought so. He knew his own dad would be downstairs in a flash. But the terror of almost getting caught had blanked his mind.

Which meant the Steve problem remained. Jack had done nothing to solve it.

He'd think of something. And soon.

Night was falling by the time he reached his house. He noticed that Tom's car was gone, but that didn't mean he hadn't left a little surprise for Jack. He waved to his parents as they watched *Falcon Crest.* Family drama was not Dad's favorite by a long shot, but Mom loved it—Jack had even heard her humming the theme music now and again.

"That was a quick trip," Dad said.

"Yeah, well, Steve wasn't in the mood."

He laughed. "You guys better get cranking. Once you start high school you're not going to have much spare time."

It occurred to Jack that tonight might have been a good time to try his new lock-picking skills on Dad's lockbox, but things had turned hectic at USED and he'd forgotten to bring home the picks. Maybe tomorrow. Anyway, he wasn't in a lock-picking mood.

Like last night, he checked his bedroom door for booby traps. Finding none, he stepped inside, turned on the light, and looked around. Unlike last night, he had no sense that the room had changed. Everything seemed just as he'd left it.

Then he remembered the Xeroxes of the tracings Weezy had given him for safekeeping. He'd stuck them in the top drawer of his desk before running off to USED this afternoon. He'd been running late and hadn't hidden them as he'd promised.

He quick-stepped to his desk and yanked open the drawer. Relief—still there. Then he wondered why he was relieved. Why would they be anywhere but where he'd left them?

But he'd promised to hide them, and his top drawer wasn't exactly hidden. Had to find a safer spot.

Safer . . .

Listen to me, he thought. I'm starting to think like Weezy.

As he began looking around for a hiding place, he noticed his open window. He checked the screen—still latched as he'd left it last night. Well, of course it would be. Who besides Tom would have any reason to want to sneak into his room.

Still . . .

He turned out the bedroom light, then pulled out the bottom drawer of his dresser and dropped the papers into the space beneath. Then he replaced the drawer. Not the safest hiding place in the world, but the best he could come up with on such short notice.

As he stepped toward the light switch by the door he remembered Weezy's remark about seeing someone in her backyard last night. Not terribly surprising, coming from Weezy. But what if . . . ?

He started tiptoeing toward the window, then stopped.

Why am I tiptoeing?

He walked the rest of the way, then crouched until the sill was at chin level.

The moonlit cornfield looked just the same as last night. Nothing moving. But he realized anyone standing in the corn rows would be as good as invisible and still have a clear view of his room. That had never occurred to him before, and it gave him a crawly feeling in his gut.

Thanks a lot, Weez.

He shook off the feeling. Silly. Nobody out there.

Still, he pulled the shade, then undressed in the dark. He crawled under the covers before turning on his bedside lamp. He wanted to let the Spider take him away from all these spooky feelings. The Spider's world was safe in that if things got too weird, Jack could always close the cover.

But real life had no covers. What did you do when life got too weird?

1

"Jack! Jack, wake up!"

Jack opened his eyes in the dark. An insistent tapping accompanied the frantic, harshly whispered words.

"Come *on*, Jack! Wake *up*!"

Where was he? He felt the pillow under his head, the sheet pulled up to his shoulders . . .

Bed.

"Jack, *please!*"

He jackknifed to a sitting position. The voice . . . coming from the window. He looked and his heart jumped when he saw a head silhouetted in the moonlight.

"Who?"

"It's me—Weezy. You've got to—"

"Weez? What are you doing out there?"

"Helicopters, Jack! Over the Pines. They were carrying some kind of equipment."

"So?"

"They're right over our mound!"

A second head appeared at the window.

"C'mon, Jack." Eddie's voice. "We're gonna go take a look."

Jack glanced at his clock radio: 1:10 in the morning.

"Are you guys nuts?"

"Yeah," Eddie said. "Nutsacious. And so are you. That's why we're here."

Weezy said, "We've got our bikes. So get dressed. Wear dark clothes. Let's go!"

"Do you know how dark it is in there?"

"We've got flashlights. Bring another. Come on. We've got to see what they're doing to our mound."

Jack thought for a second. He didn't know how Weezy knew they were over the mound, but he did know his folks would kill him if they found out he'd sneaked off into the Barrens at night.

But what were helicopters doing over their mound in the middle of the night? What couldn't wait until morning?

He jumped out of bed.

Well, why not? Not like he was going to be able to get back to sleep now anyway.

"Be right there."

2

As usual, Weezy led the way. She kept her flashlight beam trained ahead as she rode, but Jack figured she knew the trail so well she probably could have found her way by the moonlight.

He stayed close behind, holding his own light in reserve, in case Weezy's ran out. Eddie brought up the rear.

"Look," Weezy called back, flashing her beam along the sand. "Tire tracks. And recent too."

Jack saw what she meant. Some of the deeper sand stirred up by the tires was still dark and damp. The cars or pickups or whatever they were had to have come through within the hour.

At first the Barrens had been dark and silent, the overhanging pine branches blotting out all but a few rays of moonlight. But neither lasted.

The silence was the first to go.

They were passing the trapper's spong, and Jack was wondering if he'd reset the traps, when he began to hear a faint, low-pitched thrumming noise that grew steadily louder as they rode. This graduated to the unmistakable *whup-whup-whup* of helicopters.

And then Jack began to catch flashes of bright light through the upper branches. He couldn't imagine where they could be coming from until he realized the copters were using their searchlights to light up the ground.

Without warning, Weezy veered to the side and hopped

off her bike. She was leaning it against a tree when Jack pulled up beside her.

"Why're we stopping?" he said, raising his voice over the racket.

Weezy motioned her brother to get off his bike. "We should walk from here."

"Bikes are faster," Eddie said.

"And more easily noticed. We don't want to be seen."

Eddie laughed. "Why not?"

"Because then we'll be chased home."

Jack could make out Eddie's face in the light through the branches. He looked insulted.

"No way! It's a free country. We can watch if we want."

Weezy rolled her eyes. "They don't want *anyone* watching."

"That's stupidacious. And besides, how do you know?"

Jack thought the answer was pretty obvious, but he let Weezy tell her brother. She stepped closer and got in his face.

"Can you think of any other reason why they'd go to all this trouble at night when it would be so much easier during the day?" When Eddie didn't answer, Weezy looked at Jack, then back at Eddie. "So, can we all start walking?"

"Let's go," Jack said. "We're wasting time."

He took the lead now. With the lights ahead as a beacon, they no longer needed flashlights or Weezy's keen sense of direction. He kept to the side of the firebreak until he noticed a deer trail angling toward all the activity. He took it.

This path was much narrower . . . branches scraped against him as he passed. He was glad he'd worn full-length jeans instead of cutoffs, but wished he'd picked out a rugby shirt instead of this T.

As the three of them neared the site, the noise of the copters grew even louder. Ahead and above they looked invisible—black fuselages against a black sky—with their searchlights seeming to come out of nowhere.

But another sound gradually joined the mix—the throaty, up-and-down roar of diesel engines.

Construction equipment.

As they closed in on the mound area, Jack lowered to a crouch, then turned and motioned Weezy and Eddie to do the same. When he reached a break in the trees he came to a sudden stop. Weezy bumped him from behind. He heard her gasp as she saw what he saw.

Just a hundred feet away, the burned-out area of the mound was ablaze with light, illuminating the dozen or so men walking back and forth among the charred pine trunks. And among those trunks, a backhoe furiously dug up the sand.

He felt Weezy grip both his shoulders and squeeze—hard.

"Our mound!" she said softly, leaning over him, so close he could feel her breath on his ear. "They're tearing up our mound!"

Not our mound anymore, Jack thought. Pretty soon it wouldn't even *be* a mound.

He watched the backhoe systematically tearing up the ground, its yellow arm swinging up and down, ramming its bucket into the mound, pulling out a yard of sand, then dumping it to the side before backing up for another go. If a tree had grown too close, the backhoe's tractor simply pushed it aside or knocked it down.

Weezy said, "That must have been what the helicopter was carrying when I saw it."

Men followed in its wake of destruction, some with rakes, some with hoes, some with baskets. Some wore police uniforms with black leather belts that circled the waist and crossed the chest, others wore dark suits and narrow-brimmed hats. They'd poke through the turned-up sand and every so often one would stoop to pick up something. Mostly they tossed whatever they found aside, but every so often one would call the others over. They'd all cluster around and look at his find for a few seconds, then place it in one of the baskets and go back to work.

"They can't do this!" Weezy said. "They're going to ruin everything!"

She stepped around Jack and started toward the mound. He grabbed her arm and pulled her back.

"Are you nuts? You can't stop them."

"I can try. They're ruining everything! They're—"

"Hey!" said a gruff voice behind them. "What are you doing here?"

3

Eddie squealed. Jack jumped and turned to find a flashlight beam in his eyes, the glare blotting out whoever was holding it.

"Did you hear me?" the voice said, louder. "What the hell are you kids doing here?"

"We-we-we saw the copters," Eddie said. He sounded scared, his we-can-watch-if-we-want attitude of a few minutes ago vanished.

"Damn!" the man said. After a pause, he pointed to three state police cruisers parked on the fire trail. Jack had been so intent on the backhoe, he hadn't seen them. "All right, get over there." The man gave Eddie a shove in the direction. "March."

Eddie stumbled away, his path angling away from the mound. With the light out of his eyes, Jack could see that the man wore a NJ State Trooper uniform. It looked loose on him, as if he'd lost weight. After a few heartbeats' hesitation, Weezy started to follow. Jack fell in line between her and the trooper.

A state cop . . . all he could think of was how this would end: The trooper knocking on his front door in the middle of the night, his father answering, the trooper explaining where they'd found his son, Dad yanking him inside, grounding him for life, maybe longer.

Oh, this was bad . . . very bad.

As they reached the nearest police cruiser, a man in a dark suit came over.

"What the hell's going on?" he shouted over the sound of the copters.

The trooper jerked his thumb at them. "Saw the choppers. Told you we should have made a southern approach. How many more peepers we gonna have to deal with before the night's over?"

The suit stepped closer and played a flashlight over them. The beam lingered on Weezy.

"They're just kids—dumb piney kids."

Jack heard a sneer in his tone and felt a flash of anger. He wasn't a piney and he wasn't dumb.

"Not pineys," he said. "We're from Johnson."

The suit waved his hands in the air. "Ooh, now *there's* a metropolis."

"We happen to be on private land," Weezy said. "We know Mister Foster and he lets us come here whenever we want."

Jack glanced at her out of the corner of his eye. They'd never once seen Old Man Foster.

"Yeah?" the suit said. "Well, if we could find him we could check that out, but he's a hard man to track down."

"I'm sure he wouldn't like you digging up his land."

The trooper said, "Doesn't matter what he likes. This is a crime scene and we've got warrants. It's all nice and legal."

"Then why are you doing it at night?" Jack said.

Weezy chimed in, "Because you're not looking for evidence, are you. You're looking for something else."

"Enough of this crap," the suit said, sounding annoyed

and surprised. He turned to the trooper. "Lock them in your unit until we're done."

Jack's gut tightened. Locked up?

"We wanna go ho-home," Eddie said.

"You will," the suit told him. "But not till we're finished here."

The trooper opened a rear door and pointed to the backseat.

"In. Now."

Jack thought of bolting—not back down the fire trail, because he didn't know how fast the trooper was, and he might not be able to outrun him on a straight course. But he was sure he could duck into the brush just ten feet away and disappear among the trees before the guy knew what happened. With his dark clothes and the sound of the helicopters and the backhoe drowning out any noise he made, he could circle around to the bikes and hightail it out of here.

Get home. Sneak back in the window. Slip under the covers. Pretend nothing had happened. And avoid being grounded for life.

Yeah . . . he could do it.

But it meant running out on Weezy and Eddie. Sure, the distraction he provided might give them a chance to bolt too, but he couldn't count on it. If he escaped alone, he'd never be able to look them in the eye again. Never be able to look himself in the eye either. Didn't want to look in the mirror and see a guy who deserted friends.

Better to be grounded for life.

Eddie was first to go in. He resisted, whining a little, but a shove from the trooper got him moving, sliding to the far side. Weezy went next, settling in the middle. Jack was last.

"You kids wanted to see what's going on. Well, now you've got box seats."

Jack leaned against Weezy so the door wouldn't bang him when the trooper closed it.

It sounded like a prison cell door slamming shut.

4

As soon as the trooper turned his back, Jack tried the handle—it moved but didn't open the door. Across the car Eddie wiggled his.

"It doesn't work!"

"That's the way police cars are built," Jack said. "To keep crooks from jumping out. There's an emergency door release up front"—he tapped on the thick plastic barrier that confined them to the rear compartment—"but we'll never reach it."

Weezy was staring at him. "How do you know so—?" Then she nodded. "Oh, I get it. Your deputy friend."

"Right. He locked me in the back of his cruiser once—just to let me know how it feels. But he also showed me a switch on the door that can undo it."

"Well then undo it!" Eddie said.

"You can't reach it when the door's closed."

"What if they're not cops?" Weezy said in a wondering tone.

Jack looked at her. "Of course they're cops."

"What if they're just pretending to be? Those guys in suits sure don't look like state cops. What if they're some secret government agency—?"

Jack waved his hands. "Don't start with that stuff, Weez. Things are bad enough already. We don't need a conspiracy too. We've got uniformed troopers driving state trooper cruisers. Let's leave it at that, okay."

"I'm serious, Jack. You ever see a trooper with such a bad-fitting shirt? And if a government agency is high enough up, don't you think it can come in and commandeer a few cruisers for a night?"

A far-out story, Jack thought, but not impossible. That guy in the suit . . . he had an air about him that gave Jack the creeps.

"Yeah, but—"

"Let's just hope they're really going to let us go."

Jack felt his chest tighten. "What are you *talking* about?"

"Yeah, Weez," Eddie said. "Cut it out, will you. You're scaring me. You're always scaring me."

"I'm not trying to scare anyone." Her calm tone was scary in itself. "But it's pretty obvious they're not looking for evidence. So what *are* they looking for? Something they don't want anyone to know about if they find it?"

"Fine," Jack said. "But that doesn't mean they're going to keep us prisoners."

"We *are* prisoners, Jack. I'm thinking that real state troopers would have sent us home. We didn't commit a crime, so why are we locked up in a cop car?"

Good question, Jack thought. He felt his mouth going dry. Suddenly being grounded didn't seem so bad.

"Maybe—" He had to clear his throat. "Maybe they don't want us going home and talking about it and bringing a bunch of people back before they're through."

"Let's hope so," she said. "I'm just worried they might not want anyone *ever* talking about this."

Eddie started working his handle again. "It's getting stuffy in here." He sounded panicky.

Weezy leaned toward Jack and lowered her voice. "He doesn't like enclosed places. It's called—"

"Claustrophobia—I know. I may not know 'gravitas,' but I know that."

"I didn't say you didn't."

They fell into silence; the only sound was Eddie's continuous rattling of his door handle. Jack's mind raced. They had to get out of this car. But how? Possibilities popped into his head but he tossed them out one after another as unworkable. And then . . .

He grabbed Weezy's arm as a plan leaped full-blown into his head.

"Wait! Eddie, can you fake getting sick—I mean, puke-type sick?"

"If I'm cooped up in here much longer I won't *have* to fake it."

"Great. Look sick."

Jack began rapping on his window. The trooper stood a few feet away with his back to them, arms folded across his chest, watching the excavation. He didn't turn. He might have been ignoring them, but most likely couldn't hear them over the racket.

Jack began pounding on the glass with his fists.

Weezy said, "Jack, you're going to break it."

"I wish."

No way he could break auto glass with his bare hands—which were starting to hurt from the impacts.

Finally the trooper turned. His expression turned from bored to annoyed when he saw Jack pounding. After a few seconds of hesitation he walked over and yanked open the door—not all the way, just a foot or so.

"What the hell do you think you're doing?"

Jack jerked a thumb over his shoulder at Eddie. "He's getting sick! He's gonna puke!"

Right on cue, Eddie retched.

"Oh, no, he's not!" the trooper said, eyes widening. "Not in any car I'm driving!"

As Jack watched him slam the door and hurry around the rear to Eddie's side, a question nibbled at his brain. Wouldn't a real trooper have said "*my* car"?

When he reached Eddie's door he pulled it open and yanked him out.

"If you're gonna puke," he said, pointing Eddie away from the car, "you do it out here." He turned and jabbed a finger and Jack and Weezy. "Don't get any ideas."

As soon as he turned away, Jack crawled over Weezy.

She gasped. "What are you—?"

"Shhh!"

He stretched out across her lap, reaching for the edge of the half-open door, then hesitated. The trooper was behind Eddie, holding a fistful of the back of his T-shirt to make sure he didn't try to run. But if he happened to reach back and slam it closed with Jack's hand there, it could be bye-bye fingers.

Let's just hope they're really going to let us go . . .

Do it!

He stretched his arm to the limit, ran his fingers along the rear of the door edge until he found the little toggle switch. He pushed it up—no go. But a downward push clicked it into a new position—the unlocked position, he hoped.

He straightened up and looked out the rear window.

He could see Eddie bent over, retching, putting on a great show.

"C'mon, kid. Get it over with."

Eddie glanced up over the trunk and Jack gave him a thumbs-up. Eddie straightened and wiped his face with his shirt.

"I feel better now."

"You'd better be sure," the trooper said. "You mess up that car, there'll be hell to pay."

"No, really. I'm okay. I just don't like being cooped up."

"Well, get used to it. You're gonna be there awhile."

He guided Eddie back into the rear seat and slammed the door, then walked back around the car. He checked the door on Jack's side to make sure it was latched, then wandered away toward the excavation.

Eddie pulled on his door handle. The door unlatched.

"Hey! It opens!"

"Keep it closed!" Jack said.

"Why? I thought—"

Jack pointed to the light in the ceiling above their heads. "That goes on when the door's open. We've got to make this fast and time it just right."

He checked out the trooper. He was maybe a hundred feet away, talking to the guy in the suit. Both had their backs turned.

Now or never.

"Okay. When I give the word, Eddie opens the door, we all dive out, stay low, and run into the bushes. We'll circle around to the bikes and get our butts back home. Everyone okay with that?"

Weezy was staring out the window. "I wish I knew if they were finding anything."

Jack waved a hand in front of her face. "You're kidding, right?"

"No. I really want to know." She looked at him. "But I really want out of this car too. So let's go home."

That was a relief. For a minute there he'd been afraid she'd want to stay.

"Okay. Get ready, Eddie. I'll tell you when."

Jack fixed his gaze on the trooper and the suit . . . waiting . . . waiting . . .

And then pine lights appeared, half a dozen of them, swirling above and around the helicopters. Jack had seen a couple once. No one knew what they were—ball lightning, some people said—but every so often they appeared, varying from baseball to basketball size, skimming along the treetops.

What had drawn them here? The light? The noise?

Everyone around the excavation stopped what they were doing to point and look up, and then Jack realized his time had come.

"Now!"

Eddie opened the door and tumbled out, Weezy close behind him. Jack brought up the rear and swung the door closed—enough to turn out the light but not enough to latch it. With all the racket from the helicopters he probably could have slammed it with no risk of anyone hearing, but didn't want to risk it. So he leaned his shoulder against it until he felt the latch catch.

He turned and saw Eddie in a low crouch, disappearing into the brush a few feet away. But Weezy stood tall, gazing in awe at the pine lights.

"Look, Jack! I've seen one or a pair at a time, but *six*—never six!"

"Worry about them later. Let's go!"

He grabbed her arm and pulled her into the brush.

Fifty feet or so into the woods the excavation site disappeared behind them and it was safe to walk upright.

"Did you see them?" Weezy said. "Six pine—"

She broke off, whirled, and put a hand over Jack's mouth. Eddie's too.

"Don't move," she whispered, her voice barely audible.

Jack froze. What? Had she seen or heard something?

And then Jack saw it—a dark shape slinking among the pines. If it was a man, it didn't move like one. A breeze carried its sour odor their way and the smell made Jack break out in a sweat. All his instincts screamed *Run!* but he held his position. The shape slunk toward the excavation area. About a dozen feet short of the fire trail it stopped and crouched among the brush and trees, watching.

Who or what it was, Jack couldn't tell, and didn't want to know.

The excavation seemed to be attracting a lot of attention from things that came out only at night.

Weezy removed her hands and signaled them to follow her. She moved slowly and quietly away from the watcher and the excavation. The farther they got, the faster she moved. Cutting quickly through the brush and weaving among the trees on a curving course that seemed to be taking them away from the fire trail and their bikes. But Jack said nothing. He didn't see much choice but to trust her sense of direction.

He was lost.

5

Just when he thought they'd never find their way out, when he was convinced they'd wind up like those hunters who entered the Barrens and never returned, they stepped out of the trees onto a fire trail.

But which fire trail?

Jack's heart leaped as he watched Weezy hurry across to where three bikes leaned against the trees.

Yes!

He dashed after her.

"What was that thing in the woods?"

"I don't know. A big piney maybe."

"Th-that was the Jersey Devil!" Eddie said. "I just know it!"

Weezy, who bought into every other weird thing, had never bought into the JD.

She looked at Jack as they pulled their bikes back onto the trail. "I don't believe you got us out of that car."

"I don't believe you led us right back to the bikes. We make a pretty good team."

She laughed and punched him on the shoulder. "You kidding? We make a *great* team."

The way she said it sparked a flood of warmth inside him, but it didn't last. Nerves doused it. They had to get out of here.

No one needed to speak again. They all knew what to do, and where they were going.

Once they were moving toward Johnson, with the sound of the copters fading behind them, Jack's heart began to ease its pounding.

He glanced over his shoulder. No sign of headlights.

They'd made it.

Well, not completely. Not yet, anyway.

They'd be home free if the trooper remained where they'd left him. If he just stayed put, watching those pine lights, he wouldn't know they were gone. He could look all he wanted, but from that distance he couldn't see into the dark interior of his cruiser. As far as he knew, they couldn't open the doors, so he'd assume the "dumb piney kids" were right where he'd left them.

Another over-the-shoulder look—still no headlights.

Jack wished he could have hung around to see the look on that suit's face when he found out they were gone.

Where's your sneer now?

They were passing the trapper's spong. Great. Halfway home. He took another look behind and—

He almost lost control of the bike when he saw a pair of headlights bouncing down the trail, coming their way.

He looked around. Even though a car could go only so fast without bottoming out on these undulating trails, it could still beat a bike. No way they could outrun it.

"Hey!" he shouted to the others. "They're after us!"

He heard a frightened whine from Eddie and Weezy cry, "Faster!"

"No! Pull off the trail and hide the bikes!"

"They'll catch us for sure!" Eddie wailed.

"Maybe, maybe not. I don't think they've seen us yet. But they will if we stay on the trail."

Weezy angled into a stand of pines at the far edge of the spong clearing. Jack and Eddie followed, hauling their bikes into the brush and laying them flat.

"Tires toward the trail," Jack said.

Eddie obeyed but asked, "Why?"

"Because tires are black."

"Oh, no," Weezy said. "I've got reflectors on my spokes."

"Do they pop off?"

"They're screwed on."

Not good.

"Okay," Jack said, "we've got to get away from the bikes." He pointed to another copse of pines at the other end of the clearing. "There!"

Eddie's gaze was fixed on the approaching headlights. "But that's going toward them!"

Weezy pushed her brother from behind. "Exactly. The last direction they'll expect us to go."

Keeping low, they dashed for the copse and crouched among the trunks, panting, waiting. Jack's bladder was sending urgent signals that it wanted to empty. He did his best to ignore it.

He saw the wavering glow from the headlights grow brighter as the cruiser bounced closer. Finally it pulled into view.

"Move along," he whispered, wishing he knew how to use the Force. "Move along. Nothing of interest here."

If the cruiser passed the hidden bikes without seeing them, it would keep going, and Weezy, Eddie, and Jack could follow it at a distance, keeping it well ahead of them.

The cruiser bounced closer to the bikes . . . came even with them . . .

"Keep moving," Jack whispered. "Keep moving—"

The brake lights came on. The car stopped. Went into reverse. Backed up parallel to the stand of trees.

"Oh-no, oh-no, oh-no," Eddie whimpered.

"Hush!" Weezy said, then looked at Jack. "Had to be those reflectors on my spokes—sorry."

He was about to tell her it couldn't be helped when a spotlight beamed from the cruiser onto the bikes. The car backed up farther, the light shining into the spong clearing, then arcing toward their copse.

"Down!" Jack said.

They flattened themselves on the ground just before the beam swept over them. The beam swung back again, then remained fixed on their spot.

"Don't even breathe!" Weezy whispered.

As Jack lay frozen he felt something moving on his left forearm. His first impulse was to snatch it away, but that might give away their location. Slowly he angled his head until he could see. The reflected glow from the spotlight revealed a good-sized snake, big around as a plump hot dog, slithering over his arm. Fighting the instinctive urge to throw it off, he held his breath and stayed still. He couldn't see the head, but its body was mostly black with a white center stripe and yellow-orange stripes along the flanks.

It's okay, he told himself. Just a garter snake . . . a harmless garter snake.

He'd caught and played with dozens when he was younger. This was a big one, but just as harmless as the little ones.

That didn't keep him from breaking out in a cold sweat.

It kept moving and soon was gone, wriggling toward the spong.

The search beam moved away just then, giving Jack two reasons for a relieved release of the breath he'd been holding. But he stayed put until he heard voices.

Raising his head he saw the trooper and the suit standing by the cruiser's open driver door as they beamed the searchlight back and forth across the clearing. He wished he could make out what they were saying.

Leaving the light trained on the spong, they stepped into the stand of trees where the bikes were hidden. They pulled out Weezy's and Eddie's and wheeled them around to the rear of the cruiser.

"My bike!" Eddie whispered.

The trunk popped open, and then it became clear: They were taking the bikes.

"What are we gonna do?" Eddie said. "We can't let them—"

Weezy nudged him. "We're going to stay here until they're gone, then we're going to have to walk home."

"That'll take forever. And that's my racer!"

"Better than what might happen if they catch us," she said.

Jack didn't know about that, but he felt a surge of anger as he watched them throw Weezy's bike into the trunk. Then Eddie's. His would be next. How was he going to explain the loss of his BMX?

He glanced into the clearing. He could just make out the rim of the spong in the wash of light from the search beam.

And that gave him an idea.

"Rocks!" he whispered as he raked his fingers through the sand around him. "I need a couple of rocks!"

"Come on, Jack," Weezy said. "You don't really think throwing rocks at them will—"

"Not at them! Find me a couple of good-size rocks."

Jack's fingers found the edge of a piece of sandstone. He pulled it out.

"Here's one," Eddie said and handed him another fist-size piece.

The crumbly, rust-colored rock was all over the Barrens.

Jack looked again and saw the suit wheeling his bike toward the trunk.

Dirty, rotten, sneering—

He crawled to the edge of the copse, rose to his knees, and hurled one of the rocks toward the spong. It missed, landing near the edge instead. But it made a loud enough *clink!* to stop the trooper and the suit in their tracks.

"You hear that?" he heard the suit say.

He let Jack's bike fall and leaped to the spotlight, sweeping its beam back and forth across the clearing. Jack waited for it to pass the spong, then tossed his second rock.

This one sailed over the rim and landed with a loud splash.

"There!" the trooper cried, pointing. "Must be some sort of a pond. That's where they're hiding."

Leaving the light trained on the spong, the two of them ran toward it.

"It worked!" Weezy cried, grabbing the back of Eddie's shirt. "Let's go!"

"Wait," Jack said.

"*Wait?* Are you—?"

"Remember what Mrs. Clevenger said this afternoon about that trapper coming back?"

"Yeah. So?"

"Well, if she was right . . ."

"Ohmygod!" Weezy clapped a hand over her mouth. "You don't think—?"

A cry from the trooper cut her off. He staggered, yelled again, then fell, grabbing at his ankle.

Jack pumped a fist. "Yes!"

"What happened?" the suit said, starting toward him.

Then he too cried out and dropped to the ground—where he shouted again. He rose to his knees, struggling to remove the steel trap that had closed around his elbow.

He looked so comical, Jack had to bite his tongue to keep from laughing out loud. He wanted to stand up and shout, *How about another sneer for the dumb piney kids?* but thought better of it.

He turned to Weezy. "*Now* we can go."

A steady stream of curses floated from the clearing as Jack led the others to the rear of the cruiser where he helped Eddie and Weezy pull their bikes from the trunk. Then he ran around to the side and retrieved his own.

"Ready to go?"

Eddie looked ready to jump out of his skin. "Oh, man, are they ever gonna be *mad*!"

"What for?" Jack said. "We didn't set those traps. It was their idea to go wandering in there in the dark."

"Still," Weezy said, "we're going to have to cut through the trees, otherwise they'll just catch up to us again."

Jack shook his head. "No, they won't."

"Yeah, Jack, they will."

He leaned inside the cruiser and plucked the keys from the ignition, then held them up and jangled them.

"Not without these, they won't. Let's roll."

Weezy didn't move, just stood there staring at him with her wide dark eyes.

"What?" he said.

"You're scary, you know that? Really scary." She jerked her thumb toward the spong. "What kind of mind thinks up something like that?"

Jack had no idea where the idea had come from. Suddenly it had just popped into his head.

"Weez, sometimes I scare myself."

6

The sound of the lawn mower awoke him.

Jack opened one eye and looked at his clock. The blurred numbers slowly came into focus . . . 9:02. He groaned and rolled over.

That same clock had read 3:22 when he'd crawled back in the window last night. No, not last night—earlier this morning. And then he'd lain here, wide awake, too wired for sleep, too worried there'd come a knock on the door and the trooper and the suit would be standing there with their bloody, banged-up ankles and elbows and messed-up clothes, looking to haul him away.

He didn't know when he'd finally drifted off. He did know he needed more sleep, but that wasn't going to happen with the lawn mower roaring back and forth outside his window.

Officially it was his job to mow their lawn. Dad paid him to do it once a week, and usually he did it on Wednesdays. But with everything going on, he'd missed this week. He guessed Dad had decided to cut it. He did that every so often when he felt the need for a little exercise. But why today of all days?

Wait!

He bolted upright in bed. Had last night really happened? Or had it all been a dream? Could have been. More like a nightmare. Sure was bizarre enough.

He should have kept the cop's car keys. Then he'd have

proof. Instead he'd left them hanging from a branch over the fire trail. Or at least he thought he had.

He looked out the window on a sunny summer morning with his father pushing the lawn mower around the backyard. So normal, so everyday. Like something out of that old Monkees song "Pleasant Valley Sunday." And yet just a few hours ago, and just a couple of miles away in the Pine Barrens, strange men had been digging up the earth in search of . . . what?

Or had they? He couldn't be sure. How could something that had felt so real then seem so unreal now?

He noticed a small, dark-brown lump on his left forearm. A closer look showed it had little legs.

A tick.

It hadn't buried its head too deeply yet, so he flipped it on its back and pulled it out. He studied it as it crawled across his palm. A simple brown wood tick, not the tiny deer tick everybody was being warned about. Get bitten by one of those and you could catch some new infection called Lyme disease, whatever that was. What'd it do? Turn you green?

Watching the tick he realized that here was proof of sorts that he'd been in the Barrens last night—the place was lousy with ticks. But he could just as easily have picked it up during the day.

He took it between his thumb and forefinger, ready to crush it.

"You have attacked me," he intoned, holding it up at eye level. "You have bitten me. For that you must die."

And then he realized it hadn't hurt him—hadn't even had a chance to suck his blood. Just a tick being a tick.

He stepped to the window, opened the screen, and

flicked it out onto the lawn. Then he checked the rest of himself for more but couldn't find any.

Since he didn't see any more sleep in his immediate future, he decided to get dressed. He'd just put on his jeans when his mother knocked on his door and stuck her head in. She looked concerned.

His gut tightened. Don't tell me there's a trooper at the front door! *Please* don't!

"Jackie?"

"*Jack*, Mom."

"Weezy's here to see you." She frowned. "She looks upset. I asked her to come in but she said she'd wait for you in the front yard."

Weezy! She could tell him if last night had been real or not.

"Great. Thanks."

As he squeezed by her she put a hand on his shoulder.

"She couldn't be in any . . . trouble, could she?"

Jack froze. Did Mom know? But how could she? It was—

When he saw how uncomfortable she looked he realized what she was talking about. He didn't know whether to laugh or get mad.

"Weez? Are you kidding? No way! How can you even think—?"

"Well . . ." She looked even more uncomfortable. "You two do spend an awful lot of time together . . . disappearing for hours . . ."

Now he laughed. "We're just friends, Mom."

"Famous last words." She looked stern now. "Don't you go jumping into anything you're not ready for. Remember to use your head."

"Okay, okay," he said on his way to the front door. "Message received and understood."

Why'd she have to think that? Weezy got upset a lot—a *lot*. It certainly didn't mean she was pregnant.

And certainly not by me, of all people.

7

He found her in the front yard, leaning her back against the big oak. At first sight of her he couldn't help thinking of him and Weezy . . . together. He never thought of her like that. They'd known each other forever. They'd hung out in her bedroom lots of times and he'd never thought about . . .

But he remembered her kiss. Nice . . .

Jack and Weezy sitting in a tree . . .

When she saw him she ran over. For an awful second he thought she was going to throw herself into his arms. Not that that would be so bad someplace else, but not here. Because sure as Tuesday followed Monday, Mom was watching. That'd be all she'd need.

But she stopped short and grabbed his arm and began pulling him toward the sidewalk.

Jack saw what his mom had meant about looking upset. Her eyes—no liner this morning—were bloodshot and her face was blotchy, as if she'd been crying.

"It's gone, Jack!"

"What?"

"The cube! It's gone! So are those tracings I made. And the photos too. Everything is *gone!*"

They stopped at the sidewalk where she'd left her bike.

"What do you mean, 'gone'? Maybe Eddie's got them."

"He swears he doesn't and I believe him. Besides, I had

them hidden and Eddie can barely find his own shoes. He'd never find the cube."

"Your folks?"

She shook her head. "No. They were sound asleep when we sneaked out last night, and just as asleep when we sneaked back in. I know the cube was in my room when I left—I had it out, trying to open it, before I heard the helicopters."

"And you put it away before you left?"

"Absolutely."

Her face scrunched up as tears filled her eyes. She looked like she was going to break down and start bawling. Jack raised an arm to put around her shoulders, but a glance at his house revealed his mom watching from a living room window, so he settled for a hand on her arm.

He could sense how much she was hurting. That cube and pyramid meant so much to her—as if she'd been looking for something like them all her life. But he didn't know what to say to make her feel better. Was there anything anyone *could* say?

"Weez . . ."

She took a deep, shuddering breath, then seemed to pull herself together. She looked back toward the Barrens.

"Somebody took it, Jack. Someone sneaked into my room last night while we were out and stole it."

"But you're on the second floor."

"I know." She crossed her arms across her chest. "It gives me the creeps. But how did they *know*?"

"Maybe because they couldn't find it in my room."

Her head snapped around. "*Your* room?"

"When I came back from Steve's Thursday night, I sensed some stuff in my room had been moved. I thought it was Tom, looking for a way to get even for the pistachios. But now . . . I wonder."

"But only a few people knew we had it. Mister Rosen is the first one we showed it to."

"Yeah, but he wouldn't tell anybody. I mean, he hasn't got anyone *to* tell."

Weezy's eyes narrowed. "What makes you so sure? I mean, what do we know about him—*really* know about him? He comes to Johnson from who knows where, opens a store that sells junk, doesn't even live in town, and—"

"His trailer is just up the highway. You know that."

"Right, with dozens of antennas on the roof and the biggest satellite dish I've ever seen. I mean, that thing belongs at Lakehurst."

"He can't get cable out there so he pulls in the signals with the dish."

"How do we know all that stuff's just for receiving? Maybe some of it transmits. Who's he communicating with?"

Jack saw Weezy's new suspicions as good news and bad news. The good was she seemed to have pulled back from the meltdown point and returned to her old off-the-wall-conspiracy-theory self. The bad was she was talking down Mr. Rosen, and he didn't like that.

"He's a good guy, Weez, and he's not communicating with aliens."

"Who said anything about aliens? He could be—"

"He's not doing anything but watching TV. Trust me. But I'm not so sure about Steve's old man."

"Mister Brussard?"

"Yeah. Add it up: I showed him the box and mentioned that we'd found it. Since he saw me with it, wouldn't it be natural to assume we were keeping it at my place? And if he wanted it, wouldn't my room be the first place he'd look?"

"But since he didn't find it in your room," Weezy said in a soft voice, "mine would be the next best choice." She shook her head. "But wait—I can't see him climbing up on my roof to get to my room."

"Maybe he used the back door. Isn't that what you used going in and out? And you said no one heard you."

Jack realized whoever had been in her room could have used the front door as well. He wondered if maybe it wasn't such a good thing that most folks in Johnson never locked their doors at night, or even when they went away for a weekend. On hot nights they'd leave all the doors and windows open to let the air through.

"Yeah, but—"

"Wouldn't even have to be him. Could have been someone else from the Lodge."

"The Lodge?"

"Yeah. The Lodge. Every time I turn around lately it's the-Lodge-the-Lodge-the-Lodge. Mister Sumter and the other two dead guys were Lodge members, and the body we found right next to the cube was another. Mister Brussard's a Lodger—*and* he can open the cube. So as far as I can see, the Lodge is definitely involved."

"Oh, wow." Her eyes were wide. "Do you think whoever killed that man buried the cube with him? Maybe both were supposed to stay buried, but we found them." She looked at Jack with even wider eyes. "We could have had a killer in our bedrooms!"

Jack had been thinking the same thing, but hadn't wanted to mention it. The thought of any stranger in his room gave him a major case of the willies. But a killer . . .

He kept up a calm front for Weezy.

"Well, whoever it was, they didn't come to harm us, just take back what was theirs."

Weezy grabbed his arm and squeezed. "The Xeroxes! Do you have them?"

He nodded. "Safely hidden away."

"You're sure?" Her eyes bored into his. "When was the last time you saw them?"

"Um, last night."

Her grip tightened. "Last night! Then the copies could be gone too! Go check."

"Weez . . ."

She was squeezing hard now. "Please, Jack. I've got to know. I mean, what if that whole operation we saw last night was just a ruse to get us out of our rooms?"

Jack shook his head. She was getting way far out now.

"I can't see them going to all that expense and taking all that time just to get hold of our little cube."

"Maybe, maybe not. But you heard that cop say they could have come by another route, from the south, but no, they flew right over Johnson. Why would they do that, hmmm?"

"Just coincidence."

"And weren't we wondering why they locked us in the car instead of shooing us home?" She was on a roll now. "Maybe they wanted to give their operatives back here enough time to get the job done."

" 'Operatives'? Weez, do you hear yourself?"

Her tone turned angry. "Yeah, I hear myself. Now you hear this: The cube is *gone*, Jack. And since I didn't lose it or misplace it, that means someone took it."

"Okay, okay. But that doesn't mean the helicopters and the excavating had anything to do with the cube disappearing. Someone may have been watching your house, spotted you leaving, saw his chance, and took it."

"Just check for me, Jack. Please?"

He didn't feel like going back into the house, but had to admit that whoever had stolen from Weezy's room while they were out could just as easily—more easily, since he was on the ground floor—have stolen from his.

Plus he found it hard to refuse that pleading look in her eyes.

"Okay. Be right back."

"If they're there, don't bring them with you. Don't let anyone know you have them."

Wondering at the bizarre turns of events since he'd dug into that mound, Jack hurried inside. He passed Mom on his way through the living room. She was giving him a funny look.

"Is anything wrong?"

"Weezy lost something—that little cube I showed you the other night. She thinks someone stole it. That's why she's upset."

"She should report it to Tim."

On his way out of the living room, he said, "She'll probably do that." But as he headed down the hall, he thought, Then again, she probably won't.

If Jack were betting on it, he'd go with *not*. Tim worked for the county sheriff's department, which routinely traded information with the state police. And the state police often wound up working with the federal government—the "feds," as they said on TV. And the feds worked with the CIA, which was part of a network of global organizations.

In Weezy's world they all had secret agendas. Not that she didn't trust them to do their jobs; she did—as long as those jobs didn't interfere with their secret agendas. And number one on their list of agendas was guarding the secret history of the world, which included the secret history of America, which in turn involved the secret history of the Pine Barrens.

No, Weezy would expect no help from the authorities.

Jack had always laughed off her theories as wacky. After the events of this past week he was finding that a lot harder to do.

Once in his room, he closed the door, then lowered the shades, thinking, I don't believe I'm doing this.

Then he pulled out the bottom drawer of his bureau and checked the space below. Two sheets of paper lay there. He pulled them out and checked them in the dim light.

Yep. Weezy's copies, safe and sound.

He replaced them, slipped the drawer back into place, raised his shades, then returned to the sidewalk.

"Right where I left them," he said as he reached Weezy. "Want me to make copies for you?"

"No-no-no!" she said. "Someone might have copiers staked out. Just leave them right where they are."

They stood in silence, looking around. Jack was beginning to wonder if whatever Weezy had was catching.

"Well," he said finally, "at least they didn't get the pyramid too."

She slapped her forehead. "Ohmygod! I've been so crazy about the box I forgot about the pyramid. We've got to get it back!"

"So it can be stolen too? At least we know it's safe down at the Smithsonian."

"Don't be so sure. I want it back. I'll have my mother rent a safety deposit box and keep it there."

Jack smiled and nudged her. "What about the international banking conspiracy? Won't they be able to get into the box?"

She frowned. "I never thought of that."

"Weez, I'm kidding."

"I'm not."

Jack shook his head, then closed his eyes and pressed his fingers against his temples.

"I see a visit to Professor Nakamura in the near future."

Weez gave his arm a gentle slap. "Not 'near'—immediate. Get your bike."

8

A Japanese woman Jack assumed was Mrs. Nakamura answered the door.

"*Ohayo gozaimasu*," Weezy said, all sweetness and light as she made a quick little bow from the waist. "Would you please tell the professor that Jack and Louise wish to speak to him about the pyramid? He will understand."

The woman smiled and bowed back. "*Dozo yoroshiku*. Wait here. I'll tell him."

"*Arigato*."

Jack made a conscious effort to close his dropped jaw as he stared at Weezy.

She noticed. "What?"

"Since when do you know Japanese?"

"Since forever. I'm fluent in it."

"No, really."

She smiled. "Okay, after we met the professor I started thinking about it, so I picked up a Japanese phrase book at the library."

"What did you say to her?"

" 'Good morning' and 'Thank you.' "

"And what did she say?"

She frowned. "Not sure. It came out so fast. But I think she said, 'Pleased to meet you.' "

The woman was back at the door, but no longer smiling.

"The professor is out at the moment. In fact, he is away

for the weekend. He will get in touch with you next week. *Gomen nasai.*"

She looked guilty as she closed the door.

"*Sayonara*," Weezy said in a low voice, then turned to Jack, her features constricted with disappointment and concern. "Do you believe that?"

"Not for a minute."

Anger flashed through him. Nobody blew Weezy off and closed the door in her face when he was around. Suddenly he knew what to do.

He hopped off the front steps and started walking around the side of the house.

"Where are you going?"

He didn't turn. "To see the professor."

Jack led her around to the backyard. Immediately he was drawn to the stone garden, but he pulled his attention away and focused on the windows into the study. There, hunched over his desk with his back to them, sat Professor Nakamura. Jack stepped up and rapped on the window.

The professor jumped as if he'd heard a gunshot. He spun in his chair and froze when he saw Jack. They locked gazes for a few seconds, Jack giving him his best glare, then the professor took a deep breath and nodded. He gave Jack the *stay-there* signal as he rose and left his study.

A few seconds later the rear door opened and he motioned them inside.

"Oh, dear," he said as they filed past him. "I was hoping for a little more time before speaking to you."

"Why is that?" Weezy said. "Did they find something?"

"Let us not talk here."

The professor led them to the study where the three of them took up seats around the desk.

"What did they learn?" Weezy said. "Did they date it?"

The professor kept his eyes down. "Not yet."

"Then what?"

He sighed. "I had hoped this problem would be resolved before speaking to you."

"Problem? What problem?"

With a sinking feeling, Jack sensed what was coming.

The professor looked up but still did not make eye contact. "The artifact has been . . . misplaced."

"What?" In a flash Weezy was on her feet and leaning over the desk. "What are you talking about?"

"The Smithsonian . . . it appears to have mislaid the artifact."

Weezy looked at Jack with a stricken expression. "Oh, no! It's happening there too. They're everywhere!"

Jack needed more information before he climbed onto Weezy's wagon.

"How does something like this happen?"

The professor shrugged. "It will be found."

"No, it won't!" Weezy said, her voice rising. "We'll never see it again!"

"Young lady, I am sorry for this, but I am quite confident that by Monday, or by Tuesday latest, they will locate it. That is why I told my wife to say I am not here. I felt if I could put off speaking to you until then, all this unhappiness would be avoided."

"How did you find out it was gone?" Jack said.

"My colleague at the Smithsonian called me yesterday, asking the whereabouts of the object I told him I was sending. I had sent it for morning delivery; he should have received it."

"Did the delivery company get it there?"

The professor nodded. "I called Federal Express and they said they had a signature from the receiving clerk. My colleague called the clerk who said he signed for a number of packages. He put them on a cart for delivery, but the package never reached my colleague."

"And it never will!" Weezy cried. She slammed her hands on his desk hard enough to make the pens jump. "I never, *ever* should have let it out of my sight!"

With that she turned and stomped out of the study.

Shock flattened the professor's features. "Why is that one so upset? Does she not believe me? Does she think I stole it?"

Jack didn't know what Weezy believed at that moment, but he said, "I don't think so. She thinks she'll never see it again. Do you really think we'll get it back?"

"Of course. The Smithsonian will find it, I promise you. It has simply been misplaced."

Jack wasn't buying. He didn't know who ran the Smithsonian, but since it was on the mall by the Capitol, he was pretty sure it was the government. The man in the suit in the Barrens last night—he worked for the government. Jack didn't know what branch, or whether state or federal, but the way he gave orders to the state trooper made Jack pretty sure he was with some high-up agency.

High up enough to send one of its people into the

Smithsonian to steal a package between the mailroom and the professor's "colleague"?

Absolutely.

"You have our phone numbers, right?"

The professor patted his desktop. "Yes-yes. Right in here."

"Good. Please call me first if you hear anything, okay? Good news or bad news, call me first?"

"If you wish, of course. But I am sure it will be good news."

Jack was just as sure of the opposite.

He found Weezy out on the sidewalk, getting on her bike. She had an angry expression and tears in her eyes.

"This is all your fault, Jack. I just wanted to keep it, but no, you had to talk me into letting other people look at it."

"Me?" He had trouble hiding his shock. "We both agreed we wanted to find out what it was, and the only way to do that was to show it to people who might know."

She shook her head. "No. It's all your fault. I hate you, Jack! HATE YOU!"

Hate me? Jack felt as if he'd been slapped in the face. How could she hate him? He hadn't lost the pyramid.

As she started pedaling her bike back toward 206, Carson Toliver pulled his convertible in by the curb.

"Hey, Weezy," he called.

Without looking at him she yelled, "Shut up and leave me alone!" as she passed.

He blinked in surprise and looked at Jack. "What's up with her?"

"She's having a bad day."

He smiled. "Oh. I get it. I know all about that from my sister."

Jack started pedaling away. "Yeah," he said around the lump in his throat.

Let Toliver think what he wanted. Jack wasn't going to try to explain.

9

He found Weezy on the other side of 206. She'd stopped and was waiting for him.

"I'm sorry," she said, head down, staring at the ground. "That was a stupid thing to say. I didn't mean it."

Jack felt the lump in his throat start to shrink, but he kept cool. Couldn't let on how she'd gotten to him.

"So you don't really hate me?"

She looked up at him. "I could never hate you. I'm just mad at the world right now and I needed someone to blame and you were closest. I never should have said that."

Jack hid his relief. "Forget it. I knew you didn't mean it."

Not true. Crossing the highway he'd been trying to imagine life in this tiny town without Weezy to talk to and hang out with.

"Besides," he added, "it was part mine too."

"Yeah, but you don't seem upset."

He shrugged. "What's the point? Getting upset isn't going to help us get it back."

"You're too logical. Maybe that's what made me lose it." She shook her head. "There must be *something* we can do."

"You mean, like go to Washington and help them search?"

"Of course not. It's gone from the Smithsonian. They'll never find it there. It's probably back in the cube, waiting to be used for whatever it's used for, or buried again."

The cube and the pyramid . . . hundreds of miles apart, yet both stolen, and both thefts within hours of each other.

It smacked of an organization with a long reach, which fell right into line with Weezy's conspiracy theories.

"If they are back together," Jack said, "I'll bet they're right here in town."

Her eyes widened. "Where?"

"In the Lodge."

"Why?"

"Because the Lodge is involved."

Jack remembered what his brother had said about messing with the Lodge, how they had influence in high places. Tom wasn't an ideal source, but he seemed to know the score on the Lodge.

He added, "Maybe they're doing it themselves, or maybe they're just pulling the strings, but they're involved. Gotta be."

Weezy was nodding. "You're right. The Septimus Order has lodges all over the country—all over the world." Her eyes narrowed. "You told Mister Brussard that the pyramid had gone to U of P?"

"Yeah. Wednesday night when I showed it to Steve."

"The Lodge must have someone inside. They might have tried to steal the pyramid there but found out it had been shipped to the Smithsonian. So they had one of their people in Washington grab it from the mailroom. Then, after it's stolen, someone starts digging up the mound, and while that's going on, someone steals the cube and everything related to it."

"Not everything," Jack reminded her.

"Right." She smiled without humor. "I remember that look you gave me when I handed you the copies. You thought I was crazy."

"Crazy, no. But definitely . . ." He searched for the word. "Eccentric."

Another smile, this one warmer. "Eccentric I accept." She sighed. "But just say all that's true, what can we do about it?"

"Haven't a clue. No way we can get into the Lodge for a look. The place is like a fortress."

And even if he could find a way in, Jack doubted he had the nerve to make use of it. He had a feeling he might never get out.

"Helpless!" Weezy spoke through clenched teeth. "I *hate* being helpless!"

So did Jack, but he figured every obstacle had a way around it. You just had to find it. No such thing as an insurmountable object, just people who gave up too soon.

Just then, a sheriff's patrol car turned off the highway and cruised into town. Jack recognized Tim behind the wheel.

"Hey, Weez, want to report a theft?"

"No way. He could be a Lodger for all we know. And even if he's not, you can bet someone above him is. Don't waste your breath. Besides, we weren't supposed to have something from a crime scene in the first place."

She had a point. But Jack wanted to ask Tim something, so he flagged him down.

"Hey, Tim," he said as the car stopped.

"Hey, Jack. What's up?"

"Lot of commotion in the Barrens last night."

Tim frowned. "First I've heard about it."

"Yeah. Couple of helicopters with searchlights hanging over the trees. I could be wrong, but it looked like they were concentrating on that place where we found that body."

"Helicopters? Probably from Lakehurst."

"Didn't look like it. These were black." He motioned to Weezy who was hanging back by her bike. "Weezy saw them too, didn't you, Weez?"

She nodded but said nothing and moved no closer.

"And then," he added, "I saw some cop cars driving into the Pines—three state police cruisers."

That last part wasn't exactly true. The troopers had probably entered the Barrens without going through Johnson, but Jack *had* seen them in there.

Tim's frowned deepened. "Staties? The sheriff never mentioned any activity out here."

Jack faked a relieved sigh. "Well, then, I guess everything's okay. But you know how it is. People see all that commotion and they start worrying about some sort of escaped convict hiding out in the Pines."

Tim shook his head. "No worry there. No escapees running around. But I'm going to look into this. The state's supposed to coordinate with the sheriff when they run an operation in the county."

"Yeah, okay, whatever," Jack said, trying to look uninterested. "Just wondering."

As Tim cruised away Jack saw him pick up the handpiece of his police radio and start talking.

Exactly what he'd hoped he'd do.

When he reached Weezy, she said, "I don't know if that was such a good idea. What if he starts asking the wrong people and they want to know where he got his information? When they hear it's two kids, a boy and a girl, they may come looking."

He shrugged. "I woke up worrying about that, but now

I don't think it's a problem. If they want to keep that operation a secret, the last thing they'll do is come into town and cause a scene. We're just 'dumb piney kids,' remember? So who's going to listen to us anyway, right?"

"I suppose." She hunched her shoulders as if feeling a chill. "I just wonder where we'd be right now if we hadn't got away."

Jack decided not to wonder. That kind of thinking did nothing but crowd the brain with useless thoughts that went nowhere and accomplished nothing.

He preferred to think about their next step and what it could be. Then he remembered something he'd seen Thursday night.

He turned to Weezy. "How do you feel about going for a swim?"

10

They rode to Quaker Lake. Along the way Jack told Weezy about seeing Mr. Brussard throw something in on Thursday night.

She smiled. "Which Hardy Boy do you think you are—Joe or Frank?"

This Hardy Boy thing was getting annoying.

"Why does everybody have to say that?"

"Everybody?"

"Okay, just two—you and my father. But when you consider I've only told two people about what I overheard, two out of two makes a hundred percent."

"Well, what do you expect? Sneaking around, eavesdropping from bathrooms, spying on a suspected murderer through a window"—her grin broadened—"looking for *clues*. If that's not a Hardy Boy wannabe, I don't know what is."

She giggled. Weezy never giggled. A nice sound. But she was getting on his nerves.

"Okay. Fine. Swell—"

"See! You even say 'swell'! Nobody says swell anymore—except maybe a Hardy Boy."

Maybe he'd been reading too many of those old pulp magazines, but he didn't think so.

"Lots of people say 'swell.'"

She laughed. "Next you'll be calling Steve your 'chum'!"

Jack felt a sudden heaviness. "Yeah . . . Steve."

Her grin faded. "Have you done anything about him?"

"Not yet. There's been a *lot* going on."

"No argument there. Way too much going on."

They arrived at the lake and angled their bikes toward the boat area. Not a dock by any stretch. More like a patch of sandy soil where Mark Mulliner left four old canoes for rent. The charge was three dollars an hour, and renters left their payment in the coffee can sitting on the bank next to the *No Swimming* sign.

Mark lived up in Sooy's Boot but left canoes with the same setup here and there in various small Pine towns. He'd stop by every evening in his truck and empty the can.

Jack had heard there'd been some sort of trouble last fall when two guys from Trenton sneaked into town, loaded the canoes into a pickup, and took off. One of the bad things about a town as small as Johnson was that everybody knew everybody else's business. But the good thing was that people tended to watch out for each other.

Some insomniac on Quakerton Road had been sitting by a window that night and saw an unfamiliar truck go by loaded with canoes. She called someone who called Mark. Soon Matthew, Mark, Luke, John, Peter, and Paul Mulliner—their mother was really into the New Testament, apparently—piled into a truck of their own. The story went that they intercepted the thieves on Carranza Road near Tabernacle. What happened after that nobody knew, or nobody was saying, but next morning the canoes were back at their usual spot. Never a mention of the fate of the Trenton guys, and nobody asked. Piney justice tended to be swift, severe, and silent.

Weezy shielded her eyes as she stared at the canoers

already on the lake. "When you talked about swimming, I assumed you meant here."

"Uh-huh."

"You're going to go diving for whatever Steve's father threw in."

"Uh-huh."

"You'll never find it."

"Don't be so sure. I have a pretty good idea where it landed. The water's clear and not very deep. I think it's worth a shot."

"You're not the type to go looking for trouble. Wouldn't it be better to do this at night?"

"But then I wouldn't be able to see."

"Oh, right." She pointed to the blocklike Lodge squatting on the far corner of the opposite bank. "Yeah, you'll be able to see, but so will they. If they're watching, they'll call the fuzz."

The Lodge owned the pond. They let people boat on it, even fish in it—someone had stocked it with small-mouth bass—but absolutely no swimming. Jack had never understood why. But then, the Lodge never explained what it did. It didn't have to.

"I think I have a way around that. But I need your help."

"If it involves swimming, forget it. I'm not going in that lake."

"Don't worry. I'll be the only one getting wet. I'm going to paddle one of these canoes to the other side of the bridge. You're going to follow along the bank. When I get to the right spot, I'm going to become a show-off."

"That's it?"

"You'll see."

He pulled three dollars from his wallet and dropped it in the coffee can, then handed Weezy his wallet.

"Here. Keep this dry for me."

Then he kicked off his Vans. He was glad he was wearing cutoffs, so he didn't have to roll up his jeans. He dragged the canoe into the water, hopped in, and began to paddle.

Weezy pedaled along the bank, looking confused. "What am I supposed to do?"

"Easy!" he shouted. "Just look beautiful!"

Even from here he could see her blush. Immediately he wondered if he should have said it. She might take it the wrong way. A guy could say one thing and a girl would hear something else.

Weezy wasn't beautiful by most standards. Unless she changed dramatically over the next couple of years, she probably wasn't going to have a gaggle of guys following her down the street. But she wasn't bad-looking. She easily could be cute or even attractive if she gave it half a try. He didn't mean she should become a bowhead or anything like that, not that she ever would. But Weezy considered herself a plain Jane, maybe even something of a bow-wow—she'd never told him so but he could sense it—and so she never made that try. Or maybe she just didn't care. Maybe she was going to wait until she came across a Cure fan looking for a girl who reminded him of Robert Smith.

"Easier said than done," she replied in a barely audible voice.

"Nah! Just think *beautiful!*"

Ouch. That was bad—super hokey. He wished he hadn't

brought this up. But if nothing else, it made him look like he was out here just having fun.

He guided the canoe under the bridge and into the south half of the dumbbell-shaped lake. His was the only canoe on this end. To his right on the west bank he saw the big oak near where Mr. Brussard had stood when he threw whatever he'd thrown. Jack guesstimated it had landed about thirty feet out.

He backpaddled the canoe to stop it at the spot. Then he checked for Weezy on the shore. She'd leaned her bike against the big oak and stood watching him with her hands on her hips. She wore a *Now-what?* expression.

Okay, Jack thought. Time to take the plunge.

Carefully he rose to his feet. The canoe began rocking with the shift in weight. When he'd gained his balance he waved to her.

"Hey, Weezy! Look! No hands!"

"And no brains!" she replied.

Can't argue with that, he thought. Or am I just crazy?

Maybe he was. This was certainly a crazy stunt. Weezy was right about his chances of finding whatever it was. Slim to none, even if he knew what he was looking for, and he didn't.

But he had to give it a try.

He pretended to lose his balance, windmilling his arms, which increased the canoe's rocking until—

"Whoa!"

Taking a deep breath, he fell/dove off the canoe into the water. The temperature was a shock. He'd known it was fed by a cold spring, but not *this* cold. Fighting the urge to start swimming for the warm shore, he stroked toward the bottom for a look.

The water wasn't crystal clear but enough light filtered through to reveal the muddy bottom. He stayed a few feet above it, stroking gently so as not to stir up the muck. He saw some beer cans, dead tree branches, a sneaker, and some unidentifiable lumps all coated with green-brown ick. They looked like they'd been here a long time. Something down here for only a few days should stick out like Weezy at an Air Supply concert.

He kept stroking. He'd always been able to hold his breath for a long time. Knowing it was only a short distance to the surface, he pushed it to the max before kicking back toward air.

Nothing . . . he'd found nothing. On his next dive he'd search a little farther out from shore.

A shadow passed over him. He looked up and saw someone else in the water, swimming along the surface.

Who? Too big for Weezy.

As his head broke the surface he felt an arm go around his neck.

"Gotcha!" said a voice close behind him.

Jack panicked when he recognized it: Steve's father!

He heard a high-pitched scream from somewhere as he began struggling to get free.

"Don't fight me, Jack. I'm stronger than you."

Jack knew that, but didn't stop his struggles. The killer was going to drown him to make sure he never found what he'd thrown in here.

11

"Be calm, Jack," said the voice, close to his ear. "Relax. I've got you. You're safe."

Safe? He must mean his secret will be safe.

Jack took a deep breath, preparing for when Mr. Brussard forced him under. He could almost hear him later: *I tried my best to save him but just couldn't.*

But instead of pulling him down, the arm slipped from his neck to across his chest. And then he felt himself being pulled along the surface. He craned his neck and saw that Mr. Brussard was using a cross-chest carry to move him toward shore. Jack had learned this one in his lifesaver course last summer.

He thinks he's saving me.

"I'm okay, Mr. Brussard. I can swim."

He stopped stroking. "You can?"

He released him and Jack treaded water as he turned to face him.

"Yeah. I . . . I just fell off the boat."

"But you didn't come up. I thought . . ." He laughed. "You mean I got soaked for nothing?"

"Well, I wouldn't say for nothing."

"Poor choice of words. Let's get to shore. It's cold in here."

"You go ahead. I've got to get the boat."

"I'll help you."

Together they stroked out to the canoe. Then, each grabbing a side, they swam it ashore.

As they stood panting on the bank, Mr. B said, "Well, I've got to say I didn't have this in mind when I walked over to the Lodge this morning."

Jack felt like a fool. "I'm sorry."

He shrugged. "It livened up an otherwise dull Saturday." He pushed back his wet hair. "I don't know about you, but I'm heading home for some dry clothes. Boy, that water's cold." He clapped Jack on the shoulder. "Next time you're in a canoe, don't act like a jerk, okay?"

As he walked off, Jack said, "Thanks, Mr. B."

He stopped and turned. "Thanks? You said you could swim."

"I can. But you didn't know that. Thanks for trying to save me."

He smiled. "Hey, Steve needs you. If something happened to you, he'd *never* finish that computer."

As he stood and watched Mr. Brussard walk away, Weezy ran over.

"Do you *believe* that?" she said.

Jack shook his head. "He tried to save my life."

"Some cold-blooded murderer he is," she whispered.

Jack turned to her. "I don't get it. What happened?"

"I was watching where you'd 'fallen' in when I heard a splash on the other side." She pointed toward the Lodge. "I saw a pair of shoes on the bank there and someone swimming like mad toward you. I didn't know who he was until he grabbed you."

"I heard a scream. Was that you?"

She nodded. "I thought he was going to . . ."

"Yeah. So did I. But he was trying to save me."

. . . trying to save me . . .

Jack couldn't wrap his mind around that. He'd suspected Steve's father of being a murderer. But maybe he'd had it all wrong. Maybe Mr. B had been genuinely trying to protect those men, and whatever he'd been trying simply hadn't worked.

That meant someone else—or some*thing* else—was killing them.

The klazen? Or Bert Challis?

Or maybe they weren't being killed at all. Maybe it was simply a huge coincidence that all three Lodgers died of cardiac arrest within days of each other. Or, like Dad had said, voodoo.

Jack shook his head. He knew coincidences happened, but this was too much. Those men had been killed. But how? And by whom or what?

Could there really be such a thing as a klazen?

Bert Challis was a better bet.

Weezy nodded toward the lake. "You going back in there?"

"No way." Despite the warmth of the late-morning sun, Jack still felt chilled. "Besides, whatever it is, I'll never find it in all that muck."

"So this was all for nothing?"

He looked at her. "No, not 'all for nothing.' I learned something about Steve's father."

She lowered her voice further. "What? That he's not some mustache-twirling serial killer?"

"Well, what else am I supposed to think?"

"Lots of things."

Should have known, Jack thought. If there's another, darker way of looking at something, Weezy's going to find it.

"Like what?"

"Like maybe he couldn't drown you because he knew people were watching."

"Then why would he swim out at all?"

"How about to drag you away from the spot where he'd thrown the whatever?"

Jack hadn't considered that, but he saw a problem with it.

"If that was true, wouldn't he be hanging around to make sure I don't go back in?"

She crossed her arms over her chest. "Maybe."

"Can't we just give the guy the benefit of the doubt?"

"Sure we can: He saw you fall in, thought you were drowning, and swam out to save you."

"That's good enough for me."

"But that doesn't mean he didn't have something to do with the deaths of those three Lodgers. Maybe he's got a list—and maybe they're on it but you aren't. Plus you're Steve's friend. That means he does the right thing for you and for anyone not on his list. But if you're on his list, better watch your back."

"But wouldn't a guy who could plan and do the murders of three men just stand there and watch me drown?"

Weezy shook her head. "Hardly anybody's all bad, Jack. Just as hardly anybody's all good."

Jack thought of Mom and Kate and couldn't imagine anything bad about them. But he didn't mention that to Weezy. Who knew what she'd dream up? Whatever it might be, he didn't want to hear it.

He shivered. "I'm heading home to change."

"What about the canoe?"

He looked at it, half pulled up on the bank. He'd forgotten all about it.

"Guess I'll have to paddle it back."

Weezy smiled. "Best you stay away from the water for a while. I'll help you carry it."

Not a bad idea.

It turned out to be pretty light so they each carried it on a shoulder.

"This is turning out to be one bad day," she said. "Maybe the worst Saturday ever."

Jack knew what she meant.

"Yeah, we get nabbed in the Pines, the cube gets stolen, the pyramid disappears—"

"You mean 'stolen.'"

"Yeah, you're probably right. And to top it off, I take a cold-water swim and come up with nothing."

"Top it off? The day is still young, Jack. It's not even noon yet."

Swell.

12

They were riding their bikes back toward their homes when Tim pulled his patrol car up beside them. He was grinning.

"Heard about your dunking."

Man, news traveled fast in this town. Jack bet his folks already knew.

"Yeah, well . . ."

"You look like a drowned rat."

Jack needed a change of subject. "Did you find out anything about the state troopers I told you about?"

Tim's grin vanished. "Yeah. And no. I called the sheriff and he called the state, and the state said they didn't know what he was talking about. When the sheriff pressed them he was told he'd be a lot better off if he minded his own business."

Jack looked at Weezy and she looked back.

"I saw that," Tim said. "What do you two know?"

Weezy gave her head a tiny shake—*don't*—but Jack felt he could trust Tim. So he gave him a brief, edited version about the copters, the cops, the suits, and the backhoe digging up the mound. He left out the parts about being locked in the cruiser and the spong traps episode, also the theft of the cube and the pyramid. No use laying too much on him at once.

"They choppered in a *backhoe*?" Tim said. "This sounds major."

Weezy finally spoke up. "Yeah. So major no one's talking."

"And it looks like no one will. The sheriff told me it was none of our business and to drop it. And I'm supposed to pass the same on to you: Just forget what you saw. No good's going to come from yakking about it."

"Consider it passed on," Jack said.

"So whoever they are," Weezy added, her voice thick, "they get to do whatever they want, whenever they want. Is that the way it's supposed to work?"

He knew she was thinking about the pyramid.

Tim didn't reply, so Jack said, "Is that what you're going to do—mind your own business?"

Tim had never struck him as the type to roll over.

"For the record, yes. But this is my beat, Jack. So the way I see it, whatever goes on here *is* my business. And since you live here, it's your business too. Don't go snooping around, don't go sneaking into the Pines at night, don't pull any Hardy Boys stuff—"

Weezy snickered and Jack wondered if there was some sort of conspiracy to smack him with the Hardy Boys at every opportunity.

"What's so funny?" Tim said.

Jack waved a hand. "Nothing."

Tim pulled out a pen and pad and started scribbling. "Yeah, well, okay, but listen to me: You see something like that again, or *anything* out of the ordinary, you call me—and only me." He handed Jack the slip of paper. "That's my home phone. It has an answering machine that I check all the time. You need me, call and simply say, 'This is Jack.' That's all. Nothing more. I repeat: Say nothing more. I'll find you." He nodded to Weezy. "You see anything, tell Jack so he can tell me."

This sounded like spy stuff, like intrigue, like he'd stepped into Weezy's world. It made his stomach tingle.

"Okay." Jack folded the paper but thought better of shoving it into a wet pocket. "You expecting anything to happen?"

Tim shook his head. "Nah. What's done is done and that's probably it. But it never hurts to have a couple of extra pairs of eyes on the lookout. And speaking of looking, I think I'll take a ride out to the mound and see what they've done."

"Can we come along?" Weezy said.

Tim shook his head. "Sorry. Better if you don't." He put the car in gear. "Take it easy, you two. And keep those eyes open."

They watched as he drove away, heading toward the Barrens.

"Think we can trust him?" Weezy said.

"Yeah. Tim's a good guy."

Jack just hoped he didn't get himself in trouble by sticking his nose in the wrong place.

As they started riding again, Jack saw a car pull to a stop at the end of South Franklin. He wouldn't have paid it much mind except that the driver seemed so short. His head was so low he could barely see over the dashboard.

Then he recognized the man and realized he wasn't short—he was crouched low behind the wheel.

Bert Challis.

He glanced Jack's way. Their eyes met for a second, then he turned away. His hand shot up to the side of his face, hiding his profile as he gunned the car and raced down Quakerton Road toward the highway.

What was that all about?

His furtiveness made Jack uneasy. South Franklin led to Harding Street, where the Brussards lived. Was he watching the place?

This was getting scary.

13

The lock-picking set felt like a fire in Jack's pocket as he stepped through the front door. Business at USED had been unusually slow for a Saturday, allowing Jack extra time to practice on the locks around the store.

The big sale of the day had been the curved-glass China cabinet. Once it could be opened, people became more interested in it. Some lady on an antiquing junket from Princeton walked in, took one look at it, and wrote out a fat check.

A glow of pride had followed Jack home—he'd been responsible for that sale.

On the way out of the store he'd borrowed the lock picks without telling Mr. Rosen. Was that stealing? He didn't think so, especially since he didn't intend to keep the set—just use it and return it.

As he stepped in the back door his mom said, "Dinner's going to be early tonight, dear. Your father and I are going to a movie."

Yes! He could work on the lock box without worrying about getting caught.

"Oh?" he said casually. "Going to see *Return of the Jedi* again?"

She made a face. "Not likely. This time it's my choice, and I choose *Risky Business*."

Every few weeks his folks would head up to Mount Holly to catch a movie. They took turns choosing. Though

Dad complained about the way the spaceships maneuvered and hearing explosions in space—none of which bothered Jack in the least—he liked the *Star Wars* movies. Mom liked romantic comedies. For the sake of togetherness, each suffered through the other's choices.

"Tom's going out, and Kate's in Stratford. You'll be okay with nobody here?"

Jack gave her a reassuring smile. He *loved* having the house to himself.

"I'll be here with me."

Just then Tom appeared in the doorway to the living room.

"How's it going, Miracle Boy?"

Tom saying hello? Jack was immediately on guard.

"Fine. How about you?"

Tom nodded. "Life is good, but it could always get better."

Something was up.

Jack turned to Mom. "I'm gonna wash up."

As he headed down the hall to the bathroom he could feel Tom's eyes on his back. Up ahead he could see his bedroom door ajar—maybe two or three inches.

Ah-ha!

He washed his hands and threw water on his face, then stepped back into the hall. Tom stood down by the kitchen, talking to Mom but positioned so he had a clear view of Jack's door.

Something definitely up.

He returned to the kitchen and headed for the backyard.

"Where you going?" Tom said.

"Garage. Wanna come?"

"Nah. I'll wait here."

But instead of the garage, Jack ran around to his bedroom window at the rear of the house. He peeked through the screen and immediately spotted the bucket balanced atop the partially open door.

The bucket-over-the-door trick. Oh, Tom, you clever, clever guy. So original.

After half a minute of studying the setup, Jack knew just what to do.

But first he had to know if he could get into the room unseen. He tugged on the outside of the screen—had he latched it last night? He grinned when the bottom popped out. No, he'd had too much on his mind to worry about latching screens.

He trotted to the garage and pawed through his dad's toolbox until he found a couple of eye hooks. Then he pulled out his penknife and cut twenty feet or so of nylon fishing line from one of Dad's never-used rods. Goodies in hand, he scuttled back to his bedroom window to crawl inside.

Quietly as possible, he moved his desk chair over to the door and stepped up on it. He screwed one eye hook into the ceiling directly above the bucket. He threaded the end of the fishing line through the eye and tied it to the bucket handle.

Next he moved the chair to the right, to the corner by his closet, where he placed a second eye hook about six feet up the wall. He threaded the line through that, then looped it around the closet doorknob. He adjusted the tension on the line just enough to lift the bottom edge of the bucket a smidgen off the top of the door, then knotted it into place.

Moved the chair back, slipped out the window, then returned to the kitchen.

Mom was setting plates on the table. "Call your father. We're almost ready."

"Okay. Just gotta stop in my room first."

With that, Tom stepped back into the kitchen and again positioned himself where he could see Jack's door.

As Jack passed him he couldn't resist: "Wanna share some pistachios later?"

"Very funny, Miracle Boy. Your time is coming. Sooner than you think."

Hoping he'd done everything right, Jack held his breath as he pushed open the door to his room, preparing to be doused if he'd screwed up.

But no . . . he stayed dry.

Immediately he pulled out his penknife and positioned himself by the closet door to wait. He didn't think it would take long.

It didn't.

Seconds later Tom arrived, wearing a perplexed expression. As he stepped through the door he looked up at the bucket.

"What the—?"

His eyes widened when he saw the eye hooks and the fishing line, but too late. Jack had cut the line and the bucket tipped and emptied on Tom's face. He cried out in shock and rage as he was drenched with cold water.

Jack thought it was one of the most beautiful sights he'd ever seen.

The commotion brought Mom running.

"What happened? What's—?" She stopped and stared at her soaked son, then at the puddle on the floor. "What is going on here?" She looked past Tom at Jack. "Jackie! What were you thinking?"

"I did *not* put a bucket over my own door, Mom."

She turned to Tom. "Well, since I doubt very much it was your father, and since Kate isn't home, that leaves you. When are you going to grow up, Thomas? You're in law school, for heaven's sake!"

"He started it with the doctored pistachios," he said, wiping his dripping face with a wet sleeve.

"No," she said. "*You* started it when you stole his pistachios. Now, I want the two of you to shake hands and end this. Right now. You heard me: shake."

Tom stuck out a hand. "Peace, brother?"

Jack knew what Tom had in mind: He was going to trap Jack's fingers in a deathgrip and squeeze with everything he had. This wouldn't be the first time—not by a long shot. When Jack was younger Tom would squeeze and try to get him to say, "Tom is God." Jack never would—even though the crushing agony almost brought him to tears, he never said it.

Tom was still bigger and stronger, but Jack had learned a trick.

"Peace, brother," he said, forcing his hand as deep into Tom's as it would go.

Tom squeezed but it didn't hurt, because he was squeezing Jack's hand, not his fingers. He squeezed harder, the effort showing on his face, but still no pain for Jack.

"Mom said, 'shake hands,' Tom, not go steady."

Glaring, Tom released him.

"That's my boys," Mom said as she headed back toward the kitchen. "Tom, you mop up your mess."

"I'm not through with you, numbnuts," he said in a low voice.

Jack held his gaze, then slipped past him into the hall.

"Better get mopping or you'll miss dinner."

14

Tom had gone out to who cared where. Kate and another student she met were fixing up the apartment in Stratford they'd be using during the coming year at medical school. His folks were off to the movies.

He had the place to himself.

Ah, freedom.

He hurried upstairs to his folks' bedroom closet and retrieved the lock box from the top shelf. He set it on the double bed and laid out the pick set next to it. He hadn't found a lock like this in USED but he was sure he could open it.

Half an hour later he was pretty sure he couldn't. At least not at his level of experience. He needed more practice.

Frustration gnawed at him as he folded up the pick kit, returned the box to its original place, and headed back downstairs. The secrets within had become secondary. The lock . . . the lock had become his Everest and he was determined to climb it.

After hiding the pick set under the T-shirts in one of his drawers, he wandered through the house. He could read or watch TV, but neither appealed to him at the moment. He could see if he could get past the smart bombs in *Missile Command*, but he wasn't in a video game mood. Weezy and Eddie were visiting their grandmother in Baltimore.

That left Steve and the Heathkit.

15

"Steve's downstairs working on the computer," Mrs. Brussard said as she let him in.

Jack hoped so, but had his doubts.

"Is Mister Brussard around?"

She shook her head. "No. He's over at the Lodge. Why?"

"I just wanted to tell him something about the black box I showed him the other night."

Jack had wanted to see if he would have any reaction when he told him the cube and the pyramid were missing.

"He shouldn't be too late."

Jack nodded and headed for the basement. As he passed the den he slowed, looking for the humidor. He spotted it—inside the locked liquor cabinet.

Swell.

Downstairs he found Steve dozing on the couch.

Jack shook his shoulder. "Hey."

Steve's lids fluttered open to reveal glassy eyes. "Hey, man."

Aw, no. He was at it again.

"More pills?"

He grinned as he pointed to a Pepsi can and rattled the vial of pills in his shirt pocket. "Double barreled: Valium with a bourbon chaser."

"But how'd you get hold of the bourbon? I thought your father had it all locked up."

His grin broadened. "He does. Or at least he thinks he

does." He pointed to a small key lying on the end table. "But he doesn't have the only key. I had a copy made at Spurlin's this afternoon."

"Swell. So I guess you're going to spend the night on the couch."

Steve burped in reply, closed his eyes again.

Jack resisted the urge to kick him. Instead he stepped over to the end table and stared down at the key to the Brussard liquor cabinet . . . and to the humidor.

Should I?

He decided he should. He hadn't been able to learn what was in his father's lock box, but maybe he'd be able to pierce the secret of the little red boxes in the humidor.

He snagged the key and hurried upstairs. If Mrs. B was around he'd just go to the fridge for a Pepsi. If not . . .

She was nowhere in sight, so Jack hurried to the den and the liquor cabinet. His hand was shaking a little—what would happen if Mr. Brussard returned now?—so it took him a second try to put the key in the lock. As the door swung open he grabbed the humidor and lifted the lid.

One box remained. He pulled it out, then returned the humidor to its shelf. He turned the little red box over in his hands, examining it. It reminded him of a hatbox, only this was barely two inches tall and wide, and had seven sides. It was covered with some sort of fine shiny fabric, like silk.

Jack was about to lift the lid when he heard voices in the front yard. Two men . . . and they sounded like they were arguing. One of the voices was Mr. Brussard's. Coming closer.

A jolt of panic coursed through Jack. He didn't have time to put the box back in the humidor. Didn't even have time to relock the cabinet. He pushed the door closed and ran in a crouch. He'd just rounded the corner into the stair-well when the door opened.

He stood there panting like he'd just sprinted a three-minute mile.

Too close.

He heard Mr. Brussard saying, "You've just got to stay calm, Bert. Everything will be—"

"Calm? How can I stay calm after all that's happened? I go to the West Coast for a week and come back to find everything gone to hell!"

But he hadn't been on the West Coast, Jack knew. Why was he lying?

"After two years," he added, "with my nerves finally calming down, this happens!"

Two years . . . Anton Boruff had been murdered two years ago . . .

"The important thing is to realize that this will all blow over."

"Will it? I've heard that the Council is sending someone to take charge of our Lodge."

As they moved into the den their voices faded and Jack didn't have the nerve to try the bathroom trick again. So he tiptoed downstairs and checked Steve. Still out.

He looked down at the little box in his sweaty palm. How was he going to get it back in the humidor before Mr. Brussard realized it was gone?

But before he worried about that, he had to see what it held. He lifted the lid gingerly, cautiously, half afraid some-thing would jump out at him. But instead of some exotic insect or mysterious amulet, he found a small, round, white object.

A pill.

He picked it up and inspected it but could find no markings to give him a hint of what it contained. But he had a suspicion it might not be good for anyone's health. Steve's father had given three of these to three men, and all were dead the following day.

Questions swirled.

Could it be some kind of poison, something untraceable that only the Lodge knew about?

He should take it to the police and tell them his suspicions, convince them to analyze it. That seemed the most logical and direct course, but would they believe him? Or would they react like Weezy and think of him as a Hardy Boy wannabe?

But what if he was wrong? What if it was something harmless, supposed to ward off the klazen but didn't. He'd have hurt the reputation of an innocent man, a man who'd jumped into the lake to save him because he thought he was drowning.

Jack couldn't help feeling in Mr. B's debt. After all, what was Challis's role in all this?

But he couldn't ignore what he'd seen and heard. If Steve's father was guilty, Jack had to find a way to let him hang himself.

He looked at Steve, then looked at the pill lying in its box, and had an idea.

But he'd have to set the stage carefully to make this work.

16

"Listen, Bert, I've found a way to protect us from the klazen."

Jack stood outside the den, listening. He'd been about to walk in but had stopped just around the corner.

"I don't need protection from some mythical threat, I need—"

"Vasquez, Haskins, and Sumter might disagree as to how mythical it is. If I could have got to them in time they'd still be alive."

A lie. He'd given them each a pill.

That clinched it for Jack.

He's guilty, he thought. But I'm the only one who knows.

In the next few minutes he hoped to change that.

"You know what?" Challis said. "I almost wish I were with them. This is eating me alive. We shouldn't have taken matters into our own hands like that. We—"

Mr. Brussard cut him off, saying, "What's done is done. We've got to deal with now. Let me show you what I've got. I—hey. This is supposed to be locked."

Uh-oh. Time to make his move. Jack quickly stepped into the den. Mr. Brussard was squatting by the liquor cabinet; Challis, a thin, twitchy man, stood nearby.

"Mister Brussard?"

He looked around to stare at him. "Jack! How long have you been standing there?"

Jack dodged the question by saying, "I think there's something wrong with Steve."

Mr. B straightened and stepped closer, his expression concerned. "What do you mean?"

"I can't wake him up."

In a flash, he was pushing past Jack. He almost knocked over Mrs. B as she stepped from the stairs into the hallway.

"Gordon, what's wrong?"

"Steve! Downstairs!"

She blanched. "What—?"

But her husband was already to the basement steps. As he pounded down she hurried after him. Challis followed, though not as hurriedly.

Jack stayed behind and picked up the phone. He dialed 911 and reported an unconscious person at the Brussard address. Then he headed downstairs.

When Jack arrived, Steve's folks were shaking him, yelling at him to wake up. His eyes fluttered open and gave them a dazed look.

"Wha? Wha?"

His father spotted the Pepsi can next to the couch and sniffed it. His face turned red.

"You're drunk!" he cried and grabbed the front of Steve's shirt. "You've been pilfering from my—!"

Something rattled in Steve's breast pocket. Mr. Brussard pulled out the pill vial and stared at it.

"It's your Valium!" he said, turning to his wife. "He's—!"

And then he froze. Jack followed his gaze to the little red box on the cushion next to Steve.

"What's—?"

He snatched it up and yanked off the top. His red face turned ashen when he looked inside.

"Oh, no!" He turned to Steve and shook him. "Did you take this?"

Steve gave him another glassy stare. "No. It's right there."

"I mean the pill, damn it! Did you take the pill that was in here?"

Steve shrugged and slurred, "Dunno . . . maybe . . . coulda."

Mr. Brussard tossed the box aside and started lifting Steve under the arms.

"We've got to get him to the hospital!"

Just then someone knocked on the wall of the stairwell and called down.

"Hello? Is there a problem here?" A sheriff's deputy came down the stairs. Not Tim, but Jack had seen him at the car lot when the first aid was trying to revive Mr. Sumter.

He'd been counting on a deputy's arrival—the cops always responded to a 911.

"I heard the first-aid call and came over to see if I could help."

"First-aid call?" Mr. Brussard looked around. "Who—? Never mind. My son took pills and liquor! He needs to get his stomach pumped!"

"The ambulance is on its way." The deputy leaned closer to Steve. "He's still conscious. Maybe he won't need that."

"He will! He'll die!"

The deputy wasn't looking where Jack wanted him to, so he picked up the little red box and pretended to examine it. When the deputy saw it he reached toward Jack.

"May I?"

As Jack handed it over, Mr. Brussard said, "Never mind that! We've got to get him to the hospital!"

But the deputy wasn't listening. He was staring at the box, turning it over in his hands.

"I've seen one of these before. Mister Sumter had it on him when he died. And I've heard the same box was found on Vasquez and Haskins." He looked up at Mr. Brussard. "What was in this?"

"Nothing. Look, we need to—"

"Nothing?" Challis said. "*Nothing*? I just heard you ask your boy if he took the pill that was inside." His jaw dropped. "And when he said yes you went crazy. You just said he'll die." He pointed to Mr. Brussard. "It's you! You poisoned them! Sumter, Vasquez, and Haskins—you killed them!"

Mr. Brussard looked stunned. "Don't be ridiculous."

"It's true! It's all clear! You poisoned them with whatever pill was in that box! And I was next! 'I've found a way to protect us from the klazen.' Isn't that what you said? But what I need is protection from *you*!"

Mrs. B looked horrified. "Gordon, what is this man talking about?"

The deputy frowned at Challis. "Why would he want to kill you?"

"Because five can keep a secret only when four are dead, isn't that right, Gordon."

"I'm not following," the deputy said.

"We killed Anton Boruff—the body found in the Pines!"

"Bert!" Mr. Brussard shouted.

"There. I've said it. It's haunted me for two years. Now maybe I'll be able to sleep at night!" He turned to the deputy and his words spewed at machine-gun speed. "He swindled us—fake diamonds. We confronted him. Things got rough. He fell, hit his head. It wasn't supposed to happen. We didn't mean to—"

" 'We'?" the deputy said. "Who do you mean?"

"Me, Sumter, Vasquez, Haskins, and Gordon here."

Just then a heavy guy with a first-aid emblem on his shirt thundered down the stairs.

"We tried the bell but no one answered. I heard voices—" He looked at the swaying Steve. "Is this the unconscious person you reported?"

"I didn't report anyone," Mr. Brussard said, "but as long as you're here, he needs immediate hospitalization."

Jack figured this had gone on long enough. He snatched the pill from where he'd left it on the floor behind the couch, and held it up.

"Is this the pill?"

Mr. Brussard's eyes widened. "Give it to me," he said, reaching for it.

But the deputy grabbed his arm.

"I'll take that."

Jack gave it to him. He looked at it, put it in the little red box, and shoved the box into a pocket. Then he stepped back and rested one hand on his pistol as he pulled his two-way from his belt.

"This is Driscoll," he said. "I've got a situation at one twenty-seven Harding in Johnson. Requesting backup."

Jack felt a rush of . . . what? A strange, tingling fire flared in his chest as he realized he'd done it. He'd tricked Mr. Brussard into incriminating himself. He wanted to whoop and yell and do the Snoopy dance around the room.

But he couldn't. Now was not the time. Not with Steve and his mother staring in shock and fear and disbelief at the man they called father and husband. Maybe there'd never be a good time for the Snoopy dance.

Free-form guilt dulled the edge of his elation. He looked around and found Mr. Brussard glaring at him.

"You called them, didn't you."

Jack couldn't look at Steve, but he stared Mr. Brussard in the eye.

"I was worried about Steve."

And that was the truth.

"Trouble just follows you around, doesn't it."

Jack turned at the sound of the voice and saw Tim leaning out the window of his patrol car.

"What do you mean?"

Tim smiled. "You know exactly what I mean. My buddy Driscoll says you were right in the thick of things last night. Even found the pill."

"Yeah, well, just hanging with Steve."

Tim nodded toward the Brussard house down the street. "Returning to the scene of the crime?"

The whole town was buzzing with the news of the Brussard arrest and the Challis confession. Jack had wandered over, wondering if he should stop in and see how Steve was handling it. He knew he shouldn't feel guilty about exposing a murderer, but he couldn't help it.

He'd chickened out on the visit, at least on his first pass, afraid Steve would take one look at him and somehow know Jack had got his dad arrested. As he'd passed he noticed that the garbage can near the end of the driveway was full of empty liquor bottles. Mrs. Brussard was cleaning house—a first step toward helping Steve, but Jack had a feeling he'd need more.

"Brussard posted bail," Tim said.

"He's *out*? How?"

"Not much on him beyond what Challis said. But we're analyzing that pill, and if it turns out to be some funky poison, we'll have a whole different ball game."

Now Jack was doubly glad he hadn't stopped in. The way Steve's dad had looked at him last night made it clear he suspected something.

Tim went on. "Challis, on the other hand, didn't want bail. Said he felt safer behind bars."

Safe from the klazen? Or his Lodge brother?

"He give any reason for the way they—?"

"Cut him up?" Tim shook his head. "Not much. Told us Boruff was killed in a 'sacred rite' used for those who betray Lodge brothers, then clammed up. Said it was a Lodge matter and nobody else's business."

Cutting off the arms at the elbows and sewing them into the armpits . . . what kind of sacred rite was that?

"Seen any more state troopers running around?" Tim said.

Jack used the title of another book on his summer reading list. "All quiet on the western front."

Tim nodded. "It *is* sort of the western front, isn't it—the western front of the Pine Barrens."

Mention of the Barrens reminded Jack of something.

"You went to the mound yesterday. How's it look?"

Tim shook his head. "I saw it when we dug up the body. Gotta tell you, you wouldn't recognize the place now. All torn up." Another head shake. "Shame. One of the pointy heads we had doing the crime scene work-up said he was sure the mound was pre-Columbian."

Jack had heard the term before. "Before Columbus? Wow."

"Yeah. Wow. He said definitely pre-Columbian, maybe even prehistoric."

"Oh, man. Weezy will want to go back."

Jack did too, but knew Weezy would want to even more.

"Nothing left to see. Trust me." Tim poked his arm. "But even so, you two stay away from there for now . . . until things settle down. I asked one of the medevac pilots I know to snap a photo or two on one of his many runs to AC."

"Why?"

Tim looked away, through the windshield. "Not sure. Something about that place . . ."

A burst of static from his two-way interrupted with a report of an accident near Shamong.

"Gotta go. Remember what I said: Stay out of the Pines for now."

As Jack watched Tim go, he figured he could manage that for another day or two, but there'd be no stopping Weezy once she heard "prehistoric."

Good thing she was in Baltimore for the weekend and wouldn't be back till tonight. Because he wasn't sure he could keep the news from her.

2

Jack sat in the dark on a thick limb of the tree across the street from Steve's house, watching.

It had turned out to be a quiet Sunday, quieter than usual after the rain started around midday. Kate was still at her apartment in Stratford. Tom was packing to move back to his place in Jersey City. Sure signs that summer was drawing to a close. Not much shaking at USED either, so Jack did his cleanups and polishing, and practiced his lock picking when he had a chance.

After dinner, he'd watched a *Knight Rider* rerun, followed by the *ABC Sunday Night Movie*, then hit the sack. But sleep eluded him. He kept thinking about Steve, and how his friend's family was messed up now because of him.

No, he kept telling himself. Steve's father had been the one to mess up that family.

Finally he'd pulled on a shirt and jeans and slipped out his window.

He wasn't sure what had drawn him here. Guilt? Or maybe worry that Mr. Brussard might slip off into the night?

The rain had stopped earlier but the tree bark and leaves were still wet; a thick mist hung in the air, glowing in the widely scattered streetlights. The house lay dark and quiet. No sign of anyone moving about. Jack finally asked himself what he was accomplishing here. And when he couldn't come up with a good answer, he decided it was time to go.

But just as he was readying to swing down from the

limb, he saw a thin dark streak flowing through the mist along Harding Street. He couldn't call it black, couldn't call it solid. More like something colorless or invisible, displacing the mist. Tapered at both ends, maybe ten feet long and no more than two feet wide, it moved lazily, undulating on the breeze—

And then Jack realized with a start that there was no breeze.

Despite the warmth of the night, chill gooseflesh rippled over his skin. He shrank back against the tree trunk and watched as the streak angled toward the Brussard house. For some reason he wanted to shout out a warning, but his vocal cords were clenched tight. And a warning against what? Smoke? A hole in the mist?

Whatever it was, it nosed against the left side of Steve's house and then splashed out along the siding like water from a faucet hitting a sink. As it spread it thinned and broke up into tiny dark wisps that swirled and faded to nothing.

Weird, Jack thought. Really weird. But it was gone now. Time to get back.

He swung down from the branch and began walking home. As he passed the house he glanced back and saw the streak seeping out the opposite side. He stopped, his Vans glued to the pavement, watching as it reformed into the elongated shape he'd first seen. It began to drift again . . .

Toward him.

And then a light came on in the house and he heard a woman scream.

Part of him wanted to run up to Steve's door and see if he could help, but he had a feeling whatever had happened in there was beyond his help or anybody else's.

Mr. Brussard had just met the klazen. Jack was sure of it. And now it was heading for him.

No . . . angling northwest . . . across his intended path.

So Jack did an about-face and began walking the other way, taking the long way home. When he looked back he saw the streak still headed in the other direction.

Safe . . . or was he? Somehow he didn't feel safe.

He broke into a run and didn't slow until he'd reached his yard. He stopped and looked around, praying he wouldn't see a dark streak filtering through the misty cornrows of the neighboring field and heading his way.

Nothing. It must still be heading northwest.

Wait . . . the county jail was northwest of Johnson . . . and Mr. Challis had stayed there . . . because it was safer . . .

He wished Weezy were here. She'd be so into this. But Jack . . .

He crawled through the window, closed and locked it behind him, leaped into bed, and pulled the covers over his head.

He hated things he couldn't explain.

1

"Did you hear?" Kate said, rushing into the kitchen.

Jack was just finishing the Taylor ham and egg sandwich he'd had for lunch.

Mom turned from the sink. "Hear what, dear?"

"Gordon Brussard dropped dead last night."

Mom dropped the plate she'd been fitting into the dishwasher. It didn't break.

"No!"

"Yes! And so did that man Challis, the one who confessed to killing the man Jack found. Within an hour of each other. Can you believe it?"

"No," Mom said. "I can't."

Jack could. But even though he'd half expected it, he couldn't help but feel shock. Had he really been on Harding Street last night? Or had he dreamed it? How could he be sure?

Kate said, "It's true!"

"Where'd you hear all this?"

"Down at Burdett's. I was on empty and Jeff filled me in while he was filling me up."

That sort of clinched the deaths. Jeff Colton, the pump jockey at Burdett's Esso station, talked to everyone who stopped in and pumped them for gossip. He knew every-thing there was to know in this end of Burlington County.

Jack said, "What are the chances of that happening? I mean, two people arrested for the same crime dropping dead at almost the same time?"

Kate shook her head. "Astronomical, I'd think. Then again . . ." Her voice trailed off.

"Then again what?"

"Getting arrested has got to be unbelievably stressful, whether you're innocent or guilty. I can't imagine that would be good for your heart. And if you had any heart disease . . ." She shrugged. "I guess it's possible. If this were *Magnum, P.I.*, I'd be guessing they were both poisoned or something, but in real life . . ." Another shrug. "Just a bizarre coincidence."

Uh-uh, Jack thought. Maybe no coincidence. Maybe a klazen.

But no way was he mentioning that. Talk about open-ing a can of worms.

"Poor Steve," he said, and meant it. The thought of losing his own father . . . he couldn't imagine what Steve was feeling.

He *could* imagine Steve's mom using her Valium today, and Steve probably wishing he had some—*needing* some.

Jack realized then that he needed something too: fresh air. He had the day off and didn't want to spend it thinking about things he couldn't explain. Besides, Eddie had called to announce that his grandmother had bought him the new *Star Wars: Death Star Battle* video game.

"I'm going out," he said, carrying his empty plate to the dishwasher.

"Where?" Mom said.

"Weez and Eddie's, I guess."

Mom gave him a don't-forget-what-I-told-you look.

Man . . .

Jack heard cursing as they approached the spong.

He'd hung out with Weezy and Eddie for a while, the two guys taking turns at *Death Star Battle*—it looked super on the 5200—and Weezy watching morosely, saying little. She was still bummed out about losing the cube and the pyramid. Somewhere along the line Jack let slip the possibility that the mound was pre-Columbian, maybe even prehistoric.

Well, that was all Weezy had to hear. Before he knew it she was up and out and headed for her bike. Jack tried to stop her, telling her what Tim had said, but Weezy was deaf to all that. Since he couldn't let her ride off into the Pines alone, he went with her. Even Eddie tagged along, saying something about it being "fossilacious." Apparently he'd equated prehistoric with dinosaurs.

On the plus side, the road trip pulled Weezy out of her funk. She was her old self again, chattering away about her secret-history stuff as she led them down the fire trail.

The cursing grew louder, and as they reached the spong area they saw a skinny man wearing an Agway gimme cap, bib-front overalls, duck boots, and probably nothing else. He looked like he was dancing around the open area, but he was kicking at the traps, many with sticks jutting from them, and cursing a blue streak.

The three of them stopped to stare. This had to be the

trapper, and it looked like Mrs. Clevenger had been doing her thing again.

He stopped when he saw them.

"Whatchoo lookin' at?"

When they didn't reply, he started toward them. He needed a shave and most likely a bath, and his eyes looked wild with rage.

"You been doin' this? You the ones been messin' up muh traps?"

"We just got here, mister," Jack said, thinking this couldn't be Old Man Foster because he wasn't old. Forty, tops. "Are you Mister Foster?"

"Zeb Foster? No, I ain't him."

"Then what are you doing trapping on his land?" Weezy said.

He stepped closer. "Look, I don't need no little girl asking me no fresh-mouthed questions. Get outa here!"

Weezy stood her ground. "Well, if you're not Mister Foster, who are you?"

"I'm his son, dammit! Now git!" He pointed a dirty finger at them. "And you better not be the ones springin' muh traps, 'cause if you are, I'll skin you like a coon—only you'll still be alive when I do it. Now git!"

"Okay, okay," Eddie said, moving faster than usual.

"One creepitacious guy," he said when they'd moved out of earshot.

Weezy made a face. "Like I believe he's Old Man Foster's son."

"Maybe he isn't," Jack said. "But I do believe he meant what he said about skinning us alive."

3

"This is criminal!" Weezy cried as she walked among the ruins of the mound. "An absolute sin!"

Jack agreed. The mound or mounds—he couldn't be sure exactly what had been here before—had snaked among the burned trunks. Now trenches ran in all directions amid knocked-down and half-downed trees.

She kicked at the sand. "They've destroyed everything!"

"See any fossils?" Eddie said.

"Why am I not surprised to find you here?" a familiar voice called.

Jack turned and saw Tim standing by his patrol car at the edge of the burned area.

Jack, Weezy, and Eddie looked at one another, then ambled over to where he waited.

Tim shook his head as he looked at Jack. "Didn't I tell you to stay away from here?"

Jack could have said he'd come along only to keep Weezy company, but that wasn't exactly true and he wasn't about to lay it on her. No one had forced him to come along.

So he simply shrugged.

But Weezy said, "It was my idea, Officer."

Tim smiled. "Deputy."

Weezy did her *whatever* face and said, "Isn't there something you can do about this? Someone you can arrest or we can sue for desecrating this site?"

"Desecrating?" Tim frowned. "It's not like it was a church or anything."

"Could have been at one time. It might have contained secrets hidden for . . . forever."

"Secrets?"

Oh, no, Jack thought. Don't get her started on secrets. He searched for a way to change the subject.

"Did your friend ever get that photo from his helicopter?"

Tim nodded. "As a matter of fact, he did." He reached through the open window of his patrol car and pulled out a half dozen eight-by-ten photos. "Took a bunch of them from different angles on two different runs." He handed them to Jack. "Take a look."

Jack studied the top photo, then handed it off to Weezy. He did the same with all six. The last was taken from almost directly overhead. It best showed the devastation caused by the backhoe because the angle of the sun shadowed the trench. Jack studied this one the longest. Something about it tickled his brain, but he couldn't put his finger on it.

When he handed it to Weezy he heard her gasp.

"See something?" Tim asked.

Weezy stared a moment longer, then shook her head. "No. Just a shadow." She looked up at Tim. "Can I have one of these? Please-please-please?"

He laughed. "Sure."

She held up the overhead shot she'd been looking at. "This one."

"It's yours. Now, I want the three of you back on your bikes and heading for home."

He stood there and watched them do just that. He

paced them awhile, following behind, then bop-tooted and rolled away, leaving them on their own.

As soon as he was out of sight, Weezy stopped and pulled the photo from her basket.

"Jack! Did you see this?"

He stopped beside her and looked over her shoulder. Again that tickling feeling that he was missing something.

"Yeah. But obviously you see something I don't."

"Watch."

The tip of her finger traced the trench that had replaced the mound. Jack stiffened as he recognized the figure.

"That's . . . that's on the seal"—what had Dad called it?—"the sigil of . . ."

She was nodding. "Yeah. The Lodge."

4

Secret histories . . .

As he'd done last night, Jack sat in the dark, staring at a building. Only instead of on Harding Street, he was down near the bank of Quaker Lake. And not in a tree, but sitting with his back against the big oak. And it wasn't Steve's house he was staring at, but the Lodge that squatted across the water, a light on in one of its high, narrow windows.

Secrets . . . secrets everywhere.

Maybe Weezy was right. Maybe there was a Secret History of the World. The Pine Barrens probably held a lot of it—like the pine lights and that shape in the woods—but he'd bet the Lodge was well up there in what it knew and hid. Like how old it was, and how long it had existed on that spot—not the building itself, but the Ancient Septimus Fraternal Order . . . how long had it been here? If that mound was pre-Columbian, and had been built by the Lodge, it meant the Lodge had been here a long, long time. And if the mound was prehistoric . . .

That didn't even bear thinking.

Secrets . . .

Did the troopers and suits who'd dug up the mound find anything? If so, they weren't telling.

But Weezy knew of other mounds. Maybe it was time for the two of them to start some digging of their own. Maybe they'd find another cube with a pyramid inside. He doubted it, but never say never.

He still had the copies of the pyramid's symbols. What secret did they hold?

And even Weezy . . . she had a secret or two as well. Jack sensed it, but hadn't a clue as to what. Maybe it had something to do with all those Friday morning trips to Medford.

Secrets . . .

The town itself had a secret history. How had Old Town come to be named Quakerton before any Quakers existed?

Even his own family had a secret history. Why wouldn't Dad talk about the war? What had happened there to make him clam up whenever it was mentioned? And what did he keep locked in that box?

Jack realized that he too had a secret: exposing Steve's father. He couldn't tell anyone about it. Yeah, some people would call him a hero, but sure as the sun rose every morning, Steve would eventually find out. And Steve would hate him. Soon everyone in town would be looking at him strangely, and holding their tongues when he was about.

Because everybody had secrets.

Jack simply wanted to come and go as he pleased, with no one taking any special notice of him. Just another face in the crowd.

Just . . . Jack.

Movement across the lake caught his eye. He watched a gray limousine—looked like a Bentley—pull up before the Lodge and stop in the pool of light around its entrance. A uniformed driver hopped out and opened the rear door. A very tall man in a white suit unfolded himself from the passenger compartment. He had black, slicked-back hair but Jack couldn't make out his face at this distance.

The man sauntered to the front steps of the Lodge, but instead of going inside, he stopped and turned in Jack's direction. He seemed to be staring directly at Jack. But how could that be? Jack was sitting in deep shadow. No way the man could see him.

Yet he kept staring, and it made Jack uncomfortable. Finally he turned and disappeared inside. The chauffeur followed him in, lugging two large suitcases.

Was he moving in? Into the Lodge itself? Jack had never heard of anyone actually living there.

Mr. Challis's words came back to him: . . . *the Council is sending someone to take charge of our Lodge . . .*

Was that him? If so, he was one creepy guy. And why had he seemed to be staring at him?

Jack wanted to keep his distance from that place. The arrests of Mr. Brussard and Challis, and Challis's confession about how they'd killed Boruff according to "sacred rites," had embarrassed the Lodge. Better they didn't know he'd been instrumental in that.

And still . . . he had a feeling he wasn't through with the Lodge.

As for what he'd seen outside Steve's house last night . . . better not talk about that. Had he really seen *anything*? Now, just twenty-four hours later, it seemed unreal. Maybe just a trick of the light. But maybe not . . .

The uneasy feeling vanished in the persistent memory of the sensations that had shot through him Saturday night when Mr. Brussard had stepped into the trap and given himself away. All because of Jack, who had come upon a bad circumstance, a broken situation, and fixed it.

What a rush . . . maybe like what Steve felt when he drank or popped a pill. At least Steve's mother was aware of that now. Hopefully she'd get him some help.

But as for Jack . . . he was hooked on that feeling. If he saw a chance to do another fix, he'd go for it.

He could hardly wait.

• • •

A reader's guide for *Jack: Secret Histories* is available online at http://tor-forge.com/jacksecrethistories.

Coming soon:
JACK: SECRET CIRCLES
www.repairmanjack.com

THE SECRET HISTORY
OF THE WORLD

The preponderance of my work deals with a history of the world that remains undiscovered, unexplored, and unknown to most of humanity. Some of this secret history has been revealed in the Adversary Cycle, some in the Repairman Jack novels, and bits and pieces in other, seemingly unconnected works. Taken together, even these millions of words barely scratch the surface of what has been going on behind the scenes, hidden from the workaday world. I've listed these works below in the chronological order in which the events in them occur.

Note: "Year Zero" is the end of civilization as we know it; "Year Zero Minus One" is the year preceding it, etc.

THE PAST
"Demonsong" (prehistory)
"Aryans and Absinthe" (1923–1924)
Black Wind (1926–1945)
The Keep (1941)
Reborn (February–March 1968)
"Dat Tay Vao" (March 1968)
Jack: Secret Histories (1983)

YEAR ZERO MINUS THREE
"Faces" (early summer)
The Tomb (summer)
"The Barrens"* (ends in September)
"The Wringer"
"A Day in the Life"* (October)
"The Long Way Home"
Legacies (December)

YEAR ZERO MINUS TWO

Conspiracies (April) (includes "Home Repairs")
All the Rage (May) (includes "The Last Rakosh")
Hosts (June)
The Haunted Air (August)
Gateways (September)
Crisscross (November)
Infernal (December)

YEAR ZERO MINUS ONE

Harbingers (January)
Bloodline (April)
The Touch (ends in August)
The Peabody-Ozymandias Traveling Circus & Oddity Emporium
    (ends in September)
"Tenants"*
yet-to-be-written Repairman Jack novels

YEAR ZERO

"Pelts"*
Reprisal (ends in February)
the last Repairman Jack novel (ends in April)
Nightworld (starts in May)

Reborn, The Touch, and *Reprisal* will be back in print before too
long. I'm planning a total of sixteen or seventeen Repairman Jack
novels (not counting the young adult titles), ending the Secret
History with the publication of a heavily revised *Nightworld.*

*available in *The Barrens and Others*